Riverside Reverie

J.C. Hannigan

Editor: Catherine Muss

Proofreader: Jess Martin

Cover Designer: Blue Moon Creative Studios

Formatting: Heritage Creek Formatting

THE SNAP

I ZIPPED up my new hiking bag and lifted it off my queen-size bed, dropping it on the floor beside the other supplies and gear with a tempered huff. I surveyed the pile, my anxiety growing.

At any minute my best friend, Jasmine Kade, would arrive to pick me up from my parents' house in Guelph for our camping adventure. Although it'd been weeks since I'd last texted her, Jasmine was the first person I had reached out to after my recent heartbreak. Her solution was to get me away from the situation by inviting me on an already-planned camping trip. We were headed up north to spend the next several days camping somewhere along the French River with a handful of people that I didn't know and had never met before. They were Jasmine's friends she knew from college and living up north.

It had been half a year since I'd last seen her. Our post-secondary goals had taken us in different directions. I had headed to McMaster University in Hamilton, while she went north to Sudbury to study for her PhD in Human Studies and Interdisciplinarity at Laurentian University. We'd stayed in touch and met up whenever we could, but with our equally demanding course loads it wasn't that often.

But no matter how much time passed, Jasmine and I were the kind of friends that could slip back into the easy companionship we'd always had. We rallied around each other from afar, and we were always a text or call away.

My stomach rolled with nervousness. It wasn't the prospect of seeing Jasmine again that had me on edge—it was crashing her and her friends' camping trip in the wilderness. *Am I really doing this?* I asked myself, staring at the pile of newly purchased gear on my bedroom floor.

I still couldn't believe that she'd been successful in talking me into going, especially given the fact that we would be canoeing to the backcountry campsite.

Me, canoeing, when the prospect of camping was hard enough for me to digest.

There would be no electricity, no running water, and likely no cellphone service. Worst of all, Jasmine had cautioned me that most of the 250 backcountry campsites along the French River wouldn't even have outhouses.

That's right, I would be spending the next several days squatting in the woods to do my business.

I wasn't outdoorsy, not in the slightest. It's why my college choices had veered to bigger cities. I enjoyed the hustle and bustle, how the city was always alive with something happening. Despite my reluctance to spend the next several days in the great outdoors, I felt a burning need to do something different...to step outside of the person I'd always been.

Plus, it meant getting away from the drama. I would much rather deal with mosquitos and peeing in the woods than the situation I'd found myself stuck in.

A few weeks ago, my relationship with my high school

boyfriend, Scott, had ended abruptly when my sister, Brinley, had sent me a Snap of him in bed with another woman.

Brinley was the woman in the picture.

She hadn't sent it to me accidentally, either. She hadn't even *pretended* that's what happened. To add insult to injury, she'd posted the picture to her feed for good measure so that everyone else would see it, too.

I was heartbroken; less so over the fact that things with Scott had ended, and more so over the fact that I didn't think I could ever forget the satisfied smile on Brinley's face. My sister had intentionally sought to hurt me, and that knowledge cut far deeper than Scott's betrayal.

The whole thing shouldn't have come as a horrid surprise to me; Brinley and I had never had a very good relationship, but I honestly never expected her to go so far and take so much pleasure out of hurting me.

There was only a year between us, but my younger sister was competitive, selfish, impulsive, and very insecure. We were as dissimilar as day and night, not only in personality and morals, but our looks as well. Brinley was a carbon copy of our mother. She had golden blonde hair, deep blue eyes, and flawless skin that tanned in the sun. My sister had beauty going for her by the truckload, and I still hadn't been able to figure out where the body dysmorphia came from. Likely, our mother.

Mom had been calorie counting and dieting since before I could remember, always seeking out the perfect body, although to her credit she *never* put that pressure on us girls. Just herself. Still, it was easy to see where Brinley had picked it up.

My copper waves and slate grey eyes framed by thick dark auburn lashes were like our father's. I had his fair complexion, with freckles dotting my nose, upper cheeks, and my arms. During the winter months, my freckles were almost undetectable, but during the summer, the sun brought them out.

I was the book smart one, and my sister was the athletic one.

Brinley had been the star player on the school volleyball and rugby teams, but she'd struggled with her academics. In grade eleven she'd ended up dropping out. The only thing my little sister had ever wanted was to be famous, and she'd decided that she didn't need a high school education to pursue a career in modeling or acting.

I was on the honour roll in high school and in university. My program had been a partnership between Mohawk College and McMaster University that had allowed me to pursue two concurrent qualifications: an Ontario College Advanced Diploma in Medical Radiation Sciences through Mohawk College and the McMaster University Bachelor of Medical Radiation Sciences degree. I had come away with glowing recommendations from my professors and the program director of my clinical placement himself.

Our parents had always been proud of my academic achievements, and less thrilled with Brinley for dropping out of high school. In an unfair twist, Brinley resented me and blamed me for the disappointment my parents felt towards her, straining our relationship even more.

Which was ridiculous, as I'd always loved my sister regardless of our differences. It had never mattered to me that Brinley was better at sports and more popular in school, in fact, I used to envy her ease at socializing. It didn't come so naturally to me. But it mattered to Brinley, because no sooner had I graduated and packed up my dorm room to come home for the summer than I'd received the picture from her. Like clockwork, it was my sister's way of knocking me down several pegs.

I huffed out a sigh, ignoring the sting of tears while I checked my bag for the hundredth time, uncertain on exactly what I was searching for. Something to do, something to distract myself from my own thoughts. It was pointless, though. My ex's frustrating face still popped in my head, his puppy-dog eyes begging for forgiveness and absolution.

Scott had been remorseful and apologetic. I wagered that he hadn't expected me to find out about his raunchy romp with my little sister, but I had no interest in giving him another chance. I'd slammed that metaphorical door without a backwards glance and had no desire to open it again. But the intentional hurt caused by my own sister? That was the wound that festered.

Brinley had caused *plenty* of premeditated hurts over the years, but usually, those were just mean quips about me. I could brush those off easily, because what sisters didn't get into hurtful spats every now and then? Even Jasmine butted heads with her three sisters from time to time.

Of course, none of Jasmine's sisters had ever done such a voluntary cruel act, nor would they. Those girls had the relationship I'd always hoped for with Brinley—they could rip on each other, laugh with each other, and at the end of the day they could still count on each other.

I couldn't do any of those things with Brinley, and I'd never been able to count on her. I didn't think I'd be able to even try, now...unless it was just counting on getting hurt and disappointed by her.

The tears I'd been trying to ignore and control broke free, a few streaming down my cheeks. Defiantly, I wiped them away, forcing myself to take a calming breath.

This had been my tactic ever since receiving the evidence. Brinley sent the Snap a mere two hours before our parents showed up at the dormitory to bring me home for the summer, so I hadn't had time to *really* cry about it before they arrived. The clinic I did my co-op at had asked if they could hire me short term to cover a sick leave once my placement ended, which allowed me to stay away from Brinley until graduation in June. I guess that job offer was especially offensive to Brinley, and gave her extra time to work on my graduation "gift" with my ex. I hadn't let myself cry since seeing the evidence, because I was afraid that once I started, I wouldn't stop.

I tried not to let myself think about it, because any time I let those thoughts take over, it was like pressing salt into the still-fresh wound. But it was futile—I couldn't escape the thoughts, the reminders; the cruelness of Brinley's near-permanent smirk each time we passed each other in the hallway. So, I was running away into the backwoods with no toilets, but also...no Brinley.

The doorbell rang, and a moment later my mother's voice drifted up the stairs as she greeted Jasmine. Not long after that, I heard footsteps on the stairs.

"Knock, knock! Are you ready?" Jasmine's voice was muffled from behind my bedroom door. I stepped around the pile of camping gear and opened it, my face caught somewhere between a grimace and a smile.

Her easy grin faded, and she arched a dark brow. "You're not seriously thinking of bailing, are you?" she demanded. Her wild dark curls were pulled back in a high, messy bun. Her rich brown eyes missed nothing, and already she could tell that something was amiss. She shot me one of her signature no-bull-shit looks.

I might be able to lie to myself, but I couldn't lie to Jasmine.

"Maybe a little," I admitted, spinning around, eyes going once again to the pile of newly purchased camping gear. All of it was acquired from the list of camping essentials that Jasmine texted. We were going to share a lot of supplies—the tent, the cookware, that sort of thing. Jasmine had packed that stuff, having most of those supplies at home, but I'd still needed to pick up a few things for myself, like a sleeping bag and mattress.

"Why?" Jasmine's brows were knotted together in confusion. She obviously could see nothing wrong with the pile of stuff I'd wildly gestured at.

"I've never been camping before in my life, and I'm going on a trip with a bunch of people I don't even know who basically have diplomas in nature," I huffed, crossing my arms, and feeling a little sorry for myself.

I couldn't help it. I was feeling insecure and anxious about this trip, especially now that Jasmine was here to pick me up. I feared I wouldn't be able to keep up with everyone, or that I would end up making a fool out of myself.

Jasmine stepped up to me and put her hands on my shoulders, her warm dark eyes drilling into mine. "You're over-thinking things. It's going to be fine. They don't have degrees in nature, they enjoy camping. Do you *really* want to stay here with the world's most evil little sister?"

My friend's eyes travelled behind me, down the hall to the closed door of my sister's room. Brinley wasn't there, but the point was well-received.

"You're right." I cleared my throat, pushing my emotions away as much as I could. Squatting in the woods was prefer-able to dealing with Brinley prancing around like she'd won the lottery. After I'd refused to take Scott back, he'd made things official with my sister, and she was still under the belief that she'd won. As far as I was concerned, she could keep her prize.

I'd been spared Brinley's taunting smirk this morning—she had yet to return from wherever she'd been the night before. But it was only a matter of time until she was home and starting in on me again.

Her little quips about how I didn't know how to let loose and have fun, that I was far too *boring* to truly satisfy Scott, and that if I'd cared more about my appearance I might have held onto him were painful burrs embedded in my skin. I didn't give a rat's ass about satisfying Scott, not anymore—but I cared that Brinley had to taunt me. I cared that she poked at my insecuri-ties and uncertainties. Sisters were supposed to lift you up, not tear you down. It seemed like Brinley was hellbent on tearing me down every time she got the chance—always when our parents weren't within ear shot.

"I'm always right. I don't feel bad at all about steamrolling you into coming. I know you're going to have fun, and you need to get away from the drama for a bit."

"I am looking forward to *that*," I sighed. That was the silver lining right there: getting away from the drama. I hated drama, and yet I'd been forced into it every time I had to deal with my sister.

Jasmine sent a comforting smile my way, then started grabbing things from my pile of gear. With her help, we were able to carry everything down in one go.

My mother was waiting in the foyer, a bemused smile on her full lips as she watched us. Her blue eyes twinkled as she came in for a hug I couldn't return, what with my arms as full as they were. I knew before she opened her mouth that she was going to say something that would embarrass me, and I was thankful only Jasmine was around to bear witness.

"Have a fun trip! I slipped a box of condoms in your bag when you were in the shower," she sang as she pulled back.

"Mom!" I said, my cheeks heating. Shaking my head incredulously, I rolled my eyes.

"What? I remember my single days," she said, winking at me. "There might be an opportunity that you don't want to miss out on," she laughed again at the horrified look on my face. Jasmine sniggered, and I glared at her.

Mom had heard about my breakup with Scott, but she hadn't heard the reason, or that Brinley was now seeing him. That news would disappoint my parents.

They had done their best to raise us to be each other's best friend and constant source of support. Brinley must not have gotten the memo. It's not very friendly or supportive to sleep with your sister's boyfriend, or to send her a picture on Snap of yourself in bed with him.

"Okay, then. I'm leaving now. Bye, Mom."

"Bye, honey! Have a wonderful time!"

I followed Jasmine out the door to her CRV, the red canoe already strapped down to the roof. She slid the cooler toward the back of the open trunk. I placed the tote I carried inside, then tossed my hiking bag on top of it.

"Tell me more about who's all going?" I asked as we loaded the rest of my things into the back. I'd been so occupied with ensuring I had all the camping essentials I'd need, that I hadn't really had time to ask questions. Now, I was curious about the people I'd be spending the next several days and nights with.

"Looking to use those condoms?" she teased, waggling her eyebrows.

I shot her an unimpressed look. "Hardly," I rolled my eyes. "I want to have some idea of who's going to be there."

"Aside from us? Seven," Jasmine replied with a grin. "Desmond, Baz, Rhiannon, Theo, Talia, Zoey and Kai."

"That's...a lot of people." I frowned. Like, *a lot*. I only recognized a couple of names from conversations over the years. Talia had been one of her college roommates, and Desmond was one of the owners of the duplex they rented from. Theo might have been too...or maybe that was Baz, I couldn't remember. They were all mysteries to me: names I'd recognized from her mentioning them in passing, but I'd never registered any lingering details about them.

Jasmine slammed the trunk closed, her grin widening. "They're all really great people, Lux, you'll see. Stop worrying and get in the car, we've got to hit the road so we can meet everyone at the boat launch."

"All right," I sighed, looking past Jasmine at my house. The knots in my stomach had already lessened with the knowledge that I had four days away from the drama that lived there. *But what about after?* The thought tried to worm its way in, but I pushed it away, unwilling to face it. I knew I needed to figure out my next move, but it was clear I couldn't subject myself to Brinley's continued cruelty.

Walking around to the passenger side, I opened the door and climbed in, closing it behind me.

The engine roared to life and Jasmine sent an excited grin my way. "This is going to be an amazing trip, you'll see," she assured me with a confident smile before backing out of my parents' driveway.

ROAD TRIP

"So what do your parents think about the whole Brinley and Scott thing?"

"They don't know yet," I shrugged.

"And why the hell not!?" Jasmine exclaimed, her eyebrows raising with disbelief.

"I haven't told them, and Brinley certainly hasn't." My parents thought that Scott and I had broken up due to the strain the long distance had put on us, and that we'd simply outgrown each other. Both those things were true: those issues *had* contributed to our demise...but they had no clue how much of a hand Brinley had in things. She hadn't brought him around the house, she had enough self-preservation to realize that she'd catch *some* flak for that, and it was as if she was waiting for me to tell on her.

"I don't think I can handle them excusing her behaviour again," I admitted. I knew I couldn't handle yet another dismissal of my concerns or listen to them minimizing what I've always suspected could be a real problem: that my little sister needed psychological help.

"I still can't believe Brinley did that to you!" Jasmine blasted, rolling her eyes. She had caught me staring out the window with the same dejected look that prompted her to force me to come on the trip in the first place. "Actually, scratch that. I *can* believe it."

While it had been seven months since I'd last gotten to hang out with Jasmine, we fell into the same familiar pattern we'd always had with one another. I realized just how much I'd missed my best friend, and how much I was looking forward to spending time with her again.

As much as I hated to admit it, I'd been down the last few weeks. It wasn't exactly upbeat knowledge, knowing that your own family would intentionally betray you just to hurt you. My eyes started to itch, and I blinked away tears, glancing out the window and trying to pull myself back together. There was no reason why Jasmine's presence should make me feel so emotional, other than she felt and acted more like a loving sister than my own.

I'd known Jasmine and her family since grade seven, and she'd known mine just as long. Our younger sisters had been close friends too, although Camellia was so sweet compared to Brinley. None of Jasmine's three sisters were as competitive and cruel as Brinley, and Jasmine had a great relationship with each of them.

To have so many sisters, and to have such unique bonds with them all...it was something I'd longed for with Brinley. Jasmine's sisters could depend on her, and vice versa. I couldn't depend on Brinley unless I wanted to depend on getting hurt. My little sister had always been catty and mean, choosing to see other women as the enemy. She saw other girls as competition, someone to defeat, rather than the powerful allies they could be.

Jasmine had called me after seeing my Facebook relationship status change. She thought I'd be happy, celebrating having finally broken the chain that had held me back since high school. She'd thought I'd be ready for a summer of mingling. But I wasn't, I was quietly devastated. Not about the Scott thing, and once I explained the other party…she understood.

Things had seemed so wonderful at the beginning of our relationship. Scott was one of the few guys in our grade with a license and a car, and he'd picked me up every day before school, and he loved having me at his rugby games. But outside of sports, Scott didn't have many goals, and his grades weren't very good.

Scott planned on taking sports therapy after graduating. He thought it'd be cool to work on big sports teams, but he lacked the motivation and discipline, and his marks weren't high enough to qualify for the program without taking a few refresher courses first.

Which was what he was doing, refresher courses at the local community college—and my sister, apparently.

I sighed, finally drawing my gaze away from the window and to my friend. I lifted my shoulder in a weak shrug. "Brinley just…has a lot of issues."

Jasmine chortled. "Understatement of the year."

"I want her to get help for them, Jas. It's always been painful watching her lash out at those close to her, simply because she's hurting. If she got help, maybe she wouldn't."

My friend sent me a sympathetic smile. "Girl, you know I love your heart. But…people have to *want* to help themselves; they have to *want* to change. I don't think Brinley sees a problem with herself."

I nodded in agreement. She was right about that. I was beginning to see it.

Although she understood, Jasmine didn't like how down the whole situation made me feel. She'd said I wasn't acting like me, and I really wasn't. I'd let Brinley smack me down, and I remained on the ground. I had allowed my sister to dull my shine, and if I was being perfectly honest with myself, I'd been letting her do it our entire lives.

"Remember when Brinley actually stood up for me that time with Brittany Carmichael?"

Jasmine pursed her lips, shaking her head. "You mean that time she out mean-girled the meanest girl in our grade? Yeah, I remember. But that was more like a territorial fight between two mean girls."

I sighed again, knowing she was right. It had less to do with me and more to do with Brinley taking on the mean popular girls in my grade, even if she *had* said *"nobody torments my sister but me,"* before the ensuing catfight.

If Brinley wanted something, she'd stop at nothing until she got it, so I usually let her have whatever it was to spare an argument. Before dropping out to "pursue modelling", Brinley had walked the halls of our high school like Regina George herself. Her beauty allotted her popularity, and most of her peers—Camellia included—were too intimidated to stand up to her.

She didn't bother to hide her inner ugliness, but when it suited her Brinley knew how to schmooze and could put on a very convincing innocent act. A lot of the time, the adults were fooled by her; my parents, especially. Brinley really would make a great actress, as she could act out any emotion expected of her in any given situation.

But when she got angry, it was like a switch flipped. Brinley would fly off the handle, screaming and yelling, her eyes cold and raging. Her comments would slice through even the toughest of armour. Over the years, I'd learned to mask my hurt, because Brinley would only use it as a weapon to further antagonize.

I thought she'd grow out of her petty cruelties, and as adults we'd grow closer as sisters. But it seemed we only grew further apart, separated by Brinley's anger and actions.

My high school graduation was the first indication I'd had that Brinley's resentment for me had escalated from stealing my favourite clothes and purposely ruining them. She had scowled throughout graduation ceremony. In every picture our mom forced us to take together with me in my graduation cap and gown, Brinley was glaring. At the fancy restaurant my parents took us too for dinner, she had erupted into tears because everybody was making such a big deal of me graduating.

She'd next taken personal offence to my career choice, like it was somehow meant to be a slap in her face, like I was rubbing it in that I was "smarter" than her, when that wasn't the case at all. I wanted to help people. My choices weren't meant to slight my sister, and it'd never occurred to me that she'd react so combatively. I'd hoped that her pursuing her own dreams would bring her some form of happiness, and that we could bond over our differences while still supporting one another's choices and dreams. Brinley's recent cruel actions had me wondering if there was anything within in her that was salvageable. She showed no regret over how much she'd hurt me. It had put me in a dark place, wondering what I'd done to deserve such contempt from my baby sister.

I needed this trip; I needed to get away from her and regroup. I needed to figure out how I was supposed to move past the hurt she'd caused—or if I even could. I didn't know how I could ever trust her again, and I considered myself a pretty forgiving person. To know that Brinley had intentionally sought to hurt me, and that she'd relished in succeeding...well, that changed things. It might be too much for even *me* to move past.

"You're so loyal and helpful, and kind...a lot kinder than I am. You see the good in everybody, even if they don't deserve it." Jasmine remarked, keeping her focus on the road as some guy in a lifted Dodge sped past us, the engine roaring.

"Hardly," I huffed. "I see the bad in people too, I just try not to condemn them for it, and I try not to let their past choices define their future. If Brinley got help for everything tomorrow, I wouldn't hold a single thing against her."

"I know, that's the craziest part. I'd never talk to my sister again if she did half the stuff Brinley's pulled on you." Jasmine sounded impressed. "But…and I don't mean to upset you by saying this…I think you're holding your breath on something that isn't going to happen. Brinley isn't going to change, and definitely not overnight. For so long, you've held yourself responsible for her actions towards you, and you need to stop."

I nodded, releasing a slow breath. She was right.

I was no martyr, and I knew consistently signing up to be my little sister's punching bag wasn't going to help her, and it certainly wasn't helping me. But there was still a part of me that didn't want to give up on her. I couldn't turn off caring about my own sister, and I knew I could never truly escape the scope of Brinley's problems or their trinkle-down effect on me *because* I cared. At the end of the day, we were sisters. It was just in my nature to worry about her.

It seemed like Brinley had been looking for something to drive the wedge permanently between us for years. Did I want this Scott thing to be what finally pushed us apart forever? I wasn't so sure, but I did know that if she continued to show no remorse for her actions, I'd have no choice but to distance myself to protect my own heart.

I'd highly suspected my sister was mentally ill for years now—although my mother vehemently denied it whenever I voiced my concerns.

My parents were from the era of not talking about mental health, from burying it with a glass of rye or wine. They had a "stiff upper lip" approach to mental health. I don't think they even knew what to do with the possibility of my sister's mental illness, so they'd ended up minimizing it. Telling me it was just teenage angst, that Brinley had a flare for dramatics. My mother assured me Brinley would grow out of it, and to not take it so personally; all sisters fought.

Something in my gut told me otherwise, and things only got worse when she dropped out of school to be a social media influencer. The moment Brinley realized that people no longer needed an agent to be discovered, she'd invested all her time on social media cultivating a following.

Brinley had a knack for doing makeup and hair and making herself look flawless. She'd inherited the same gifts from our mother, who'd done some modelling work in her early teen years. The more followers Brinley got, the more her cruel nature reached new heights. I couldn't help but worry that the pressure of maintaining that carefully cultivated image was worsening her mental health struggles. She'd sneer and scoff, tell me that her only problem was me, then she'd toss a couple of insults my way and storm off.

"I think she's hurting, and instead of addressing why...she lashes out." I shrugged, toying with my hair. That knowledge didn't make it hurt any less, but it helped me understand her.

I'd read somewhere that people who feel disempowered lash out because they lack the skills that make them feel better when they feel bad, and it's the only way they know how to get that boost. Brinley coped with her issues by being cruel and attacking, and this latest offence was just another example of her pattern, a pattern my parents had ignored and excused for our whole lives.

On the flip side, if they *did* finally acknowledge there could be a problem after all these years...what would change? Would they insist she finally see a therapist? Would it benefit Brinley in the long run to come forward about her discretions? Was my silence perpetuating harm?

"Brinley has made *a lot* of bad choices, but she's my sister." I pointed out, weakly trying to defend my...defensiveness of her, and Jasmine sent me a look over the top of her sunglasses briefly before her attention returned to the highway. "It feels wrong to just give up."

Jasmine sighed. "You're too close to the problem, here. She'll never be able to see you as anything but the enemy, the competition. At least not until she learns how to deal with her issues herself. You've gotta let go of the idea of being the one to save her. Brinley needs to save herself."

It was a hard truth to hear, but Jasmine wasn't wrong.

"She's family, and family is supposed to be there for each other, to help each other." It was the internalized expectation I'd been brought up with, and no matter how mad I got at Brinley, that expectation was rooted in me.

"She slept with your boyfriend, Lux—and now she's dating him. Worst of all? She doesn't see a problem with it. How could you forgive something like that?"

I sent Jasmine a sad smile, appreciating her willingness to stand up for me. She was more like a sister to me than my own blood. "Well, yeah, it hurt. But Scott wasn't my forever, I guess I knew that, but I was..."

"Afraid to rip off the Band-Aid?" She arched a brow and tilted her head. She had been saying for years that I should break things off with Scott and be single for a while, enjoy college life to the fullest. She never really liked him.

"Yeah. I guess you could say that. I should have ended things with Scott years ago, but I was afraid to." All the excitement I'd once felt for him seemed to have remained behind in the halls our old high school, and that was perfectly alright.

Even before Brinley had sent the photo, I'd been considering breaking things off with Scott.

My patience for his laziness and lack of interest in our relationship had already worn thin. I just hadn't been sure how to go about breaking up with him. Confrontation wasn't really my forte, and my aversion to drama had me dreading it.

Our relationship had never been the stuff of romance novels, but Scott had been more creative about dates when we were in high school. At least then, he'd taken me out for meals and to the movies. After graduating, his idea of a date had been to have me watch him play Call of Duty until three in the morning. He had zero interest in going out when I was home, unless it was to drag me along to one of his friend's parties.

"You really should have; he was never at your level," Jasmine said, shooting me a knowing glance before turning her attention back to the road.

"Tell me about it," I sighed. "He never put in the effort." When I first started university, I'd made frequent trips back every other weekend to do laundry and to see him, but Scott had put zero effort in us. I'd ended up spending my time with him doing homework while he played videogames and all but ignored me.

At first, I'd been so focused on my studies, I hadn't even realized what was happening between us. Not consciously, anyway —or perhaps I knew, but again, just didn't know how to end it. Eventually, I'd stopped going as frequently, opting to stay at the dorms instead and save my parents' the trip.

I didn't think Scott would be bothered by this, after all—he never called me out for it or asked *why* I'd stopped coming as much. Our relationship really hadn't really felt like a relationship in years, and as he'd tossed that at me, I couldn't blame him for finding something else to fill that void. We both knew it never had to be my sister, though. That was one betrayal he could have spared me.

"He didn't deserve you, that was obvious from the beginning," Jasmine said, shaking her head. "I feel bad you wasted all that time with him."

"He didn't distract me from my studies or my goals." I

reminded her, pausing to collect my thoughts. "He complained about that, you know, when I told him things were officially finished between us. He said, 'Good, you cared more about school and your future than you did me anyway.'"

"Because he *wasn't* your future, and you both knew that. You just didn't want to admit it." Jasmine scoffed. "Forget about that loser. You need to find someone adventurous, someone to sweep you off your feet and give you the experience of a lifetime."

"I'm not looking for someone to sweep me off my feet, and I'm not even adventurous!" I pointed out with a laugh as I tucked my copper hair behind my ear. My finger brushed against the gold of my heart shaped daith piercing. Jasmine had one too, we'd gotten them the summer we'd turned sixteen. It was the most 'adventurous' thing about me.

"Not yet, but after this trip you will be," she said confidently. "You'll get the camping bug—then you'll want to do it all the time!"

"Don't count on it," I sighed, rolling my shoulders. I detested bugs and dirt, and I was certain there'd be plenty of that where we were going.

"Just you wait. You'll be eating your words by the end of this trip," she giggled. "You're going to love it!"

"We'll see." Secretly, I hoped that Jasmine was right. I hoped that I'd love every minute of it, that it'd be the distraction I needed away from the crummy bits of my life. I hadn't felt like myself lately.

But I was determined to not sulk this weekend. I wasn't about to allow Brinley another win. Me spending the next several days away from her miserable would be just that, letting her cruelty have the upper hand—again.

"I think," Jasmine drawled, wiggling her eyebrows at me, "that you'll love the experience so much, you'll decide to move to Sudbury and be my new roomie. Wouldn't that be fun?"

"You're looking for a new roommate?" My curiosity was a little piqued.

"Actually, yes. The student renter moved out at the beginning of July, and the room is still available if you want it. They don't usually start looking for new renters until closer to September, but I could talk to Desmond, tell him to let you have it."

"I don't know..." Rooming with Jasmine would be easy—we'd always gotten along. She was just as serious and focused as I was when it came to school and work, but she knew how to unwind, too. I'd forgotten how to do that, and living with Jasmine would remind me how to have fun again.

It sounded like a better option than my current predicament. I didn't want to commit to the idea, but I could always check out local job listings and see if any clinics or hospitals were hiring. It wouldn't hurt to broaden my job search several hundred kilometres, especially if it meant putting more distance between myself and Brinley.

THE DRIVE to the French River was a long one from Guelph, where we'd grown up and where both of our parents still lived. We filled the rest of the time with reminiscing conversations, laughter, and music. She updated me on how her parents and three younger sisters were doing, and we laughed about the time the two of us had stumbled in after a few too many drinks at a semi-formal after party when we were in grade eleven.

Jasmine was the eldest daughter of the Mayor of Guelph. The Kade's had been politicians for many generations, and although Mayor Kade was about as modern and chill as politicians came, it had been a risky thing for us to do. Even though we had been honest about where we were and we'd returned before Jasmine's curfew, we'd gotten into a lot of trouble afterwards. If our giggles hadn't been the thing to give us away, Jasmine's parents could smell the alcohol on us, and they weren't impressed. As the eldest of four girls *and* the daughter of a politician, an example had to be set. For the rest of that summer, Jasmine was grounded and had to do community service. She chose to volunteer at a sleepaway camp up north.

The Kade's had informed my parents of my misdemeanour too, but mine were laxer about it. After all, Brinley drank in excess; every weekend, she'd stumbled home past curfew, drunk. My minor drinking experiments had always seemed so tame, comparably.

Jasmine's punishment had worked more effectively to discipline me, as I'd had to spend an entire summer without my best friend, and she'd had the best time at the sleepaway camp. After that incident, the two of us got a hell of a lot wiser about drinking.

My phone dinged with a message, and I absently picked it up. It was a new Snap from my sister. It wasn't even nine o'clock and she'd already started in with sending Snaps directly to me. She'd sent Snaps of her and Scott together so often that seeing them together had lost some of the initial sting.

The Snaps were always cross-posted to her stories, adding double the fuel to the gossip mill. Back home had been churning with Brinley's latest escapades. I'd received more "hey girl, just checking in" messages from former high school classmates than I cared to admit, all of them fishing for information on the latest Kennish sister drama. Some were my old friends, curious but authentic, relating to the pain of being betrayed, but most were Brinley's minions, fishing for insider information that I wouldn't give. She was looking for a public reaction, but she wouldn't get it.

I dropped my phone into the centre console without checking her latest Snap. There was no sense in giving Brinley power when she wasn't even here. It felt like a waste of energy,

energy that I could spend worrying about all the uncertain things this trip would undoubtedly contain instead.

Like *all* the unfamiliar people, and variables. My stomach churned with nervousness. "Let's see how this trip goes first, I might not like you by the end of it."

Jasmine cackled, like what I'd said was the funniest thing she'd ever heard.

3

PATH OF THE PADDLE

Lux

WHEN WE HAD BEEN DRIVING for over four hours, Jasmine started to squirm in her seat. "Oh man, I have to pee so bad," she exclaimed, squeezing her legs together, her face pinched with discomfort.

"Me too. How much further?" The urge wasn't too bad for me, but if Jasmine was going, I might as well, too. I didn't know when I would get the opportunity to use an actual toilet again.

"Until we reach the marina? Twenty minutes, but I can't hold it. We're going to have to stop." Jasmine answered, flicking her turn signal on. She waited for a break in traffic, then turned into a tiny old gas station. There was a long line spilling out of the door of the gas station, running along the entire length of the small building.

"This is going to take forever."

I frowned at the line, the pressure on my bladder increasing.

Having to pee was a lot like yawning—once someone really had to go, everyone in the vicinity seemed to have to go.

Jasmine found a parking spot and surveyed our surroundings. "Come on," she said, opening the door and stepping outside. I reluctantly followed her while she walked around the back of the gas station. She led me away from the potential prying eyes of other travellers, close to the treeline, then she started undoing the button on her shorts.

"You're seriously peeing out here?" I asked fretfully, glancing around with a somewhat horrified expression on my face. Anybody could look over and take a good guess at what we were doing here.

"You realize that we'll *all* be peeing in the bush, right?" Jasmine laughed, squatting. "You can hold it if you want, but who knows how long the lineup for the outhouse at the marina will be. Probably twice as long."

I mulled it over, debating. My friend stood, pulled her shorts up, and waited for me to come to my decision. Sighing, I began to unbutton my black shorts, shaking my head and pursing my lips. "Keep an eye out, I don't want anybody to see me."

Jasmine obeyed, standing guard with her back to me. It wasn't as hard as it had looked, but I wasn't looking forward to squatting like that the whole trip. My thighs were already protesting.

We walked back to the car quickly, wanting to get out of the crowded rest stop and to our destination as soon as possible. The last twenty minutes of the drive seemed to fly by, and each second that we got closer to the marina, my anxiety surged.

I had dealt with mild anxiety over the years by doing my best to repress it and maintain my sunshine and rainbows disposition, but it was harder to quiet that voice when I had no idea what to expect, and I had *no idea* what to expect from this camping trip. I was an organized planner, and when I couldn't plan my days down to the minute I felt a little squirrely.

Jasmine turned right onto a dirt road and drove for a minute before the boat launch came into view, pulling up to the large wooden building. There were *a lot* of people around, I was surprised to see how many. Close to fifty, at least. Jasmine had been right about the outhouse lineup—it was double the length of the gas station one.

There were two boat launches; one was between the two large docks, and to the left of the far dock was the second launch for canoes and kayaks. People were moving in synchronized groups, getting kayaks and canoes down from roof racks and placing them in the water, or taking their turn to direct trailers into the river at the boat launch.

"We need to go in and pay for our tickets and parking, then we can start unloading. Let's go say hi to the others first." Jasmine said.

My gaze went back to the canoe launch. Immediately, my attention was drawn to the attractive man carrying a kayak effortlessly over his left shoulder. His dark blond hair curled around his white baseball cap, and he wasn't wearing a shirt. He had the *yummiest* back I'd ever seen; ogling was an unfortunate side effect of his tanned muscles, and I couldn't even bring myself to feel sorry about it.

Forcing my eyes away from him, I distracted myself by assessing the other people in the group as they approached. One couple was loading up their canoe on the shore of the rocky beach. Another girl with short black hair was already sitting in her kayak, waiting in the water for everyone else. She was the only one to notice our approach, and she grinned widely and waved, calling out a hello to Jasmine that prompted everybody else to turn around.

The guy carrying the kayak turned, too. He was even more gorgeous head-on. He had dark green eyes that seemed infinite, lips that looked like they knew how to kiss, and a strong jaw dusted with facial hair, like he'd already spent a week in the wilderness without access to a razor. The scruff along his jaw suited him and made him even more compelling.

He was tall, too, and still blessedly shirtless. Part of me seriously hoped he'd stay that way.

When he stuck his free hand out to shake mine, my heart jumped up into my throat from the feel of his warm skin on mine. My hand seemed to disappear within his, and I gathered from his grip that he was as strong and steady as he looked.

"Hi, I'm Theo. You must be Lux. Jasmine's told us a lot about you," he said, smiling politely. Even his *voice* was sexy. I felt myself melting a little.

"Oh, that's promising," I said dryly when I finally found my voice. His eyes seemed to twinkle, and my heart stumbled again. "Did she tell you that I've never been camping before in my life?"

Theo's lips curved into a beautiful, bright smile, and he laughed a little. I wanted to fall into the sound. "Yeah, she might have mentioned it once or twice."

"I felt like they needed fair warning," Jasmine glanced between me and Theo, looking rather self-satisfied, before giving me a playful smile. Noticing the look on my face, she patted me on the back. "Kidding! You'll be fine, Lux. It's really not that difficult."

"She speaks from experience," a guy standing to Theo's left said with a slight chuckle. He had approached while we were talking, and he gave me a welcoming smile. "When Jasmine joined us for the first time, she didn't know how to set up a tent. Now, she's a pro."

"Thanks for the reminder. Lux, this is Desmond," Jasmine said as I smiled back at him.

Desmond was a little shorter than Theo, with a thicker build than him. He had dark brown eyes, brown hair and a thick, kept beard. His nose was a little large for his face, but it suited him. He shook my hand too, his eyes flitting back to Jasmine for a moment before returning to me.

"It's good to meet you," I told them both.

The couple that had been loading their canoe on the beach when we walked up approached us, their orange canoe half on the shore, packed and ready to go. As they walked, the guy reached out to hold her hand. He was tall and lean, with strawberry blond hair and light blue, smiling eyes.

She was a head and a half shorter; a tiny, slender little thing with dark wavy hair that reached below her shoulders. Her eyes were warm pools of hazel, and her smile was illuminating and friendly.

"Lux, this is Zoey and Kai!" Jasmine explained, grinning as her friends swarmed me.

Kai nodded in greeting, lifting his free hand to wave. Zoey smiled warmly at me. "Hey! It's so nice to meet you!"

"You too," I replied, smiling at the warmth and ease behind the group. They all appeared to welcome my crashing of their camping trip with open arms.

"Where are Rhiannon and Baz?" Jasmine asked, peering around the launch. I realized two were missing from her original count.

"They're already at the campsite," Desmond answered. "They got here yesterday, so they were able to secure the best one."

"Ok, great. You'll meet those two soon," she assured me. "I guess that leaves Talia, over there, in the kayak," she added, gesturing to the girl in the kayak.

"Hey!" Talia called out and waved when she heard her name, the friendly smile still in place on her lips. She was covered in tattoos, and her pixie cut was edgy, somehow. I waved back, returning her smiling. Talia had an infectious smile that evoked one in response.

I'd felt Theo's eyes on me the entire time Jasmine had been

making introductions. I stole a glance, to see if he really *was* looking. When our eyes connected, my body thrummed in a way it never had before.

It was disorienting.

Turning my head, I fixed Jasmine with a telling look. "Don't we still have to go pay for our permits?" I asked, arching an eyebrow.

"Yes," Jasmine replied. "Do you want to go pay while I get the canoe in the water?"

I wasn't satisfied with this suggestion. I'd been hoping to pin Jasmine down and find out what my wicked friend was up to. I sincerely hoped that it wasn't a matchmaking attempt, but the way she had watched while Theo introduced himself had me questioning her intent with this trip. Plus, the odd things she'd said about how much I was going to enjoy this trip.

If it *was* a misguided matchmaking attempt, I had to nip that in the bud before Jasmine could run with it.

While my belief in love hadn't died, I was reluctant to jump into anything new. It was the first time I'd been single in years, and I wasn't exactly sure what that meant for me yet. I wanted the time to figure it out, though.

There were enough changes on my horizon as it was. I had begun the process of job hunting, and that would mean a move. I couldn't be picky about where, either. I needed a job sooner rather than later, and my own place.

But Jasmine had a solution for that, too—and she'd already laid down the groundwork. I looked at her suspiciously.

"Yeah, sure," I said, smiling lightly at the people I'd just met to mask the wariness I felt before I turned around and started walking.

"Don't forget to take down the license plate number! They'll need that inside," Jasmine told me. I backtracked to take a picture of Jasmine's plate before walking toward the store alone.

When I was a few steps away from the wooden porch, I

glanced back over my shoulder, making the briefest eye contact with Theo. Butterflies took flight in the depths of my stomach, swarms of them—all in response to his arresting smile.

I forced myself forward, worrying every silly little schoolgirl emotion he'd made me feel had been reflected clear as day on my face. It was the curse of the redhead—our emotions and reactions were so easily displayed on our faces.

My footfalls echoed on the old wooden planks as I climbed the porch steps leading to the store. I walked through the open door and paused inside of it, taking in my surroundings. To my right was a long counter with the cash register, and to the left was rows of shelves filled with all kinds of supplies. Dry foods, snacks, cases of water bottles, tarps and anything else one might need.

It was like a genuine general store from the frontier days—with newer products, mind you. I couldn't help but take my time, soaking it in. I loved places like this; places that felt like you were in another time completely.

I headed towards the counter, and the woman behind it smiled at me as I approached.

"Just parking, or are you camping?" she asked.

"Both," I replied, leaning against the counter.

"How many of you, and how many nights? Will you be renting a canoe or kayak?"

"There are two of us for four nights, and we brought a canoe." I answered pleasantly, and the woman set to filling out a ticket receipt.

"License plate number and vehicle type, please?" she asked.

I pulled up the picture and recited the plate number and vehicle type. While I waited for her to write it down, I glanced around the store.

"Have you ever camped along the French River before?" the woman asked, making friendly conversation.

I laughed lightly. "I've never camped at all, actually. This will be a first for me." I replied. "But I'm going with a bunch of experts," I added hastily when I noticed the alarm on the woman's face.

"Oh, that's good then." She relaxed and went back to filling out the permits. While she did that, I continued looking around with interest.

The thick hardwood floors and wooden embellishes added to the aesthetic of an old general store. It was exactly like taking a step back in time. Even the postcards in the rack sitting on the counter by the register had an old-timey charm to them. On a whim I grabbed one, tossing it down on the counter.

The cash register dinged as the woman rang it in. "That'll be ninety dollars and thirty-five cents," she said. After paying, I accepted the permits from her outstretched hand. "Enjoy your trip! I'm sure you'll love it, it's such a beautiful place."

"Thank you!" I replied over my shoulder.

By the time I returned to the boat launch, Jasmine and Theo had already gotten the canoe down and were loading it up with the camping supplies.

"Put the parking permit in the car, Lux! We'll need to bring the camping permits in case someone comes by to check that we have them."

Nodding, I veered off to do as Jasmine had instructed. I opened the passenger door and reached in, placing the parking permit against the windshield. I tucked the postcard into the glove box and straightened, closing the door before bringing the camping permits over to the canoe.

Jasmine took the papers from my outstretched hand and put them in the small waterproof container along with her phone. I'd been tempted to leave mine behind in her car, but worried about the potential of someone breaking in and taking it—or missing an important email.

Turning, I headed back to the car to help finish unloading it, ignoring my phone—still buzzing and overwhelmed with Snap updates—in the centre console.

There wasn't much left, and I was able to carry the rest of it over to the stony beach by myself. Theo met me there.

"Here, let me get that for you."

His voice was decadent, filling me with saccharine sensations. Our eyes made contact yet again, tension of the sweetest kind building. Theo smiled again, his white teeth flashing against his lips as he took the last of the bags from me. I turned on my heel, feeling a little off balance, and went to go move the car while he loaded the supplies into our canoe.

I slid behind the wheel and started the engine, moving the car to an open spot in the parking lot. Getting out, I hesitated by the door for a moment, staring at my phone. The likelihood I'd get a signal while camping was low, but I couldn't imagine letting the next several days pass without once checking my email. I wasn't planning on being on it the whole time, but I wanted the option of checking to see if any of the jobs I'd applied to responded. I knew I might want to take a few pictures, too, since it had been so long since Jas and I had last hung out.

But I didn't want to be bombarded with Snaps. My amusement of the app had died on the spot the moment I'd received that Snap of Brinley and Scott together. Reaching back in, I grabbed my phone from the console and deleted the stupid app without any further hesitation.

Instant relief came with that choice.

My moment of celebration ended when I looked up and realized the majority of the group was watching me. I was that city girl, holding them up by playing on my phone. Cheeks flushing, I walked quickly, not wanting to delay the others any longer.

"Everything okay?" Jas asked me when I reached her.

"Yeah, everything's fine." I smiled, showing her that I was, indeed, fine.

"Good. Put the keys and your phone in here," she passed me the waterproof container. I did as she asked, putting the keys and my phone in the waterproof container along with the permits and Jasmine's phone. I passed her the container and she tucked it beneath the bench.

Our canoe was so packed with supplies, I couldn't see how it'd stay afloat once we were in it too, but Jasmine didn't seem concerned. She climbed into the back of the canoe, leaving the front for me.

I slipped my lifejacket on, eyeing the canoe with mistrust. Taking a deep breath, I put one foot inside. It wobbled and my heart jumped at the unfamiliar motion.

Strong, incredibly attractive hands came to grip the nose of the canoe, steadying it. I looked up, meeting Theo's eyes.

He smiled at me encouragingly. The darker flecks in the irises of his deep green eyes made them seem endless. He had the kind of eyes I could willingly get lost in.

Shaken, I dropped my gaze and smiled tightly, gripping onto the side of the canoe as I climbed the rest of the way in. The exchange had taken but seconds, a moment suspended in time that was as arresting as it was fleeting. A moment that seemed more significant than most others; permanently etched in time. But before I could ponder too much on it, Jasmine began to paddle. She gave me instructions on how to do it, and I did my best to listen.

It wasn't so bad—in fact the way the paddle cut through the water was soothing, although I knew Jasmine was doing most of the work. I tried, but my arms were slow and cumbersome.

Plus...I was a little distracted. Under the guise of taking in the rather beautiful surroundings, I turned my head and was blessed with the sight of Theo cutting through the water gracefully, his muscles working with each powerful stroke as he paddled alongside Desmond. He said something to the bearded man that made them both laugh.

Even Theo's laugh was enticing—rich and free.

His eyes caught mine, and his smile grew, calling out to something inside me. My lips twitched, and I gave him the tiniest smile back. I felt silly for having been caught staring yet again. I forced my gaze forward instead, refocusing my attention on the sights ahead of me.

We'd already paddled beneath a large bridge and through a channel of rocky cliffs that lined the river. We passed some cottages with wooden steps leading to old, rickety docks, and an abandoned picnic table dangled precariously on a rocky bluff.

It was breathtaking. The air up north felt different from the air down south; clearer, somehow, and everything seemed brighter, even behind my sunglasses. The energy around me was mellow. The group I travelled with wasn't boisterous, but they chatted merrily amongst themselves with a familiarity that both calmed and entertained me.

It also made me painfully aware that I'd let things like friendships and connections fall to the wayside in recent years, I had been so focused on finishing school. I used an old relationship as a security blanket, letting it put a buffer between me and my new classmates. I'd refuse invites out because I had a boyfriend, and eventually the invitations had come less and less. My peers realized I wasn't going to take time off studying to join them.

Looking at the friendships Jasmine now had with people she'd met throughout college, I regretted not taking the time to make any new lasting friendships of my own.

But I had been so outside of my comfort zone, that the only way to press forward had been to wrap myself up in what was comfortable and familiar. Studying, schoolwork—that was familiar, I could do that. So was remaining in a relationship I wasn't even happy with, simply because it was all I'd known for so long.

I'd stumbled across a quote by George Santayana recently, about how familiarity breeds contempt only when it breeds inattention. It made me realize that inattention had killed my relationship with Scott long before my sister had taken him to bed.

About an hour into paddling, my arms began to ache. "Can we stop for a minute? I need to put sunscreen on," I asked. Jasmine nodded and set her paddle over her lap. She reached beneath her feet and grabbed a bottle of sunscreen, tossing it to me.

I miraculously caught it and began to apply it. My fair skin always burned, so I'd become an expert at applying sunscreen I was done within seconds and went to toss the bottle back.

"Keep it up there," Jasmine grinned, grabbing her paddle again. "We're almost at the campsite. Besides, you have shitty aim."

"I do not," I frowned, rubbing gingerly at my biceps.

"Have you forgotten the incident with Trina?" she snorted, and I stuck my tongue out at her over my shoulder. Trina had been a girl at our high school. I'd broken her nose in grade ten— accidentally of course. We'd been forced to play volleyball in gym class, and when it was my turn to serve, the ball took an unscheduled journey of its own and smashed into Trina's face. I'd felt so terrible, I'd cried more than she did.

Jas was right, though. My aim wasn't the greatest, and the sunscreen would end up in the water if I attempted it, but it was a relief to hear we were nearly there. I picked up the paddle again, bringing it through the water with a determined—albeit *painful*—steady stroke.

Theo and Desmond had passed us some time ago, and were up ahead with Talia, leading the group in their kayaks, which seemed to cut faster through the water. Kai and Zoey were a little way ahead of us, seemingly in their own little world. Her occasional laughter at something he'd said would drift back over the water.

Jasmine and I were lagging, held back due to my inexperience. I wasn't as precise with the paddle as she was. My arms weren't used to the vigorous workout, but never-the-less I persisted, too stubborn to quit, pushing my aching biceps until we reached a segment in the river divided by rocky cliffs. We stayed to the left of the river, paddling past three of the large rocks.

More glaciated rock cliffs lined the river, sloping downward to the forested area in behind. At the top of one steep-walled gorge, two people stood: a lean, tall man wearing swim trunks and a small, pixie-like woman with long blonde hair holding a camera that obscured most of her face. A large brown and white dog stood beside the woman, his tail wagging. The couple waved, and the dog barked—although the wind carried the sound of it away.

"That'd be Baz and Rhiannon! You'll love them." Jasmine reassured me. "Rhiannon is a photographer—don't mind the camera. She brings it everywhere."

Unease settled in my stomach. "Great. I hope she doesn't plan on taking any of me."

Jasmine sent a sympathetic look my way. She knew I could be weird about photos. That little quirk of mine could be traced back to my mother, and her obsession with the perfect photo. Mom was used to modelling, so being in front of the camera felt natural to her the way it felt natural to Brinley. Dad and I were awkward, one of us always blinking or smiling not quite right. Christmas portraits were always a feat and a half, and Mom never seemed satisfied with the end result.

It was silly, but things like that had put a lot of pressure on me. Pressure to be perfect and happy, even if I wasn't feeling that. It'd set Brinley on a path of self-destruction, too, as she vied with other influencers for likes and attention.

Although I had social media accounts, I didn't frequently post to them or check them. They were locked down and private, I didn't care for likes or views. I mostly had them to peek in on what my friends and family were up to. It was a convenient way of keeping up with everybody's lives when I was too busy with school to make calls. In fact, the last photo I'd posted had been taken with Jasmine when we were at the Eaton Centre in December.

I watched as the three kayaks disappeared around the side of the latest cliff. A few minutes later, Kai and Zoey followed suit. Finally, a sandy beach came into view. From what I could see, beyond the sandy beach there was a lot of pine covered hills and rocky cliffs.

"We're here!" Jasmine declared.

"Really?" I arched a brow, wondering where we were going to set up our tent. Didn't you need flat ground for setting up tents? The hills looked far too steep, and the beach too sandy, the rocks too...rocky. But I bit back my questions, forcing myself to release some of my tedious need for control. Jasmine and her friends knew what they were doing, I just had to trust them.

"This is the best campsite on the river. I wasn't sure it would be available, but I'm glad it is! It's a good thing Baz and Rhiannon got here early enough to snag it for us. You're going to love it," she promised, steering the canoe toward the beach. "There's even a thunderbox!"

"What's a thunderbox?" I asked, glancing at her over my shoulder.

"It's a box over a hole in the woods that you do your business in," she explained. "Like an outhouse, but without the coverage."

I turned forward, blinking with reluctant acceptance. I suppose it *was* better than trying to squat. I hoped it was far enough off the beaten path that I wouldn't have an audience, yet close enough to camp that I wouldn't get lost or eaten by a bear.

Feeling my anxiety rising, I drew in a controlled breath, focusing on the sound of nature around me; at the waves lapping gently against the side of the canoe and the birds chirping. Instantly, I felt the anxiety decreasing.

It really was beautiful; I could see why Jasmine was so sure I'd fall in love with camping. I still didn't believe *that* was possible, but the landscape and the scenery already had my heart. I'd marveled at the natural rock formations as we'd paddled in, having never seen anything quite like it in person. Perhaps in pictures, but never looming so impossibly tall over me.

It made me feel incredibly small, and a part of something huge.

The rest of the group had reached the beach before us, and they'd all set to unpacking.

Theo stood on the beach beside his kayak. He'd tossed his life jacket into his kayak and still hadn't bothered to put a shirt on. Not that I wanted him to—it was distracting in the best way possible, but I still would need to work on not gaping at him. We were camping, and I'd be gifted this sight of him shirtless more often than not.

My eyes tracked across his golden chest on their own accord, appreciating the hard lines and curves of his body. I turned my head when he looked up, not wanting to get caught. When he went back to unloading his supplies, I snuck another look; he caught me. Turned out he was watching me as much as I was watching him. This time, I didn't avert my eyes.

The front end of the canoe hit the sand, and it came to a stop. Before I could blink, Theo was there, effortlessly tugging the canoe so that the nose was fully on the beach. He held out a hand, offering to assist my climb out.

I smiled my thanks, but chose to ignore his outstretched hand—even if a part of me wanted to touch him—just because.

Although this was new to me, I was a quick learner, and I'd adjusted to the rocking motion of the canoe during the long trip down the river. I was no longer scared of it, and there wasn't much to fear anyway now that we'd made it to the beach.

Not wanting to appear like a damsel in distress, I hopped out on my own, my flip-flop covered feet splashing into the two inches of water.

4

THE LURE

I DREW MY HAND AWAY, a bemused smile on my face as I watched the stubborn determination play in Lux's eyes. Those eyes—I'd never seen eyes like hers before. They were the colour of fog over the lake on a rainy day, and the moment I'd looked into their depths, I felt something stir and take shape within me, making me feel complete.

She was out of her element. Even if Jasmine hadn't told us in advance, as experienced as I was, I could always tell a beginner. The way Lux's face had paled when she put one foot into the canoe had been indication enough. I'd wager she'd never set foot in a canoe until that very moment. My response to steady the canoe for her had been automatic, and I would have done it even without being immensely attracted to her.

But it appeared Lux didn't need my help this time. She jumped out, her feet splashing in the two inches of water the front of the canoe rested in. Jasmine hopped out too, the water going up to the middle of her calves, and the two of them began to pull the canoe the rest of the way onto the beach.

I could tell when my services weren't needed, and it didn't bother me any. I went back to my kayak and started grabbing my gear; my tent, mattress and sleeping bag, my cooler and food, and set them on the beach. Once my kayak was empty, I carried everything over to the wooded hill on the left side of the beach. I found a spot and began to set up my small two-person tent.

My hands and fingers worked blindly out of habit, as I'd done it hundreds of times before. My love of camping had been spurred from my nature-loving father and grandfather. My father worked at the nickel mine—like his dad before him, and his dad's dad. Whenever Dad did have time off, we'd spend it outside, be it fishing or camping. My grandpa and little sister, Olivia, would usually join us, too.

Over the years, we'd camped in all the provincial parks in Ontario. Although Dad loved the outdoors, he wasn't as knowledgeable as my grandpa had been about the land.

It was because of my grandfather that I'd decided to be an environmental geoscientist. Now, I got paid to collect rock and mineral samples for an international consulting firm. I still worked in the mining sector, travelling to different mines to test ground and rock samples. I mostly worked out of our facility in Sudbury unless they needed me to travel to a site.

My job was rewarding and challenging, but it consumed a lot of my time. I couldn't remember the last time I'd taken a trip for pleasure, not work.

I arranged my sleeping bag and pillow inside the tent, then tossed my hiking bag inside and zipped it up. With that task completed, I stood up and stretched, working the kinks out of my back and shoulders, and risked another glance in Lux's direction.

She was remarkable; and for some unexplainable reason she

felt like both a memory and a premonition. If I were a betting man, I could count on the fact I was looking at my future.

I'd never bought into the whole love at first sight thing before, but then again…I'd never been struck quite like this upon meeting someone before. I wanted to get to know her, to find out why she called to me.

I thought about offering to help but it looked like they were catching up, and I didn't want to intrude.

With my tent set up and nothing else to keep me on the hill, I made my way to Desmond's tent. He'd already finished setting up his one-person tent and was sitting on his cooler in front of it, drinking a beer. He spotted me coming and stood up to open his cooler, fishing one out for me.

"Thanks," I said, grinning. We were on vacation, and vacation beers were always a good idea. He tossed me a can, and I caught it, popping the tab. I took a deep sip, the cold liquid refreshing in my dry throat, and looked over to where Lux and Jasmine were setting up their tent.

Lux was fluid in her movements, like a dancer. Gracefully crouching and standing, reaching and pulling. It was hard to believe she'd never set up a tent before, what with the easy way she moved, but I could hear Jasmine giving her instructions.

Her tank top rode up enough to reveal a sliver of porcelain skin, and I felt the blood rushing south. I turned back to Desmond and tried not to focus on the sound of her voice.

"How's work been?" I asked him, before taking another sip of my beer.

"It's good." He replied, shrugging. "Back on nights next week."

"Brutal." Desmond worked as an operator in the mines— another generational miner. His dad had worked there, too.

Lux let out a laugh, the sound of it light and airy and free. I looked over, watching her fight to recover from whatever funny thing Jasmine had said. Even from twelve feet away, I could see the dimple appear on her right cheek above the corner of her pink lips.

I caught her watching me, her grey eyes raking across my chest before they dropped slowly, following the trail of dark blond hair that disappeared into my swim trunks. When she saw that I was watching her, she turned her head quickly, the apples of her cheeks flushing with embarrassment at having been caught.

The slow slide of her eyes across my skin had done little to ease the heat I felt for her, and I couldn't stop the grin from spreading. Clearly, Lux was affected by me, too. Affected, but still hesitant.

"Let's see if Talia needs any assistance getting firewood," I joked, doubting it. Talia was more than capable of getting the firewood chopped on her own.

We headed toward the beach, passing Kai and Zoey as they set up their tent beside Baz and Rhiannon's. Rhiannon was discreetly creeping around the campsite with her camera, getting candid shots of everyone setting up while her two-year-old dog, Moose, roamed about beside her with the happiest dog grin on his face.

He spotted us and wandered over to me, sitting at my feet, his large tongue hanging out the side of his mouth as he panted. I stroked his soft head for a few minutes, until he caught sight of a chipmunk and took off after it, bolting away without a second glance.

It wasn't the first time he'd joined us for a camping trip, and I knew he wouldn't go far. He always had to be within five feet of Rhiannon, or at least have her in his line of sight, and she'd made her way up to the top of the hill to talk to Lux and Jasmine.

I resumed the short walk to the beach. There was a fire pit on the beach, and another one halfway up the rocky hill. When we used this site, we usually used the beach fire pit.

Talia was chopping logs that the previous campers had left with a small axe. She'd already ditched her shirt and was soaking up the sun in her bikini top and shorts. Baz sat in his camping chair, music pumping from a waterproof speaker ball with a cord attached to his phone. His head was bopping in time to the beat, but his eyes were fixated on his girlfriend, a slight smile playing on his lips as he watched her do her thing.

It wouldn't be long now before Baz was popping the question, too.

"Already set up?" I asked Talia, watching while the head of the axe split a piece of wood in two. Talia left it in the stump and looked up at me with a wide grin.

"I cheated and brought the pop-up tent," she shrugged. "Figured the less time I spent on set up and take down, the more time I'd have to drink and jump off cliffs."

"Jump off cliffs?" I turned at the sound of her voice. Lux, Jasmine, and Rhiannon had joined us on the beach. The corner of Lux's lips pulled in a concerned frown, and she looked to Jasmine for explanation.

"Yeah, cliff jumping," Jasmine explained as she set up her chair. "It's a lot of fun. There are a couple spots you can jump from here, but the really good cliffs are down the river."

"Oh," Lux said, setting up her own chair beside Jasmine's. "Is it safe?"

"Well..." Jasmine hesitated. "I guess it can be dangerous, but we know what we're doing. We know the safe spots to jump."

"Don't be scared, Princess!" Talia grinned, straightening up as she wiped the sweat off her brow. She wedged the axe into the stump.

Lux frowned upon hearing the nickname, unsure of whether or not it was meant to be a dig.

"In fact, I'll show you how it's done. Right here, right now! There's nothing to be afraid of. Anyone else in?"

"Fuck yeah, I'm in!" Baz shouted, hopping up from his chair.

Jasmine smiled warmly at her friend. "You don't have to jump if you don't want to, Lux, it's not mandatory," she added, reaching into their cooler and grabbing two cans of hard cider. She tossed one to Lux, who caught it easily, the concerned frown still etched across her pretty lips.

We made our way up the rocky hill. The incline didn't seem steep from the beach, but once we'd made it to the top of the hill, the drop was drastic—at least for novice eyes.

Jumping from the top of this cliff would mean broken limbs if not a broken neck, but to the right of the cliff, there was a small pathway that led to a ledge halfway down. You had to press your back against the rocks and move sideways to reach the narrow ledge. It wasn't as high as the other cliffs down the river, but it was still fun for a quick swim. The better cliffs would come tomorrow, when we'd rested enough to make the paddle down river.

I followed Baz, Talia, and Desmond, gripping the edge of the rock with my hand before dropping easily to the lower level. I moved along the lower ledge, my toes easily finding purchase against the narrow rocky ledge.

I swore by water shoes for this reason alone. Water shoes felt about as close to bare feet as you could get, and the textured grip prevented my feet from getting cut up and helped me find tenure on the slippery rocks.

Glancing up, I caught sight of Lux's copper hair billowing in the wind as she stood at the top of the cliff, looking down, Jasmine and Rhiannon beside her. I knew she was watching us, and I couldn't help but show off a little, kicking off the edge of the ledge with my feet and racing Talia to the water.

I couldn't tell who broke the water's surface first, as we'd jumped at the same time, but when I came up for air, I couldn't see Lux anymore. Letting out a sigh, I waded for a moment, eyes closed against the sun's rays.

"So...the new girl is hot," Talia's voice came from behind me, and I cracked open an eye at her. She was treading water beside Baz, her eyes focused on the rocky edge Rhiannon, Jasmine, and Lux were carefully walking. There was a perch about half a foot from the water for those who didn't feel like lunging off the side of the cliff.

"Yeah. And?"

"And it seems like you've got your eye on her. You gonna make a move, or can I?"

I snorted, which brought water into my nostrils and made me cough. "I don't think she swings that way."

Talia grinned. "I overheard Jasmine and her talking; she's just broken up with her boyfriend."

"So?"

"Perfect time to get beneath someone new," Talia's grin widened with mischief, and she waggled her eyebrows at me. "It's also the perfect time to experiment with…well, the other team. Who knows, she might *really* hate men after her heartbreak. I can offer her comfort."

"I wouldn't bet on that," I said, thinking about how Lux's eyes had raked over my body. "Besides, aren't you with Eliza?"

"We're not official," Talia replied, shrugging and trying to act indifferent. I could tell that mentioning Eliza upset her, but she seemed to shove that thought from her head.

I looked back at the cliffs. Lux, Jasmine, and Rhiannon were waiting on the lower ledge, looking up to the ledge we'd jumped off. Kai and Zoey were perched on it, waiting to jump in.

Zoey had her attention on Kai—worry and concern in her eyes, although she worked to keep her smile unaffected. Kai had epilepsy, and although he was on anti-seizure medication, Zoey had to keep a close watch on him. Sometimes, he'd forget to take his meds, or a seizure would happen anyway. Zoey was well versed in reading the signs, and she could always predict when he was going to have another seizure.

I'd known Kai since we were kids, and he was as independent as they came and didn't like having his epilepsy hold him back. Kai liked to experience all the adventures life had to offer. Zoey knew this well, and did her best to give him his space, but I knew she worried.

A couple of years ago, Kai had a stroke and had fallen off the roof of a house he was working on with Baz. He'd broken his leg and terrified us all, especially Zoey.

Zoey watched him closely as he pushed off the ledge and jumped into the water below. She didn't seem to breathe again until he'd resurfaced and swam out of the way. She waited until it was clear before jumping in herself.

On the lower ledge, Jasmine, Lux and Rhiannon hung out. Lux was finishing up putting sunscreen on—the sight of her hands rubbing it over her shoulders made my throat constrict. I looked away, and immediately got splashed in the face by Talia.

"Thought you needed help cooling down," she told me, pausing to splash herself in the face. "I know I did," she added with a wicked grin.

A splash sounded, and when I looked back over, Rhiannon had jumped in, with Moose following right on her heels. Moose swam while still managing to hold onto his stick, heading straight to Rhiannon.

Baz saw how hard he was working to catch up with Rhiannon and raced him, swimming toward her as fast as he could. Moose barked around the stick as he swam, almost losing hold of it.

When Baz caught up with Rhiannon, he wrapped his arm around her waist under water. She let out a squeal as he pulled her toward him that quickly dissolved into laughter. He tugged her away from the cliffs, swimming out a little way from the rest of us. Moose swam quicker, finally losing the stick with his attempts at reaching them.

I turned my head to avoid the large dog as he splashed by, and when I looked back, Lux was testing the water by dipping her manicured toes in. The white string bikini she wore gave me heart palpitations.

Jasmine crept up behind her and shoved her in, and Lux let out a startled yelp before disappearing in the water. She resurfaced, teeth chattering.

"You asshole! It's freezing!" she laughed, swimming toward the ledge. She tried to hoist her body up, and when she couldn't find purchase on the slippery edge, she lunged forward, reaching for Jasmine's legs.

But Jasmine dodged her hand, leaping over her head into the water, splashing the rest of us. Wiping the water from my eyes, I was greeted with the affecting visual of Lux biting her lip as she watched me.

Lux swam out to join us, stopping in front of me. She treaded water, her face low in it, her eyes to the left behind me. Jasmine let out a squeal and tried to swim away when she realized Lux was coming for her.

And she was. There was a determination playing in Lux's eyes that sparked a fire in my blood. That determined spirit was such a turn on for me. Lux swam after her, splashing her a little before relenting when Jasmine started reverse kicking water at her. They broke out into fits of laughter.

"Okay, okay! I give. No more revenge," Lux giggled, swimming away from Jasmine and back towards the ledge. "Right now, anyway."

She swam past me, her eyes meeting mine once more. When she reached the ledge, she tried to climb out, struggling to find purchase on the slippery ledge.

I swam up beside her. "Need a hand?"

She eyed me with consideration, arching a delicate auburn brow. "Sure."

I moved closer to her, my fingers splaying out to cup her rear. My fingers tingled where they made contact with her skin, as if I was touching an electric current.

As much as I wanted to linger, I pushed her forward, holding her while she found her footing on the ledge and scrambled up.

"Thanks."

"No problem," I told her. She smiled at me over her shoulder, wringing out her dark red curls, the water cascading down her body to pool at her feet.

As tantalizing as the view was, I had to force myself underwater to stop from staring greedily at her. She wasn't putting on a show for me, so why did I want to watch her like she was? Like every movement, no matter how slight, was designed to capture my attention?

The cold and momentary lack of oxygen zapped some of my senses back, and when I came up for air, Lux was gone from the ledge and so was her towel.

5

FIRE AND FOG

BY THE TIME Jasmine and Lux rejoined us on the beach, it was after five o'clock and we had the fire roaring. Several sausages and an aluminum tray of homemade mac and cheese were cooking on the wire grill placed over the hot coals.

Desmond patiently tended to the sausages with metal tongs, turning them every so often so they'd brown while Zoey sat on the other side of the fire, stirring the mac and cheese with a wooden spoon. Her legs were crossed, her expression peaceful as she rested against Kai's knees. He sat behind her in a camping chair, sipping a beer, bobbing along to The Tragically Hip, his favourite band.

With the distant echo of the loons down the river, a sense of peace settled over me. We'd gone camping as a group many times before. Most of us had grown up together in Sudbury, spending a lot of the weekends in our late teens camping on

Baz's family's extensive property near Whitewater Lake, or one of the local provincial parks.

The French River was a group favourite, and we'd been camping here many times before. We knew the best routes, the best places to jump off cliffs, and we knew where all the best campsites were.

We'd done this so many times together that we'd learned how to work in sync for a more effective trip. It was easier when everyone brought a little bit of something. Less supplies, no duplicates, and we were able to make the ice last a hell of a lot longer. It felt less like work this way, too.

It was a tradition of ours to get together at least a few times throughout the summer for portage camping trips.

Lux brought down a camp chair, unfolding it beside Jasmine's, across the fire from me. I stood with one foot on the stump we'd used to chop wood, trying my hardest not to stare in her direction. I didn't want to make her feel uncomfortable, like the pretty new toy at the playground, but she was damn hard not to look at.

"Feels good to be back here, huh?" Desmond remarked quietly, following my gaze. I glanced back at him.

He wasn't usually much of a talker, and when he did talk, it wasn't about superficial things like how attractive someone was. But he was observant, and he'd caught me checking out Lux a hundred times already today. This was his subtle way of calling me out for it, his knowing eyes missing nothing.

"It does." I nodded, letting him know that: *yes, I do think she's pretty.* I was still looking at him when his gaze moved from Lux to Jasmine, and the look in his eyes changed slightly. It was almost completely undetectable, but I'd caught on to him. He had feelings for her, although I doubted he'd ever act on them.

I'd known Desmond my whole life—our dads had worked together, and we'd gone to elementary school together. We'd later met Baz, Kai, and Zoey in high school. After graduating,

Desmond went to trades school for welding, and I went to Trent to get a degree in Environmental Geoscience before heading to Laurentian University to get my PhD in Mineral Deposits and Precambrian Geology.

Shortly after graduating, Desmond started working for the same mining company as our fathers, while I landed a job as a junior environmental geoscientist at an international consulting firm. The firm provided a broad range of engineering, geosciences and environmental services to the mining, water resources, hydropower, geotechnical, oil sands, oil and gas, and government sections.

In the last six years, I'd gained a lot of invaluable experience in acid rock drainage and metal leaching, as well as mine waste hydrogeochemistry and geochemical sampling. I lived and worked primarily in the Greater Sudbury area, but sometimes my job brought me to our many other locations in other countries.

I'd just got back from checking in on one of our mines in British Columbia, and in three weeks' time, I would be flying out to one of our mines in Peru to run some tests on the soil. I was scheduled to be there for at least a week.

I loved my job. There was something new to do every day, even when I wasn't travelling outside of the province on contracts. The money for a junior geoscientist was good, so good that I'd been able to pay off my student debts and go in on a duplex with Desmond.

Of course, the duplex had been in dire need of repairs when we'd purchased it, so we'd gotten it for a steal. It took a year for us to tackle the extensive—and expensive—renovations, hiring Baz and Kai to do most of the work. Desmond and I worked on the project too, whenever we had a spare minute.

After we'd finished renovating, we began to rent out one side of the duplex to university students. That was how Jasmine and Talia had joined our group of friends, they'd both rented rooms off us five years ago, and we'd all hit off.

Another laugh brought my attention to her again. My gaze collided with Lux's, and I felt the pull and could taste the tension between us, like an impending storm. There's nothing I loved more than a good storm.

Desmond flipped the sausages over the crackling flames. I drew in lungfuls of fresh, northern air, appreciating being back in Ontario again.

I had done a lot of travelling since I started working for the firm, but out of all the places I'd been, nothing compared to my home province. It was good to be back, among friends and family.

I was happy we'd chosen the French River for our trip this year. Nice and secluded, it allowed us an opportunity to appreciate nature and be boisterous about it. The sites were so spread out that we could play music without disturbing other campers, and it was close to Sudbury, where we lived.

We'd all gotten busier with each year that passed; between new jobs, demanding careers, and life in general—our group trips were slowing. Hell, Zoey and Kai were engaged now, and getting married in the fall.

They'd be the first in our circle to tie the knot, and I couldn't be more excited for them. Zoey and Kai had overcome a lot in their relationship, with Kai's seizures and the stroke. Things had been difficult for them, but their love had always come easily.

If two people deserved a happily ever after, if it was them. But watching them together now had me thinking about my own destiny. I wasn't sure what that was, yet, but...

My eyes were pulled back to the siren across the fire. She was so damn gorgeous, a seductress with those lips and curves —curves I wanted to escape in for hours. But there was something sweet and unassuming about her. Angelic, even. It was difficult not to want to know her, to know exactly what it was about her that called to me. Was it just her looks, or something more?

I wasn't afraid of my immediate attraction to her, not the way I would have been a few years ago. Now, it felt like I'd been waiting for her—or waiting for the feeling like the one I got when I looked at her. It was a feeling of...*more*. Of endless possibilities.

And I knew that was a crazy thought to have after just having met someone, but there was something different about her. Something potent and essential, something elemental. She'd bewitched me, and I found I wasn't even mad about it. Instead, I was fascinated by not only her, but my reaction to her. My thirst to know more about her was similar to my thirst to learn about naturally occurring inorganic elements and compounds. I wanted to learn about her internal structure, about all the chemical compositions that made up her breathtaking form.

Lux leaned forward and whispered something to Jasmine, her eyes aglow with conspiracy. I grinned, wagering they were probably talking about me. At least, by her smile and the glow in her cheeks I'd hoped they were.

"Dinner's ready! Dig in," Zoey sang. Lux held back, waiting until everyone else had grabbed something to eat. She filled her plate with mac and cheese and a sausage, sitting down in her seat across the fire.

Everyone dug in, and for several moments nobody talked. The crackling fire, lapping water, and the call of a loon on the river were the soundtrack to our meal. Zoey's salty, cheesy mac and cheese hit the spot, and the companionable silence made me feel at ease with the world.

Once the food had been consumed and the mess cleaned up, we stayed seated around the fire, drinking and catching up on the things we'd missed in each other's lives. Although most of us had stayed local, our jobs and daily demands meant we didn't get together as much as we used to.

Back when everyone had lived at or near the duplex, it was easier to get together. We'd have a bonfire in the backyard every weekend. About a year ago, Baz and Rhiannon had purchased their first house together and moved. They now lived in a bungalow twenty-minutes north of Sudbury.

So, it was good to sit down around a fire, share a few drinks, and catch up. One of the most interesting stories of the night came from Rhiannon.

Earlier this year, she had photographed a celebrity wedding. She and Baz had signed an NDA and couldn't talk about it until the couple announced the wedding. Rhiannon was officially free to talk about it, and show off her photos. It was *huge* news.

In an exclusive five page spread with Music Magazine, Travis Channing spoke about falling in love with the girl of his dreams. Rhiannon's photographs of the couple's small, intimate wedding in Banff, Alberta made the front page.

"It's crazy how many followers I've gained since they published the magazine. And how many inquires I've gotten for weddings! I'm booked up for next year already, and I've started taking bookings for two years from now!"

"That's so cool! How did you get the job?" Lux asked, captivated by Rhiannon's story.

"Through Baz's mutual friend." Rhiannon answered. "The job fell in my lap. Gordon, Baz's friend, arranged for me to meet with the wedding planner. Her name was Elle Thompson. I only ever communicated with her; I had no idea who the mystery couple was that I'd be photographing until I arrived to shoot their wedding."

"I had my suspicions," Baz claimed with a smile. "Gordon doesn't know many celebrities. Of course, he does work on a lot of rich people's cottages, so it could have been a rich client."

Jasmine was on her phone, on Rhiannon's Gram account, showing Lux the photographs.

"Oh, these are stunning!" Lux gushed.

"I can't believe we're going to have the same wedding photographer as Travis Channing," Zoey said dreamily, looking up at Kai over her shoulder. He was whittling one end of a stick, and he paused what he was doing to press a kiss to her lips.

"I can't wait for your wedding." Rhiannon grinned. "I have some ideas in mind!"

"Oooh! Tell me!" Zoey squealed, shuffling closer to Rhiannon so they could talk wedding stuff.

"So, Lux. You just graduated, right?" I asked, trying to make casual conversation—and learn a little more about her. I tried not to appear overly interested, but it was so hard for me to not show my hand when faced with an exciting new discovery.

"Yeah…with my degree in medical radiation sciences."

"What made you want to get into that?"

"When I was seven, I broke my leg falling off the monkey bars. I had to get x-rays, and I remember being so afraid of the machine. There was a radiology technologist that calmed me right down. She took the time to teach me a little about the machine, so I would know how it worked and wouldn't fear it."

"That was really nice of her," Rhiannon remarked, her face softening. Rhiannon had spent a lot of time in hospitals as a child, she had a bunch of her own stories about medical professionals.

Rhiannon had Ehlers-Danlos syndrome, a rare inherited condition that affects connective tissues such as skin, tendons, ligaments, blood vessels, internal organs and bones. When she was a child, she'd had a major surgery to straighten her spine and put in rods.

"Yeah, it was." Lux nodded with agreement. "I always knew I wanted to do something in the medical field, like my dad—he's a cardiologist. But, I don't know. That one experience stuck out in my head…and when it came time to pick a program, I read up on that one and just knew."

"That's cool. Now the fun part of job hunting begins," Zoey chuckled.

"Yeah, I've already started that fun process," Lux laughed lightly. "I'm hoping I can find an entry position somewhere soon. I'm not picky about where I have to go, so I've been applying all over the province."

"Hopefully something will come up soon for you," Rhiannon said.

"Thank you." Lux smiled.

"Speaking of x-rays…" Kai said, a mischievous grin on his face. "What's one body part you wouldn't mind losing?" he asked Zoey, and Lux's eyes widened in surprise.

"Oooh are we going to play campfire questions?" Zoey exclaimed, clapping her hands.

Noticing Lux's confusion, I leaned forward. "It's a game we all started playing when we were teens while camping in Baz's backyard. Basically, you have to come up with a question and the person to your left has to answer before asking their own question to the person on *their* left, and so on and so forth."

"I think I'd be okay with losing a toe." Zoey said, after I'd had a chance to explain the game to Luz.

"You can't pick a toe," Kai frowned. "That's so lame. Anyone can live without a toe."

"Toes are actually pretty important for your balance, so. I stand by my answer," Zoey said firmly. She turned to look at me. "What's a nickname you've had that you secretly hated?"

I narrowed my eyes at her, resenting her question—and the rules of the game. If you wanted to omit answering a question, you had to take a drink. If you couldn't *think* of a question, you had to take a drink. It was essentially a fun drinking game, and a fun way to pass the time.

I drank the contents of my beer instead of answering. There

was no way in hell I was going to announce to Lux that my nickname in public school had been Chubster. I'd been a chunky kid, but the nickname had come from the unfortunate time I'd popped a boner while in front of the class reading my speech on the difference between rocks and minerals. It was one of those pre-pubescent involuntary boners, but it happened in front of our entire homeroom so...yeah. Not my finest moment, or memory, for that matter.

Zoey cackled in delight, knowing full well why I wouldn't answer.

"Which famous person do you do the best impression of?" I asked Talia.

Talia arched a brow, grinning before launching into the best impersonation of Jim Carey from Ace Ventura, strolling over to the fire to grab another sausage.

Then it was Talia's turn. She turned to Lux, her eyes twinkling with mischief. "So, Lux. What do you prefer: tacos or sausage?" she asked, waiting for Lux to fall into her trap.

"Well, these were very good but I think I prefer tacos," Lux answered, thinking Talia was referring to food.

"Me too! I *love* tacos. Are you single?" Talia questioned. She was bold and abrupt, and not one to shy away from intrusive questions—and she was baiting me.

I'd met Talia while at Laurentian University, and she'd quickly become a close friend of mine. She'd started renting a room from us after we finished renovations on the duplex, and she still lived there, working as a Wetlands Research Assistant for the Lake Laurentian Conservation Area. One of Talia's favourite pastimes throughout our time at university was trying to pick up the girls I was interested in before I could whenever we went out together. She'd place a wager, enticing me to participate in her shenanigans.

It was her way of prying me out of my natural state of awkward shyness when it came to the opposite sex, her way of challenging me to go for what I wanted. Sometimes, it worked in Talia's favour, and sometimes I got the girl. Talia was an excellent wingman.

I knew her intention this time around came from Talia wanting to push me into making a move. There was interest in Lux's gazes, in the shy smiles she'd given me each time I caught her looking—and vice versa.

"Um, yes…I'm single," Lux answered, her gaze moving from Talia to me. Likely wondering what tacos and sausage had to do with it, or if Talia was fishing for information on my behalf. But I didn't need Talia to talk to her for me. I was letting her get settled in. It was easy to see that Lux didn't feel fully comfortable around us yet, and I wanted her to feel comfortable before I made a move. Even if she kept looking at me with those smoky quartz eyes.

"Lux is all about the sausage, Talia. Sorry!" Jasmine teased, answering for her friend.

"That's too bad," Talia said flirtatiously.

Lux, who'd been in the midst of drinking, coughed, her eyes widening with surprise, like she wasn't accustomed to being blatantly hit on. The blush returned, this time deeper. Once again, the attention seemed to make her uncomfortable.

I couldn't help but take in every little detail about her. The way her embarrassment coloured her cheeks, the way she smiled politely, like she was wishing the ground would open and swallow her whole. I wanted to know why she shied away from being the centre of attention, despite being as captivating as the setting sun over the river.

"But I honestly wouldn't blame you if you changed your mind about men and want to do a little taco experimenting!" Jasmine added with a cackle. Lux leveled her with a serious look before she burst out laughing, too.

"Oh, this sounds good. What did he do?!" Talia leaned forward, sensing there was a story.

Lux's laughter died. "He cheated." Jasmine went to say something, but Lux kicked her chair in warning.

"Damn, that sucks. I don't get why people cheat. There's no need for it anymore, not when there are so many people who want to be in polyamorous relationships. There are entire dating websites dedicated to it."

"Is there really?" Kai sounded surprised.

"Well, yeah. There are entire websites dedicated to all sorts of kinks," Talia informed him. "The Internet is a vast place."

"I'm really sorry, Lux. How long were you guys together?" Zoey asked.

She looked like she didn't really want to answer the question, but she did.

"Since high school."

Talia let out a low whistle. "That's a long time. I don't think I've had a relationship that's lasted longer than three months. But I think relationships are overrated, anyway. You don't need to be in one to be happy!"

Lux's gaze slid to me, then away just as quickly. I could make out the flush of her cheeks from the glow of the fire; she was embarrassed, either by the subject itself or the attention she was garnering from everyone else around the campfire. I didn't blame the others for being interested. We'd heard each other's stories before, but she was a mystery—one I wanted to unravel.

"Now that you're finished with school, where do you plan on going next?" Zoey asked Lux. The game of campfire questions had fallen to the wayside as everyone else seemed more interested in getting to know Lux.

She brought her beer to her lips and took a sip before replying. "I'm not sure, I've applied for a bunch of jobs in a bunch of different areas. It'll depend on where I get a call back from. I'm not really picky and I'll work at a medical clinic, but I'm hoping for a hospital position."

"I'd love to be a registered nurse and work with little kids. Right now, I'm just a PSW," Zoey remarked.

"Don't downplay what you do, babe," Kai lectured, placing a hand on her shoulder. "You know those old ladies you take care of would be lost without you."

Zoey peered up at him, an amused look on her face. "Only until they forget about me," she corrected with a light laugh. Then she looked back at Lux. "Dementia is a hell of a disease. A lot of my patients suffer from various stages of it. Some don't even know who their own family members are."

"That's sad," Lux looked like she wanted to weep. "My grandma had dementia. I don't remember much about her, she died when I was eight, but I remember how she forgot who I was by the end of it."

Zoey nodded, the two of them sharing a moment.

"I miss school—just the environment of learning. I graduated from the photography program a few years ago. Running my own business has been fun, but a huge learning curve," Rhiannon said.

"Finishing school does seem to be the easy bit. At least I'm not the only one struggling to figure it out, though!" Lux replied, grinning at Jasmine. "My little history buff."

Jasmine stood up and took a bow. "Thank you, thank you. It was dicey for a bit there—many times I wanted to throw in the towel and join an off-the-grid commune—but I have achieved what I set out to do. I now have my PhD in Human Studies and Interdisciplinarity!"

"What are you going to do with it?" Baz teased.

"I don't know yet," Jasmine answered honestly. "But hopefully, good things."

"Well, I for one hope you *do* go into politics. At least you'll remember the working poor and the most vulnerable," Zoey commented, earning a small smile from Jasmine.

Jasmine's father had been the Mayor of Guelph, and he'd

done a lot of good during the years he served. He was now the local MPP for Guelph. He often clashed with Dudley Wadsworth, the Premier of Ontario, but he got things done and he had the general respect of his constituents.

I'd met him a few times, and I'd liked him. It was easy to see where Jasmine got her huge heart from, and her desire to create positive change.

"Tomorrow we're going cliff jumping. You gonna join us, Princess?" Talia asked, leaning forward to poke at the fire with a stick.

Lifting my beer, I watched her, waiting on her answer while I took a sip.

"Yes," she replied, looking from Talia to me briefly before moving her gaze on to Jasmine. "I'm not sure if I'll actually jump, but I do want to see the cliffs."

"Excellent choice," Talia said, raising her beer to the air in salute. "I bet you'll jump. That, or Jasmine will shove you in."

"I wouldn't," Jasmine assured her, eyes wide with innocence. "No really, I wouldn't Lux. It's too high; I'd never do that to you. Anything less than five feet and its go time, though."

"Less than five feet?" Lux repeated, brow arching. "How tall is this cliff, and how do we climb up it?"

"There's a pathway to get to the top, it's a little steep but it's not too bad. There's about a fifty-five-foot drop," I replied, poking at the fire with a thick stick I'd found and whittled into a poker.

The colour faded from Lux's complexion.

"Moose can manage the path easily enough, so you'll be alright," Rhiannon supplied helpfully.

"Moose has four legs," Lux deadpanned, and Jasmine laughed at her look of discomfort.

"Don't worry, it's not as bad as it sounds." Zoey assured her. "The hike up, I mean. If you don't like heights, you won't like the fall."

"I don't jump, it's too high for me. You can keep me company if you'd like," Rhiannon offered, and Lux sent her a relieved smile, relaxing a little.

"Okay, that sounds fun. I'll get a camera's-eye view of the action that way."

"Ah, you noticed. Sorry about that," Rhiannon giggled. "I'm always looking for that perfect shot, you know? It's the curse of a photographer."

"I get it," Lux laughed lightly. "I always strive to get the right shot, too. Especially the first time around. Nothing sucks more than having to re-do x-rays because they turned out blurry."

"Ha! That's true. Well, I'm excited to get some shots tomorrow of everyone jumping."

Lux winced. "I'll try to stay out of your way. If you took my picture, you'd get endless captures of me being awkward—I'm not perfect shot material."

I found that hard to believe. She was too beautiful to not be the focal point in the room, any time she went anywhere.

"You're far too graceful to be considered awkward." I found myself commenting.

"Theo's right. I snuck a few shots of you and Jas setting up the tent. You definitely don't look awkward, you're a natural!" Rhiannon assured her. "But I get it, a lot of people aren't comfortable in front of the camera."

"How long have you been into photography?"

"Since I was twelve. My poppop was really into photography, and gave me my first camera," Rhiannon said, pausing to take a sip of her drink. "I've always loved documenting moments, so I specialize in weddings and lifestyle photography."

"You can officially call yourself a high-profile wedding photographer now," Baz bragged, and Rhiannon playfully slapped his chest with the back of her hand.

"Hardly!" Rhiannon giggled.

"What! It's true. Travis Channing *is* high-profile."

"Baz is right, Travis is one of the most popular country musicians right now," Jasmine added.

"Yeah, he's pretty cool, and his wife is a sweetheart."

"They covered travel expenses and I was even able to go as Rhi's assistant," Baz grinned with pride. "She nearly fainted when she saw who was getting married," he added, and we all laughed.

"Actually, *you* nearly fainted. I was fine," Rhiannon argued, rolling her eyes, although the smile never left her face.

WHISKEY WHISPERS

 *ux*

WE CARRIED ON, discussing work and life and other random topics. Close to midnight, Talia brought out a bottle of whiskey. My brow furrowed; I didn't usually drink hard liquor. I didn't usually drink at all, really.

Jasmine leaned over and whispered, "Again, it's not mandatory, Lux. But try to remember you're on vacation!"

"Want some?" Talia asked, grinning benevolently, and offering me the bottle.

I studied it for a moment before lifting my eyes, finding Theo watching me. His heated gaze made my throat dry. "Sure," I said, surprising myself as I reached for it.

Bringing it to my lips, I drank from the bottle. The harsh liquid hit the back of my throat and burned the whole way down—it was disgusting. I passed it to Jasmine, who did the same before handing it to Kai. I watched the bottle go around the fire until Theo took it.

His eyes locked on mine, his larynx working as he swallowed. The fire crackled and burned like the desire beneath my skin.

My skin prickled with awareness and arousal, the burn from the whiskey intensifying. I'd never felt seduced by a look before, and it was the most pleasantly peculiar thing. Still, I wasn't sure I wanted to act on the palpable attraction between us.

I tilted my head to break the connection as the whiskey went around the campfire again. Music pumped from the speaker ball, and conversations were happening all around me. Jasmine was talking to Desmond, animatedly moving her hands while she spoke, and Talia had her eyes closed as she sang along to her tenth most favourite song. She'd proclaimed every song that came on was her favourite.

Kai and Zoey seemed to be in their own little world, one where little existed outside of each other. Zoey was nestled in his arms, sitting in front of him. He held her close, whispering something in her ear that made her smile. My heart pulsed painfully, and I had to pull my gaze away and look at the fire before my eyes could well up. In all the years I'd spent with Scott, he'd never held me like that.

I don't even know *where* the sudden urge to cry came from. I wasn't missing Scott in the slightest. I suppose it was borne from the whiskey, and the loneliness I felt in that moment. The realization that I'd never *not* felt that same loneliness, even when I was with him, was more difficult to swallow than the whiskey.

What a colossal waste of my time.

Of course, I'd known, even if I hadn't wanted to admit it. I used my relationship with Scott—as lifeless as it was—as an excuse to not have to get wild in college the way my program peers were.

I hadn't made any new lasting friendships the way Jasmine had when she'd moved to Sudbury for college. She'd managed to find an entire new group of friends, ones that seemed to match her ideals, ones that seemed kind and friendly and fun. Friends that seemed like they were there to stay. Long-haul friends.

Jasmine was my one and only long-haul friend, but seeing how this group interacted had me wishing for more of them. Perhaps then my sister's betrayal, and my parent's indifference, wouldn't sting so much.

Movement drew my eyes from the flames, and I watched as Theo walked around the fire, adding wood, and poking at it with a sturdy stick, his concentration completely absorbed with the task. This allowed me a brief interlude to study him without notice.

He really *was* good looking, and for a moment my thoughts drifted to the box of condoms in my bag. My cheeks heated, and I was immediately thankful for the cover of the darkness. The last time I'd blushed so much had been in high school. I had a tendency of doing so whenever I felt embarrassed, and there had been *a lot* of embarrassing moments in high school. I don't know what it was about this group that had me blushing consistently—it wasn't that I was embarrassed. Theo's attractiveness alone was probably to blame, and the way he kept looking at me.

I wasn't forward or confident, like Brinley. I didn't know how to do casual hookups with men I'd just met—even if the idea of it intrigued me. But...this trip was all about pushing myself outside of my own comfort zone. It wouldn't be the worst way to do that.

Theo turned, catching my perusal, and flashed me an enticing grin that made me almost feel like he knew what I'd been thinking. "Holding up alright there?"

"Yeah, sorry," I straightened, fighting the urge to yawn. "I'm a little tired. I guess canoeing took a lot out of me."

"You did great," he remarked, his gaze warm and considerate—the smile on his lips playful and daring. "A born natural."

"Thanks," I laughed lightly, my cheeks heating again beneath his examination. His eyes were so alluring and having their focus on me did strange things to my heart. "Hopefully my arms will cooperate tomorrow," I added, lifting them meekly. They felt as limp as cooked spaghetti noodles.

Theo grinned, his smile lighting up that previously achy spot in my heart. "I brought some extra strength Tylenol and muscle pain reliever cream, if you need some."

My lips twitched, pulling into a bemused smile. "I guess I shouldn't be surprised that the environmental scientist came prepared." Jasmine had told me what he did for a living while we set up the tent; "*A lot of geoscience and a lot of travelling,*" which was another reason for my hesitation. It seemed like Theo was bound to leave again, and I had no idea where I was headed.

But if Theo was surprised that I knew his profession, he covered it well.

"I always come prepared," he replied with a wink, his grin cheeky. The racing of my heart was difficult to ignore, and I knew if I continued to expose myself to Theo's undeniably attractive good looks and charm, I'd make a complete fool of myself before dawn. I stood abruptly, nearly knocking my chair back in the process.

"Well, I'm going to call it a night," I said, stretching and letting an exaggerated yawn out.

"Night, Lux! I'll be there within an hour," Jasmine said, shaking her half-full beer and gesturing to the fire. I nodded, smiling at her, my eyes sliding back to Theo for the briefest moment before I caught myself.

"I'll grab that cream for you," he said, stabbing his poker stick into the sand.

"Thank you. Good night," I said, waving at everyone else.

"Night Princess, sleep well." Talia said, while the others waved. Turning, I started to walk up the hill, with Theo right behind me. I could feel the warmth of his breath as he exhaled.

One of his steps brought him to my side, and we exchanged a timid—on my part—look. Then, we reached his tent. Theo opened the zipper of his tent and disappeared inside it. I waited while he unzipped his bag and rooted around. When he found what he was looking for, he stepped back outside, closing the tent behind him.

"Apply a thin layer over your sore muscles, and when you wake up you should feel a lot better," Theo explained, passing me the tube of cream. Our fingertips touched together as I reached for it, shocking me with a warm, electric current.

"Thanks again," I said, pulling my hand, and the cream, away from his. He smiled, passing me the Tylenol and a bottle of water he'd also grabbed.

"My pleasure," he said, the words carrying a deeper meaning. Or at least, my hazy mind *felt* like they carried a deeper meaning. Who knows if there actually was, or if it was wishful thinking on my part. "And hey, if you want…I could help you apply it."

I gaped at him, momentarily speechless. Theo slapped his hand over his eyes and groaned. "I can't believe I said that, that sounds so creepy. I meant I could help you if you wanted."

Now it was Theo's turn to blush. It was endearing, and although a very large part of me desperately wanted to accept his offer, I chickened out.

"You're not creepy, Theo. But I should be okay on my own." Theo ran his hand across his chin and nodded. "I'll see you tomorrow," I added, turning on my heel and marching straight for my tent, not giving myself an opportunity to find out what his hands felt like on me.

Where my sister wouldn't have hesitated, it wasn't like me to be that bold, and the prospect of facing yet another rejection didn't exactly appeal.

And really, having Theo Whitmore's hands on me in any capacity might be the worst idea. I'd felt the electric heat of his touch when he helped me out of the water earlier—I'd nearly had a coronary when he effortlessly lifted and pushed me up onto the rock.

Theo seemed to be a very deadly combination: attractive, strong, funny, kind...and I knew myself well enough to know that this little crush could quickly develop into a case of the feels, especially if the large quantities of alcohol had anything to do with it.

I felt his eyes on my retreating back, and the pull to stay up along with it. But my body was depleted. If I wanted to make it through canoeing to the cliffs, I'd need sleep.

Theo

I WAITED until Lux had safely reached her tent before returning to the beach. On my way back, I passed Kai and Zoey, who were also calling it a night. They were off in their own little world, barely noticing me as I passed.

My thoughts ricocheted back to the pretty redhead at the top of the hill, and the desire that had flashed in her eyes when our hands touched as I'd given her the cream. She'd bitten her bottom lip, tugging it between her teeth. I couldn't believe I'd offered on the spot to apply it for her, internally I cringed at how awkward that had been. I didn't blame Lux at all for darting off with a quick goodbye.

I couldn't help but watch her as she crouched to unzip the tent. She didn't look back, and it was a good thing too—or she'd have caught me full on checking out her ass. I had it bad for her, and if circumstances were different I would have made a move.

But she'd *just* broken up with her long-time boyfriend.

When I got to the beach, things were beginning to wind down. Talia was sprawled out in her floaty, which was doubling as her mattress, still controlling the music, her head bobbing to the beat. She'd hit the whiskey harder than anyone else, but she appeared to be feeling no pain. I sat down in Lux's recently vacated chair, turning my head to Jasmine, who watched me expectantly.

"So?" she asked eagerly, waggling her eyebrows at me.

"So what?" I responded gruffly, pulling my gaze to the fire.

"What'd you think? Of Lux?" she whispered, leaning forward so I could hear her.

"She seems nice."

"Really? That's it? 'She seems nice'?" Jasmine repeated, scoffing, as Desmond stood and walked away, heading to the grass along the beach to relieve himself.

"If I didn't know any better, I'd say you were trying to set us up," I replied, addressing her sternly.

"I'm not trying to set anybody up," Jasmine argued stubbornly, folding her arms across her chest. "I picked up on all the longing glances and lip biting. The sexual tension between the two of you is unmistakable."

Talia grunted in agreement. "It really, *really* is. You should do something about it, Theo. I'm pretty sure I saw some balls beneath your tube sock."

Before I could respond, Jasmine interjected. "I give you my permission to ravage her and show her what multiple orgasms are all about, because I'm not all that sure she's had that experience before. You're a good guy, I trust you not to break her."

"How much have you had to drink?" I countered, cocking a brow.

"Probably too much," she laughed. "But that's not the point.

The point is…" Jasmine trailed off, her nose wrinkling with concentration. "I can't remember the point."

Talia cackled with laughter, tipping her floaty backwards. Her feet went over her head and she tumbled, her laughter reaching uncontrollable levels as she attempted to detangle herself from the bush and stand. Desmond sauntered over and grabbed her hand, helping her up effortlessly while Jasmine lost it laughing.

"I rest my case," I sighed, shaking my head.

Still, I'd be lying if I said the idea hadn't occurred to me already.

Lux

THE PRESSURE on my bladder was too strong to ignore anymore. Rolling onto my side, I lifted my head to peek at Jasmine. She was snoring softly with her sleeping bag pulled up over her head, only her curls were visible.

I didn't know what time she'd ended up coming to bed—I'd fallen asleep the moment my head touched my pillow, my body so worn and exhausted that my head didn't even put up a fight about it.

I moved about quietly, dressing in a pair of denim jean shorts and a tank top. I ran a comb through my tangled waves and grabbed my bag of toiletries before ducking out of the tent.

The campsite was quiet, save for the symphony of snores coming from a few of the tents. Some were soft, but they were drowned out by the louder, more nasally snores. From the top of the hill, I could make out the top of Theo's capped head as he crouched in front of the fire, getting it started. With one day of ogling him from afar, I'd grown familiar with the shape of his muscular shoulders and back.

Desmond sat across from Theo, cutting potatoes on a wooden cutting board he'd placed over what he affectionately referred to as his "cooking stump". Neither one of them had noticed me yet, so I made a quick and quiet escape down the pathway to the thunderbox.

It was, quite literally, a wooden box over a deeply dug hole. If it wasn't as new as it was, I would have hesitated about sitting on it, but Jasmine told me the year before they had brought supplies to fix it.

I opened the lid, doing my best to ignore the smell. I mean, it wasn't the Ritz, but my burning thighs hated the idea of squatting when I didn't have to.

Breathing through my mouth, I relieved my bladder, wiped with the biodegradable toilet paper I'd snagged specifically for this trip, and quickly shut the lid. I washed my hands with the antibacterial hand sanitizer; also purchased for this very occasion.

The pathway was far less scary during the light of day, and I took my time walking back to the tent. I reached inside for the water bottle I'd left in it, brushing my teeth quickly before I slid my toiletries bag inside and reached for my sweater. Jasmine groaned, turning over, but didn't wake up as I poked her gently with my foot.

She was dead to the world and would be until she woke herself up. Jasmine had always slept like that; so deeply, nothing could disturb her. I grabbed the muscle cream before I zipped our tent back up and stood, stretching the kinks out of my back.

With the sun not fully risen in the sky yet, it was a little chilly. I pulled my sweater over my head, collecting my hair from the nap of my neck and tugging the long strands through the collar. I slipped the muscle cream into my sweater pocket, hearing it knock against my cellphone.

I'd forgotten I'd placed it inside the pocket last night. I'm not sure why I thought bringing a cell phone with me as I trudged up the dark trail to the thunderbox was a good idea; I suppose I was thinking I'd use it to call for help if I encountered a bear. Of course, that was before I realized I got no reception—a blessing, and a curse.

This meant I hadn't heard back from any of the jobs I'd applied for, but I did my best not to stress about that. I'd know soon enough.

As I walked down to the beach, I could hear Baz and Rhiannon moving about in their tent. The zipper opened as I walked by, enough to let Moose out to relieve himself. He peed on a nearby tree, spotted me, and then raced over with his tail wagging ferociously. Licking my hand, he followed me the rest of the way to the beach.

Hearing us, Theo looked over his shoulder. He'd gotten the fire going and was boiling water in a percolator.

"Good morning," he grinned, and the way the simple greeting fell from his lips caused my heart to trip over itself.

"Morning," I repeated, sitting in the chair I'd left the night before.

"Do you want some coffee?" he asked, straightening. When he stretched, the hem of his shirt lifted to reveal a sliver of his perfectly sculpted abdomen. He was in peak physical form; even his muscles had muscles.

The tantalizing mental image of my fingers—and tongue—running along those muscles had my mouth watering.

"Coffee sounds good," I managed, tearing my gaze away from him, but not before I caught the secretive grin. He'd caught me looking again. Hiding my attraction to him wasn't exactly working. Of course, it'd help if I'd stop *staring* at him.

When the coffee finished percolating, Theo poured it into a tin mug and held it out to me. "There's creamer in my cooler, and the sugar is beside Desmond."

"Thank you." Our fingers brushed together as I took the mug from him, and another electric current zinged through me at the connection. I smiled a tentative smile and stepped over to the cooler he'd directed me to with a tilt of his chin. It would have been easy to find on its own: his last name, Whitmore, was written in capitals with a sharpie on the lid.

As I fixed my coffee with a few splashes of cream, Baz and Rhiannon made their way down to the beach. They carried more breakfast supplies, and I instantly felt silly for not thinking of it.

"I should go grab some more food," I said hesitantly.

"Don't worry about it, we've got more than enough to cook up right now," Desmond said softly, giving me a warm smile and holding out the container of sugar to me.

"Thanks," I said gratefully.

"Is Jasmine still asleep?" he asked.

"Yeah," I replied, laughing lightly. "I don't know what time she ended up coming to bed, but it must have been late. She's completely out cold." I glanced at him again as I returned the container of sugar to the log. I almost missed the fondness in his eyes, before he dropped his gaze to the potatoes in front of him and nodded. I got the sense there was something there: that Desmond's feelings for Jasmine were a little more than friendly.

"Talia's still snoring, too." Rhiannon remarked with a yawn of her own, holding out her travel mug for Theo to fill and smiling at me. "How'd you sleep?"

"Good," I admitted, pushing my hair behind my ear. I tried to avoid watching Theo; even though I could all but feel his eyes on me. "It was so peaceful, I passed out as soon as my head hit the pillow."

"I love that first night—when the fresh air and all the exercise hits you. I always sleep so well," Rhiannon said dreamily. Baz planted a kiss on her cheek as he passed by, headed for the percolator.

"How are your arms today?" Theo asked me. I had no choice but to look at him, and I prayed my cheeks weren't as red as they felt.

"A lot better. The Tylenol and cream helped a lot. Oh, speaking of..." I reached into my pocket and grabbed the muscle cream, passing it to him. He took it, our fingers making the briefest of contact. "Thank you."

"You're welcome."

The warm timbre of his voice blanketed around me, and the tug of his lips into a half grin magnetized me. I let out a breath I hadn't realized I'd been holding and pulled my eyes away from his, feeling a little disoriented.

I hadn't felt this way since high school; this jittery attraction that seemed to swell and grow with every second I spent in his presence was different from the timid butterflies I'd felt for Scott all those years ago. I was slightly irritated by this—the timing was all wrong, but my intrigue outweighed the irritation.

It had been a long time since I was in this position. Single, free, and attracted to someone who seemed to be just as attracted to me, unless I was imagining the lingering glances and the interest in each of his smiles...

Something told me that I wasn't imagining it. He smiled at me again, his lips curving around his mug before he took a deep sip. I lowered my chin, flushing a little as I wondered if I could truly let go of all my reservations and dive into something fun and new, even if it didn't last forever.

Could I let go of my meticulous need for control, if it meant an escape like the potential one Theo could provide?

The sudden drop of a body in the chair beside mine startled me from perusing him more. Jasmine had finally risen—although she looked anything but awake.

"Ugh. I should have gone to bed *way* earlier," she said, her voice raspy with lack of use.

"Yeah, me too. I went too hard for day one," Talia practically whimpered, collapsing onto the floaty she'd dragged back with her to the beach. She must have slept on it last night in her tent. She pulled her sweater up over her face, hiding from the sun and groaning with regret.

Still, the group was up early, beginning their day despite the hangovers Jasmine and Talia seemed to nurse.

Desmond let out a chuckle as he poured coffee into two more mugs and offered one Talia and another to Jasmine. She blinked up at him, as if surprised by the gesture, and accepted the mug from his hands. Their fingers connected for a fleeting moment. Jasmine swallowed, mumbling her thanks as she avoided looking directly at him.

There *was* a connection between the two of them. Buried beneath their easy friendship. I wouldn't have been able to pick up on it if I wasn't paying attention. I arched a brow, sipping at my coffee, and made a mental note to ask Jasmine about it later.

We ate breakfast on the beach around the campfire, laughing and talking. Somehow, each morsel tasted better than if it had been prepared in an actual kitchen. I slipped easily in and out of the conversations happening around me, enjoying learning new tidbits about the group.

Like how Zoey, Kai, Baz, Desmond and Theo had gone to the same school together, south of Sudbury. Talia had met Theo in college and now rented a room off them, and Rhiannon had met Baz when she was shooting his older sister's wedding at the Tempest Resort in Parry Sound and joined the group shortly after they started officially dating.

Since I hadn't helped with the cooking, I'd decided to do the dishes. At some point, someone had set up a makeshift table on the bench, placing two bins full of lake water on top of it. I made my way over with mine and Jasmine's dishes and two of the dirty frying pans. One of the bins was full of soapy water, while the other was clearly for rinsing. Beside the bins was a container of dish soap, a dish cloth and a towel.

I washed the dishes first, setting them aside in a soapy pile before starting on the frying pans. Once I'd washed everything, I rinsed them in the rinsing bin and dried everything off, stacking them in a neat pile, thinking about Theo's smile the whole time.

CLIFFS AND CLIMBS

IT HAD BEEN hard to keep my attention off Lux throughout breakfast. My eyes were drawn to her, like a moth to the flame —and I knew it wasn't because she was new and interesting— and gorgeous. Her beauty was undeniable, but there was something about her soul that called to mine.

She sat across from me, same as the night before, her body slightly inclined towards Jasmine as they talked about the impending day. When she offered to clean up after breakfast, I had to resist the urge to jump up and offer to help too. I gave her some time at the wash station, trying to calm my eagerness at the prospect of standing near her.

I hadn't felt this excited to be in someone's company in far too long, and I hadn't felt this strong of a pull of interest in someone—ever. I knew Desmond and Talia noticed my eagerness. Desmond was too stoic to call me out again, but Talia kept wriggling her eyebrows at me and grinning widely anytime I caught her eye.

"Go talk to her," she urged, her voice bordering on a whisper. "You know you want to. Stop torturing yourself—and by proxy, the rest of us."

While Lux was absorbed in drying, I got up and went to carry my dishes over, but Talia stopped me, stacking hers on top with a wink.

Lux saw me approaching. "I can wash those," she offered, holding her delicate hand out to take them.

"It's alright, I've got them," I smiled, stepping closer beside her, and setting the dishes in the wash bin.

"It's the least I can do, really. I didn't have to cook," she tried to insist, tucking a strand of her red hair behind her ear, her eyes not quite meeting mine.

"You don't have to earn your keep, We're on vacation here and everyone leans into their strengths. I know it feels like the division of labour isn't equal, but we're a team. Some of us excel at getting the fire started and keeping it going, while others are way better cooks and handle the meals. Trust me, you don't really want to eat anything Talia makes, but she's excellent at chopping wood." I assured her, a smile growing on my lips. I held out my hand and gently took the cloth from her, our fingers brushing yet again.

Something sparked in me, like it had all the times before, and I could tell by the way she bit her lower lip that she felt it too, this connection between us.

I'd only just met her, but she felt familiar. She felt *right*. It was the strangest feeling, but one I didn't mind embracing. I started washing the dishes, my focus not really on the task at hand. She lingered, unsure of whether she should stay. I didn't want her to go, so I decided to engage her.

"So, what do you think so far?" I asked, gesturing with my head to our campsite while I ran the washcloth over the dishes in the bin. She dried them while I washed, the two of us falling into harmony.

"I like it," Lux admitted, sounding surprised. "I actually slept great last night, even if it felt like I was going to slide off my mattress and down the hill."

"It's all that fresh air," I grinned. She smiled back, a little shy, but I could see the intrigue dancing in her irises. "It's good for the soul, even at that angle."

"Yeah. I'm glad I came. I mean, I might change my mind if Jasmine throws me off the cliff today, but for now, I'm really glad I let her talk me into coming."

"I'm really glad you let her talk you into coming, too," I told her, trying to keep my tone light. Even if what I was feeling was…heavier. An attraction I couldn't deny, an intrigue I couldn't ignore.

Lux's smile brightened, her eyes catching the glow of the morning sun, and I swear my heart tripped over its beat in my chest.

"Well, I better go get changed," she said, moving away from the wash station. I nodded, watching her go.

AFTER BREAKFAST CLEAN UP, we packed some food for our day excursion and then Desmond, Baz and I set to securing the coolers. We tied them off with thick ropes, hoisting them up in the trees out of reach so no animals would be lured over while we were gone.

We had never come across a bear while camping along the French River, but none of us wanted to take any chances. Even squirrels and raccoons could ruin a trip if they got into our food, so we didn't want to risk it. The nearest grocery store was an hour-long paddle and a forty-five-minute drive away.

With that task complete, we started getting ready. Everyone

changed into their swimsuits, and then the canoes and kayaks were packed and pulled out into the water.

It wasn't a long paddle down the river to the best cliff jumping spot, but we took our time, enjoying the sights along the way.

Desmond kept pace with me, and for the first half of the trip we lingered behind. I knew he was keeping an eye on everyone. He was the protector of the group. The fixer. He might be slinging back cold ones like the rest of us, but he always kept his senses about him.

I hadn't seen him drunk in years—hell, I was pretty sure the only time I'd *ever* seen Desmond drunk was the first time we'd raided our parents' liquor cabinets before a camping trip at Baz's, way back when none of us knew our limits.

But Desmond was even more quiet than usual, his gaze kept focusing on Jasmine. Each time she laughed as she teased Lux, he'd smile.

"You really should tell her how you feel," I said quietly, careful to not let my voice carry over the water. Desmond looked at me, his brow furrowing.

"It's not that simple. Whether she feels the same or...whether she doesn't, it'll change everything."

"You say that like it's a bad thing," I cocked a brow at him.

He shrugged. "It could be. Especially if she doesn't feel the same. Then everything changes for nothing. I could lose her friendship, and I don't want that."

I nodded slowly, absorbing his worries. I couldn't promise him the ending he desired, but I knew him; keeping it to himself was doing them both a disservice. I'd caught Jasmine watching him a few times, too. There was something there, but they were both too afraid to peel back the layers and see what it was.

"Remember Stacy?" Desmond said out of the blue. Stacy was a friend we'd had back in middle school. Desmond had developed feelings for her that went beyond friendship, and was crushed when he'd asked her to the grade eight graduation dance and she'd said no.

"Stacy wasn't destined to be in your life, or mine, for long." I shrugged. "And furthermore: Jasmine isn't Stacy."

"I know," Desmond nodded, his gaze going back to her. "She's so much…more. And I don't want to lose her friendship or make things awkward."

"What if she feels the same?" I challenged. "You could be missing out on *the one*."

Desmond lifted his shoulder in a shrug, a contemplative look on his face.

Lux

I STARED up at the rocky cliff with my jaw slack, my throat impossibly dry. "You guys jump off of *that*?" I asked, my fingers clinging to the paddle I'd rested over my knees, craning my neck to look up.

"Yeah, it's a straight drop, and the water's really deep." Jasmine shrugged with a grin.

"Okay," I nodded, taking a few deep breaths to steady my racing heart. "Yeah, I don't think I'm participating in that madness." I dropped my gaze, my eyes landing on Theo. He'd stopped in front of us, turning and offering me a smile that calmed the frantic beats of my heart, rebooting it, making it beat rapidly for an entirely different reason, one that wasn't all that unpleasant.

"You don't have to," Jasmine assured me. "None of this is compulsory. Just enjoy yourself."

I picked up my paddle again, slicing it through the water. Theo's paddle cut through the water with powerful strokes, his muscles taut and glistening with water droplets as he rowed away. He looked back at me as he passed, and I felt it thrum throughout me, a resounding echo.

Heaving a breath, I tore my gaze away from him, steely determination keeping me from stealing another peek at his back, although it was *really* tempting. He was every bit as breathtaking as the scenic backdrop.

Talia stood on a flat rock near the shoreline, waiting while Desmond climbed out of his kayak, using the blade of his paddle to keep it from drifting. He'd tied it off with the long rope attached to Talia's kayak and moved it aside, tossing his paddle in while Theo pulled up parallel to the flat rock.

Purposefully, I tore my gaze away, not wanting to get caught gawking at him by Talia.

"You know, it's okay to have a thing for him. He's a nice guy," Jasmine said, low enough for only me to hear.

"I thought you were pushing the single lifestyle."

"I am," Jasmine shrugged, a conniving glint in her eyes. "Dip your toes in the water, experience a little living. Kiss a cute stranger on a camping trip, because you're single and he's single and you both can."

I bit my lip, my head turning forward again. Theo was out of his boat now, his kayak tied off to the rest of them. *Could I?* Looking at him, every part of me shouted yes, I could. I had to stop being so afraid of every ripple effect.

Jasmine steered us to the flat rock where the others waited. "Toss them the rope, Lux!" she instructed. I scooped up the wet rope and tossed it toward them. Theo caught it, and Desmond held the canoe parallel with the rock, keeping it steady for us.

Jasmine stood, tossing her hiking bag onto the flat rock. She and Desmond exchanged a glance that lingered a little longer than necessary before I tossed my bag out and inadvertently broke their connection. She climbed out of the canoe, grabbing her bag, and moving toward the group gathered at the base of the cliff.

Curious, I thought. Jasmine had never mentioned having a thing for anyone; but of course, I knew my friend better than most. Commitment was something that had always made her antsy…which was a little ironic, considering her parents were still happily married after nearly thirty years together.

It wasn't a topic Jasmine liked to get into too much. She always said she had plenty of time to settle down, and now wasn't it.

But those brief few moments had shown me that Jasmine was definitely interested in Desmond; and she was fighting that interest with everything she had. I didn't even think Desmond had a clue. Jasmine was pretty good at concealing her true feelings. After all, she had a politician for a father—and a grandfather. But *I* knew. I could detect it. It became more and more apparent with each of their interactions.

Jasmine waited for me on the ledge. I stood up, the canoe wobbling as I climbed ungracefully out and scrambled onto the rock. Theo reached for me, steadying my elbow with his hand. He released me when I found my footing, and I sent him a grateful smile.

He returned it, winking before he jumped into the water, the rope to our canoe still in hand. He swam toward the row of kayaks and tied it off, making room for Kai and Zoey to pull up to the ledge. Kai tossed him the rope, and once they'd climbed out onto the ledge, he swam over and tied their canoe to Jasmine's before swimming back.

I couldn't help but watch as Theo pulled himself out of the water. His muscles working in tandem was a mouth-watering sight, and when he straightened—his deep green eyes rooted on me—I let out an internal sigh before mentally slapping myself.

I adjusted my bag and turned to Jasmine, ignoring her as she raised her eyebrows at me. We started up the steep incline, trailing behind Talia, with Theo and Desmond behind us and Kai and Zoey making up the rear.

The dog, Moose, was trotting alongside Rhiannon, occasionally falling a little behind when he stopped to sniff along the trail.

The sun's hot rays beat down on the back of my neck, and by the time we reached the top of the trail, I was ready to jump off the cliff just to get to the water quicker to cool off. My tank top stuck to my back, and my skin was slick with sweat.

Shrugging my pack off, I let it fall to the ground as I pulled my tank off, revealing another one of my bikinis—this one was black and the ties more secure. The slight breeze against my sweaty skin was a temporary respite from the heat, but soon even that wasn't enough, and the water below began to look appealing.

The drop, though? Not so much.

The others moved to set their own packs down on the pink and grey granite, beneath the shade of cedars.

Theo made his way up beside me, his body coming close to mine as he passed. He put his bag down beside the fire pit and rooted through it, grabbing a bottle of water. "Want one?" he offered me. I nodded, moving closer to him so I could accept the proffered drink.

We sat around for about twenty-minutes, rehydrating and talking.

Talia was the first person to jump off the cliff. She ran for the edge as soon as she finished her beer. Her "yew-yaw!" followed her all the way down, until she broke the water's surface. Baz followed right after her, with little fanfare. One moment he was there, the next he was gone.

As the others gathered near the edge of the ledge, I lingered back with Rhiannon. She was taking photos of the group in rapid succession. She focused on Kai and Zoey as they ran and jumped holding hands.

"What does it feel like?" I asked Jasmine, who stood on my

other side, as we watched Desmond take a running leap and disappear over the edge.

"Kind of like falling off a swing, but a little longer." She lurched forward suddenly, jogging away from me to join Theo at the edge. She said something to him before jumping over, her dark curls fanning out behind her.

I bit my bottom lip, wondering if I could do it. Theo glanced back at me over his shoulder, and I heard the shutter of Rhiannon's camera as she moved closer to capture his jump.

I crept forward too, peering down, watching as Theo disappeared into the water. My heart started to pound a little quicker as I waited for him to resurface. He did so a moment later, already swimming away from the cliffs.

"Want to see what it looks like from below?" Rhiannon asked. "I'm going to go get some shots of them jumping from down there."

"Sure." I was thankful she hadn't pressured me to jump too. I followed her back down the hill—losing my footing a couple of times. I could see how jumping would be easier, but I didn't think I was ready for that. Moose ambled along behind us.

We passed Talia, Kai and Zoey on our descent. Desmond, Theo, and Jasmine were pulling themselves out of the water when we got to the bottom.

"So much fun!" Jasmine grinned, squeezing the water out of her hair.

"Invigorating," Desmond agreed, momentarily held captive by her. He quickly caught himself before she noticed, dragging his attention to Moose, who'd knocked the stick he found against his leg. Desmond threw it into the water for him, and Moose took off after it.

"You gonna try?" Jasmine asked me.

"I think it might be a little high for me," I admitted. "I'm happy to watch you crazy kids."

Jasmine nodded. "Okay, well. I'm going to jump again!" she said, following Desmond back up the path.

Baz was getting their canoe ready, a grin on his face, like he instinctively knew what Rhiannon wanted before she even said anything.

"We're going to take the canoe so I can get a better view. Want to join us?" Rhiannon asked.

"Thanks, but I'll watch from here," I smiled.

"Suit yourself," she nodded, expertly stepping into the canoe and sitting down. Baz helped Moose in and paddled them out, leaving enough space for everyone to keep jumping safely.

"Want some company?" Theo asked me.

"Don't you want to jump again?"

"I can later," he smiled as he sat down on the rock, submerging his legs in the water. I hesitated for a moment before sitting down beside him and dipping my legs in the river too. The water was cool and refreshing, but sitting so close to him had me feeling heated in other ways.

We watched as Talia jumped again, this time shot-gunning a beer while she fell. I watched, wondering how someone could be so fearless and adventurous.

"Not a fan of heights, huh?" Theo asked.

"Not particularly," I admitted with a wry grin. "I'm also not a fan of rollercoasters."

"I don't like rollercoasters either," he laughed. "I always end up wondering how frequently they check all the bolts and replace parts."

"Yeah. Final Destination really messed me up for rollercoasters. I also don't like driving behind log trucks," I let out a self-deprecating laugh.

"Who does?" Theo grinned. "That franchise is to blame for a lot of our generation's fears, I think."

"What franchise did what now?" Talia asked, swimming over to us.

"We were just talking about Final Destination," Theo explained.

"Ah, yes. Messed up movies. I love a good horror movie, but those movies gave me the heebie jeebies. I couldn't go to the dentist for *years*," Talia grinned. "Flat out refused to get braces 'cause I was convinced I'd end up dying. My parents were so thrilled." Her teeth were a little crooked, but perfectly white.

"I still won't start a barbeque," I admitted. Not that I'd been given many opportunities to do so—barbequing was my dad's forte, and we didn't have one at my college dorms. But even if given the opportunity, I don't think I would be able to get the barbeque death out of my head. With my luck, I really would explode.

Talia laughed and hoisted herself out of the water. "Well, I guess we can either succumb to our fears, or push past them. I no longer hide from the dentist, but opted against braces now that my parents won't pay for them." She gave me a cheeky grin.

I bit my lip, considering her words. She was right, after all. For so long, I'd erred on the side of caution, sticking to what was familiar and comfortable. I didn't push myself outside my own comfort levels, didn't push the boundaries of that familiarity. I stuck to what I knew, even if it hurt me, even if it didn't bring me joy.

Scott was a testament to that. I'd never felt for him a fraction of my attraction to Theo, and yet I'd stayed for so long with him. I couldn't even say the relationship brought me comfort, it had been more or less a mask I'd worn.

With that mask gone—and with Theo's dark green eyes on me—I felt like an entirely new person.

"So, are you gonna jump?" Talia added, smiling like she knew I was *kind of* considering it. Theo was still watching me, his eyes full of intrigue and patience. The corner of his lip lifted in a half-smile that sent sparks up my spine.

"I don't know, but I'll go back up with you guys," I replied, standing up and brushing the debris from my thighs. I still wasn't sold on jumping, but I sensed Theo was keeping me company instead of jumping himself.

The three of us walked back up the pathway. Before long, we came to the top of the cliff. Zoey and Kai were near the fire pit, coaxing the flames to grow. Zoey had a package of hotdogs beside her, and Kai was taking a couple of pills, washing it back with a bottle of water.

I tensed, worried about what type of pills they were. I didn't *think* Jasmine would be friends with anyone illegally doing drugs, but I didn't relax until I noticed the medicine container beside him on the rock. He closed it, tucking it away in his bag before pulling out a granola bar and saying something to Zoey that made her laugh and shake her head.

Jasmine and Desmond stood near the edge of the cliff, locked in a conversation I couldn't hear. They pulled apart when they saw us, and Jasmine waved at me before launching herself over the cliff. Desmond watched her with an unreadable expression. He waited until she'd resurfaced before he jumped too. There was definitely a vibe between the two of them, but nobody else seemed to be picking up on it.

Talia went over to the cooler bag, grabbing three beers, and walked back over to us, handing one to me and another to Theo.

"Feel like shot-gunning while we jump?" she asked Theo, but her eyes slid to me, too, including me in on the invitation.

"Sure," Theo grinned, his eyes moving to me, awaiting my answer.

"I don't think I'm ready yet," I admitted.

Theo's hand briefly touched my elbow. "No pressure," he assured me.

I looked down at the contact, unsurprised by the pleasant jolt it sent coursing through my nerves. All too soon, it was over. Theo removed his hand and ambled over to the edge of the cliff with Talia. I followed to watch them jump.

Talia cracked her beer open and Theo did the same. Talia started counting down, and when they got to one, they launched themselves over the edge of the cliff at the same time, lifting the beers to their mouths and drinking as they fell.

I watched from above, a smile tempering my lips, and shook my head. What would it feel like to have zero hesitation launching yourself off a cliff? I couldn't imagine. Even thinking about it had my stomach rioting with nerves. From my position on top of the cliff, it looked like a steep fall.

But I couldn't help but wonder: *how would it feel?* To have the wind whipping through my hair? To let myself fall? To give in to the desire to do something reckless and foolish just because a small part of me wanted to?

What if I gave into that small part, for the sake of trying something new?

Theo and Talia broke the water's surface. I wasn't sure how much of their beers they were able to drink, but I laughed when they resurfaced and Talia crushed her empty can in her hand victoriously.

8

JUMPING IN

*L*ux

"YOU WANT TO DO IT, I know you do," Jasmine's voice startled me, almost making me lose my footing on the edge of the cliff. I whirled to face her, my heart pounding, and placed my hand over it to try and steady its uneasy beats.

"Jesus, don't do that," I laughed.

She smiled apologetically. "Sorry, but I'm right—aren't I? You want to jump."

I bit my lip, looking back over the edge of the cliff. Talia and Theo were still down there, but they had swum towards Baz and Rhiannon's canoe. Theo's arms rested on the edge of the canoe while Talia floated on her back.

"I mean, a little bit."

"What's holding you back?" Jasmine cocked her head, her eyes daring me.

"The height," I pointed out, arching a brow. Jasmine knew I wasn't a fan of heights.

"So, close your eyes!" she grinned. "I'll jump with you, we'll hold hands the whole way down if you want."

"I don't know..." my heart still hadn't settled, but the urge to let go and do something reckless was growing.

"Think of it as crossing something off your bucket list of things you've never done before." Jasmine challenged me. She knew I had several lists: things I wanted to do, things I'd never done. Although I'd never thought to add "jump off a cliff" to the list, it would be fun to do so.

"Alright, fine."

"Really?" Jasmine seemed surprised, her eyes brightening.

"I'll jump—if you tell me what's going on with you and Desmond," I tilted my chin towards the fire pit where Desmond had joined Kai and Zoey. He was immersed in conversation with them, his back to us, and couldn't hear us.

Jasmine glanced over her shoulder, her brow furrowing as she considered my wager. "Fine, deal. Now, do you want to run and jump, or just jump?" She grinned like she didn't think I would go through with it.

"Run and jump." My heart sped up at the prospect, but for some reason, I felt empowered to do it.

Jasmine took my hand and we walked back several feet. My palm started to sweat, but Jasmine didn't seem to care.

"Ready?"

"As ready as I'll ever be..." I swallowed hard, already regretting my decision. Still, it felt too late to turn back now.

She squeezed my hand in comfort. "You've got this. You're going to love it, trust me. It feels so freeing."

I nodded, unable to say another word, and we started running toward the edge of the cliff.

The thing about me was, once I set my mind to doing something, I did it. Even if it terrified me. And I was *terrified*. My heart was pounding as we launched ourselves off the edge of the cliff.

For a second, we really were weightless.

For a suspended moment in time, all the worries of my life, all the pain my sister caused, left me.

Jasmine let out a holler of elation, and I closed my eyes tight, focusing on the feeling of the wind whipping through my hair, rather than the water's surface getting closer and closer.

I couldn't even scream, not in fear or elation. It was like my voice was trapped in my throat, the rush of the fall exploding in my ear drums. It was over before I knew it, the whole thing taking less than thirty seconds before my feet hit the cool water and I was submerged completely.

Theo

"SHE'S DOING IT!" Talia said gleefully, "Lux is jumping."

Rhiannon grinned, picking up her camera and aiming it at the cliff. I turned to watch, catching Lux and Jasmine mid-jump. They were holding hands, Lux's long hair flowing out behind her in the breeze. I couldn't make out their expressions from where we were, but I could hear Jasmine's excited hollers.

They disappeared underwater, and a moment later their heads broke the surface. I could hear Lux's laughter mixing with Jasmine's as they high-fived each other.

"You did it! I knew you could!" Jasmine cheered, her voice carrying across the water as they swam toward the rocks. I started swimming to join them, lured in by the elation rolling off the two of them.

They had already climbed out by the time I reached the rock, and Lux was ringing out her hair, a triumphant smile making her glow from within.

"See? That wasn't so bad, huh?" I grinned, pulling myself up onto the rock. I couldn't help but notice the way Lux's eyes lingered on my forearms. She drew in her bottom lip, her eyes sparking with the same desire thrumming in me.

Jasmine gently elbowed her, and Lux shook her head, her cheeks burning.

"It was okay," she managed.

"Planning on doing it again?" Talia asked. She'd swum up behind me. "I'll hold your hand this time."

Lux laughed lightly, tucking a strand of wayward hair behind her ear. "I might later. I think I need to hydrate and rest a little. My legs feel funny," she admitted.

"We should all eat something," Jasmine said. "I bet Desmond and Zoey have food ready up there."

"Let's go see what mom and pop made for us," Talia grinned. The four of us made our trek back up the cliff. True to Jasmine's prediction, Desmond and Zoey had prepared a bit of a meal for us—hotdogs with buns. No condiments, they were back at the campsite, but it hit the spot.

We sat around the makeshift fire, drinking bottles of water and eating and talking about life. Lux was quiet, listening, but she looked more relaxed than she had when she first showed up. The tension was gone from her shoulders, and her expression was peaceful as she leaned her head back, basking in the sunshine.

Jasmine caught my eye, and arched a knowing brow, a secretive smile playing on her lips. I grinned and shook my head, rolling my eyes. But her words from last night crept back into my mind.

"I give you my permission to ravage her and show her what multiple orgasms are all about, because I'm not all that sure she's had that experience before."

I took a swig of water, trying to push her words out of my mind and ignore the pull I felt to do that.

After we all finished eating, we cleaned up and put the fire out using Moose's collapsible water bowl. We stuck around a while longer to make sure the fire didn't start again.

"Will we be coming back here?" Lux asked, eyeing the edge of the cliff like she was debating on jumping again. Kai, Zoey, Baz and Rhiannon had already started walking down the pathway with Moose, leaving the rest of us at the top of the cliff. I'd planned on jumping once more, so did Talia. Desmond was waiting to make sure everyone got back down safely…or maybe he was waiting for Jasmine.

"It's supposed to rain tomorrow, so we'll stick around the campsite," Jasmine answered. "If you want to jump again, I'd do it now, who knows if we'll be back."

Lux nodded, considering Jasmine's words.

"It's the fastest way down," Talia remarked, launching herself over the edge of the cliff with an excited yip.

Lux took a breath, stealing herself. "Alright, one more time. Just to say I did it twice." She grinned at Jasmine.

Jasmine was already pulling her cellphone out of her bag. "I'll record it, so you've got proof," she smiled back.

"I don't want to do it alone," Lux said, her brows creasing with concern.

"Theo, want to jump with her?" Jasmine asked, arching a brow at me.

"I could if you want me to, Lux."

Lux looked at me, biting on her lower lip. "I guess you're a safe option to jump with, what with your diploma in nature."

I chuckled. "I don't have a diploma in nature, but close enough." I held my hand out to her, and I was surprised when she took it. Jasmine was recording, but Lux didn't pay a lick of attention to Jasmine, her eyes were on our connected hands. "Ready?" I asked, hearing how affected I was by her in my own voice.

"Yes," she said, looking at me. Her eyes sparkled like the

ancient crystalline rocks of the exposed Precambrian rock around us.

We ran towards the cliff and jumped, the air rushing loud in my ears and around us as we fell. We kept holding hands, even when we hit the water and swam back up to the surface. I came up first, seconds before Lux re-emerged, water cascading down her face. We treaded in place, still holding hands.

Lux let go so she could push her wet hair out of her eyes. She was breathing heavily, like she was trying to catch her breath, her eyes finding mine as we coasted closer together.

"You alright?" I asked, and she nodded, a smile gracing her lips.

"It was more fun this time, less scary," she admitted.

"You knew you'd be okay," I grinned. "It gets easier every time. Soon, you'll be an expert."

"Oh, I doubt that," she laughed. But despite her doubt, she seemed to bloom.

"I don't." I said, sincerely. For a moment, she stared unblinking at me. Those gorgeous eyes full of endless possibilities. We were so close to one another now, a mere inch separating us. All I had to do was move my head forward a little more, and I could capture her lips with mine.

"You guys coming?!" Talia called out. She'd already untied her kayak and was waiting for the rest of us with Baz and Rhiannon in their canoe and Kai and Zoey in theirs. The five of them wore similar grins, like they'd been watching us and were entertained by what they saw.

Lux blushed, swimming away. I shot an unimpressed look at Talia and then swam after her.

By the time we reached the kayaks and canoes, Desmond and Jasmine were headed down the trail. I climbed out first, then turned to find Lux struggling a little to pull herself out of the water. "My whole body feels like Jello," she giggled. I held out my hand, but she managed to pull herself up without taking it.

Then she lost her footing, tripping a little into me, a surprise sound escaped her lips when my arms went around her to catch her at the same time her hand splayed out across my chest.

"If you wanted to touch each other, you could have done so without the dramatics," Talia teased from her kayak. Lux's cheeks flushed, but she didn't immediately pull away. Her hand flexed over my chest.

"Shut up, Tal," I said, not breaking eye contact with Lux. She felt right in my arms, like she belonged there, and having her hands on me was enough to stun me.

"What's going on here?" Jasmine asked with an amused lilt. Lux pulled away, tucking a strand of hair behind her ear, her cheeks still pink with embarrassment.

"I tripped," she shrugged, reaching for her bag that Jasmine had carried down for her.

"Hmm," Jasmine said thoughtfully, glancing between the two of us with that secretive look on her face. "Are you okay?"

"I'm fine," Lux insisted as Desmond set our stuff down and hopped into the water. He swam over to where we'd tied off our kayaks and Jasmine's canoe, grabbed the rope, and swam back over to the ledge. He untied our kayaks and handed me the rope to Jasmine's canoe so I could hold it in place for the girls to climb in.

Lux's gaze went to me briefly, the smallest of smiles gracing her lips before she climbed into the front of the canoe and set her bag down in between her legs.

Jasmine didn't really need my assistance, but I held the rope anyway until she was settled. Then I tossed the rope into the canoe with them. Jasmine used her paddle to push away from the rock.

9

CAMPFIRE SONGS

AFTER WE GOT BACK to the campsite, the group had a quick swim to cool off before it was time to start making dinner. Jasmine had brought all the fixings for tacos, and I helped set up a taco station on the bench with Zoey and Rhiannon. Jasmine had pre-cooked the seasoned ground beef but was heating it up over the fire in a cast iron pan.

When the ground beef was warm, we made our tacos and sat around the campfire eating. I hadn't realized how ravenous I was until I was consuming my second taco and still hungering for more. Luckily, Jasmine had made *a lot* of ground beef. Everyone was able to put away three tacos before we ran out of ingredients.

Once we'd cleaned up and all the dishes were washed, the temperature started to drop. Jasmine and I went to our tent to change.

"I think Theo's into you," Jasmine commented as I pulled on

99

a pair of comfortable sweatpants. The mosquitoes were bad, and I didn't want to deal with the bites.

I glanced at her and lifted a brow. "Oh?"

"What do *you* think of him?" she pressed, pulling her sweater over her head, and obscuring the coy smile on her lips.

"He's nice," I shrugged, grabbing my sweater. I tugged it on, pulling my hair out from under the collar and arranging it in a messy braid.

"And? Do you think he's attractive?"

"Sure," I tucked my phone in my sweater pocket and sent her a look. "But I don't know why we're talking about *this* when you promised you'd tell me about what's going on between you and —" before I could finish my sentence, Jasmine had taken a step toward me and put her finger over my lips, silencing me.

Casting a glance at our closed tent as if she was worried someone would overhear us, she shook her head. "It's complicated, and I'll explain later," she promised, assuring me with her eyes.

"What's complicated about it?"

"He's my friend, and technically my landlord," Jasmine whispered. "We have a great friendship. I don't want to ruin it with feelings."

"But if you already *have* feelings for each other, how can you ruin it?" I replied in a hushed tone.

"Like I said, it's complicated. You and Theo—there's no complications there. Besides, *I'm* not the one that needs a rebound."

"I don't *need* a rebound," I frowned, crossing my arms.

"No, but you could use a good distraction, or should I say, dick-straction!" Jasmine grinned.

I opened and closed my mouth, finding no lie in her statement. I *could* use a good distraction from all the drama and betrayal in my life.

"What if he's not up for being a distraction?"

"Trust me, he is." Jasmine's smile turned knowing, and I narrowed my eyes at her.

"How do you know? Did he say something?"

"I've known Theo for years. I can tell he's attracted to you, plus I *may* have given him permission to ravage you last night when we were talking, and the smile he tried to contain said it all. He'd be game for that."

"Jasmine!" I said her name louder than I intended, mortified. The butterflies in the pit of my stomach took flight at the idea, and I tried to suppress them in vain. The idea was already brewing on its own within me, and each time I caught Theo looking at me, that desire grew. I didn't need Jasmine encouraging that madness.

"I think you should go for it," she told me. "Seriously, Lux. When was the last time you did something for yourself just because you *wanted* to?"

"I'm here, aren't I?"

"Yeah, but you didn't really *want* to come on this trip. I sort of pushed you," Jasmine said with a cheeky grin. "Aren't you glad I did?"

"Actually, yeah." I glanced out the mesh tent window, trying to fight the smile. "Theo aside, it's been the perfect escape."

Jasmine nodded in agreement. "And if you go home with a few orgasms under your belt, you'll be able to face Brinley's bullshit without wavering. It'll roll off you like water on a duck's back."

I looked back at my friend, shaking my head a little. "Interesting theory."

"Why don't you test it?" she challenged.

"Why don't *you* test your feelings for Desmond?" I retorted, giving her a challenge of her own.

"Touché," Jasmine sighed, looking out the tent window. Everyone else was gathered back at the beach, hanging around the fire. It was doubtful they'd be able to hear our conversation.

"I can't do that, though. Desmond is a forever kind of guy. And I'm, well…" she paused, looking conflicted.

"You don't think you could do forever with someone?" I asked, surprised. Jasmine seemed to have such a solid example with her parents, so why the hesitation? I knew she hadn't dated anyone seriously ever—but I figured that was because she was focused on her education.

"I don't know. I don't know if I'm even ready for that," she worried her bottom lip. "All I know is I can't risk ruining our friendship. I value it too much."

"How would you ruin your friendship?"

"What if I get bored, or crave change? What if I let him down? What if he *is* forever, but I'm not ready for that yet?"

"Fair enough," I frowned. It seemed like Jasmine had given it more thought than I initially suspected. She wasn't the type of person to toy with other people's emotions, nor did she make rash decisions. Jasmine made calculated choices. After all, she had been raised by a politician who'd drilled it into her head early on that her every action could be misconstrued later.

"Anyway, I don't want to talk about that anymore. I want us to focus on *you* having fun, and experiencing all the things you've missed out on, okay?" Jasmine arched a brow.

"Okay, fine," I sighed.

We went back down to the beach, pausing long enough to grab a few ciders from the cooler, sitting down in our chairs around the fire. Baz was perched on the cooking stump with an acoustic guitar on his lap, strumming the intro to a Counting Crows song.

"I love it when Baz brings his guitar," Jasmine sighed happily.

Rhiannon grinned, her eyes raking over Baz with appreciation. "I know! I love a guy that knows his way around an instrument."

"It's not the only thing I know my way around," Baz grinned at his girlfriend cheekily, and she blushed.

"Yeah, yeah. You're skilled. Now deflate that ego and keep playing!" Rhiannon instructed, relaxing into her chair.

Baz's smile grew wider, and he kept playing. When he started singing the lyrics to *Round Here*, I was surprised at how *good* he sounded. His voice rivaled that of Adam Duritz's: it was gravelly and confident, working in perfect harmony with his guitar as he played with a skill I didn't expect him to have.

He held everyone around the campfire captive, everyone except for Theo. Theo's gaze was fixed on me, a smile lifting the corners of his lips as our eyes connected. I felt that swell of attraction in the pit of my belly, sizzling through my bloodstream.

I couldn't help but wonder what it would feel like, to—as Jasmine so eloquently put it—use Theo as a dick-straction. I couldn't deny it; the idea held a serious allure, and judging by the heat that smouldered in his irises when I bit my lower lip at the thought, Theo was thinking something similar.

But I'd never done anything so rash, and I didn't know what steps to take to signal that I was interested in exploring the heat between us. I wasn't brave enough to outright say something to him about it, and I felt frozen with my own uncertainty.

Baz finished the song, the last of the chords disappearing into the night, replaced with the crackling of the campfire and the subtle sounds of the night.

"That was incredible," I complimented, still blown away by his unexpected talent. "Do you play professionally?"

"Thanks! And no," Baz laughed, "Definitely not. Just something I picked up growing up with a family that loves music." He set his guitar down and stretched.

"I keep telling him he should do something more with it," Rhiannon wrapped her arms around him from behind, pressing a kiss to his cheek.

"I don't want to turn it into a job I'll end up hating," Baz shrugged, placing his hand over Rhiannon's. "Besides, I'm not good at writing songs, I'll stick to building shit and leave that to the real musicians."

"You are a real musician to me, babe," Rhiannon whispered. He turned his face towards hers, meeting her lips in a reverent kiss. I looked away, giving them privacy.

While Baz was distracted with Rhiannon, Talia hooked her phone up to the speaker ball and started playing background music.

The atmosphere around the group tonight was a lot more relaxed. After a day spent jumping off cliffs and paddling, everyone seemed tired. Everyone was still drinking, but at a more leisurely pace than the first night, and without the intent on getting drunk. Conversations seemed more relaxed too, the group breaking off into clusters.

Long after the sun set, Zoey got up and disappeared. She returned a moment later with a bag of marshmallows and a s'more kit.

"Who wants to make s'mores?" she asked.

"Hell yeah!" Kai exclaimed with elation, jumping up along with Desmond and Theo to look for sticks in the bush that would be suitable for marshmallow roasting. They returned ten minutes later with a handful of sticks. Theo took a pocket knife out and started carving the bark away, making the ends more pointed.

They were only able to find five sticks, so we had to take turns.

"I can't remember the last time I had s'mores around a fire," I murmured, taking the proffered stick from Theo. The marshmallow bag went around the group, and Jasmine grabbed a handful for us. "Not since we were in high school," I added, looking at her with a wry grin.

"Oh yeah! I remember that," Jasmine laughed. "You nearly set Camellia's hair on fire."

"Hey! That's not true!" Jasmine gave me a look. "Well, I guess it's sort of true," I blushed.

The last time I roasted marshmallows was at Jasmine's cottage during one of her parent's yearly Canada Day celebrations when we were fifteen. The Kade's Canada Day parties were something to marvel at. They hosted their Canada Day blow out at their cottage in the Muskokas, and Jasmine and her sisters were always able to bring a couple friends.

My family never did stuff like that. We didn't have a cottage, although every few years, my parents would rent one for a couple weeks and my dad would take a much-needed vacation from the hospital. But we never did campfires—heck, I wasn't even all that sure my dad knew how to start a campfire. He was a city boy through and through.

My mom was also a city girl, she had zero interest in anything outdoorsy—she said she hated bugs too much. They only ever rented cottages that also had pools, because my mother hated seaweed as much as she hated bugs. Essentially, it was a fancy and expensive change of scenery for a few weeks.

I blamed my lack of expertise of roasting marshmallows on my family's inexperience with anything to do with nature. I'd panicked when my marshmallow caught fire, and tried to wave it around to put it out. Obviously, that meant that I was waving around a gooey flaming marshmallow that ended up flying off my stick and narrowly missing Camellia's head by a few inches.

"Maybe I'll roast them for you," Jasmine teased, and I handed over the stick without complaint.

"That's for the best. I don't want to set the forest on fire, or our tents." I said sheepishly, watching as she popped a marshmallow on the end of the stick and stood to hold it over the flames.

Theo chuckled, drawing my attention to him from across the fire. He was roasting marshmallows with ease. The man seemed to do *everything* with ease. Once his marshmallow was perfectly golden, he put together a s'more and offered it to me.

"Thanks," I said, taking it from him. I wasn't even all that hungry for it—I wanted an excuse for our hands to touch again. But the s'more was the most delicious thing, and I hummed with appreciation as the flavours exploded on my tongue.

Theo cleared his throat, forcing his gaze away from my face. His expression was…affected, and it stirred the desire that had taken up residence in me.

Jasmine nudged me with her elbow, waggling her eyebrows at me. She'd caught it too, so I *wasn't* imagining it. I fought a smile, popping the rest of the s'more Theo had given me into my mouth.

Once everyone had a couple of s'mores and the remaining marshmallows, graham crackers and chocolate were put away, Talia busted out a bottle of tequila and plastic shot glasses.

"Let's play a game," she suggested with a mischievous smile, her eyes glinting in the firelight. "Never Have I Ever?"

Zoey groaned. "I hate this game. It makes me feel so inexperienced."

"You're not inexperienced, babe. Trust me," Kai teased, kissing her forehead. Zoey grinned at him and giggled.

Talia chuckled as she poured tequila into the small plastic shot glasses. She handed them out, and when everyone had their shot glass, she put the bottle down on the cooking stump and returned to her floaty.

"Alright, I'll start," she said, getting comfortable. "Never have I ever…Googled myself," Talia began the game, her gaze going to Jasmine with amusement.

"Ugh," Jasmine tilted her head back, polishing off her shot. Back in high school, she would sometimes Google her name to make sure the press wasn't talking about her, especially back when her father was running for mayor for the first time. They were looking for any dirt on him and his family.

Rhiannon surprised me by tossing her shot back too. "What? Ever since Travis Channing's wedding, I've been curious about what people are saying about my photography."

"I don't think that counts," Jasmine said thoughtfully, standing up to refill her shot glass. "You're essentially looking up reviews on your business, not Googling your name."

"But my name *is* my business," Rhiannon replied, tilting her empty shot glass at Jasmine so she could fill it too.

"Touché," Jasmine giggled. "Well, I'm sorry in advance then. Never have I ever met a celebrity!"

Baz and Rhiannon both took a shot, and Jasmine handed Baz the bottle and went back to her seat.

"Hey, not so fast Jas," I raised a brow. "What about that time we met Everly Daniels backstage?"

"Ah shit, I forgot about that!" Jasmine laughed, linking her arm around mine to take the shot like we practiced when we were in high school and trying to look cool. I laughed and took my shot, spilling a little of tequila out onto my chin in the process.

Baz passed us the bottle and we refilled. "Your turn, Lux."

"Never have I ever..." I thought for a minute, my mind going blank. "Had a friend with benefits!"

"Woo, shit's getting interesting now!" Talia grinned before tossing her shot back. Zoey and Kai also took theirs, and so did Theo, Baz, and Rhiannon. Once everyone's shot glass was topped off, it was Theo's turn.

"Never have I ever...been in love," he said. It wasn't surprising to me that Rhiannon, Baz, Kai and Zoey all took a shot, but Talia and Desmond also tipped their shot glasses back. Jasmine hesitated with hers as she watched Desmond, like she wasn't entirely sure about herself, but she didn't lift it to her lips. I didn't lift mine, either. I knew I hadn't been in love with Scott. Theo was watching me, though, and a small smile appeared on his lips.

"Never have I ever...kissed a friend's ex," Desmond grinned wryly, his focus on Theo. Theo shook his head, an ashamed expression befalling him, and tossed his glass back, taking the shot. I couldn't help but wonder what the story was there. Had Theo kissed the person Desmond was—or had been—in love with?

"We were in grade seven, I don't think it really counted," Theo explained, catching my curious gaze.

"Oh, it counted," Desmond assured him.

"Never have I ever...kissed someone I just met!" Zoey exclaimed. Rhiannon and Baz groaned, both tossing back their shots. Talia, Jasmine, and Kai also drank theirs. Theo's eyes met mine across the fire again, and I swear I had this feeling that the next time that question was asked during a never have I ever game, I'd be answering differently.

The bottle of tequila was empty after that last refill, most of the group was really feeling it. I'd only had to take one shot of tequila, so I was feeling alright.

"Last question of the night!" Baz declared, shaking the empty bottle at Kai. "Make it a good one!"

"Never have I ever...gone skinny dipping!" Kai grinned. Every single person took a shot, but me.

"Really? Never ever?" Talia asked me.

"Yeah, never," I laughed, feeling even more inexperienced.

"It's so fun!" Talia exclaimed. "Let's do it now, cross that off your Never Have I Ever list."

"I don't know..." I said, my face heating with embarrassment.

"Come on, Lux! It's dark and Talia's right, it really is fun!" Jasmine urged me, her eyes pleading with mine. She tilted her head a little to Theo, daring me.

I bit my lip, considering. "Alright, fine. Let's do it!"

"Hell yeah!" Talia whooped, jumping out of her floaty and nearly stumbling into the fire. Baz caught her by grabbing the back of her shirt and yanking her away from the flames. Talia barely skipped a beat, propelling herself toward the water, taking her clothes off as she went.

"Are you sure it's safe, with most of you guys as drunk as you are?" I asked with concern, eyeing Talia in particular. I think she drank to every question asked.

"Safer than the fire," Baz pointed out, standing up and holding his hand out to help Rhiannon. Kai and Zoey were racing to the water to join Talia, who was already running in stark naked. Chapter Ten: Starlight Secrets

Theo

I COULD TELL Lux was a little uncomfortable with the idea of skinny dipping from the way she hung back, apprehension clouding her expression—but Jasmine wasn't taking no for an answer.

"Come on, it's so much fun! Finish your shot and let's do it!" Jasmine urged, handing Lux her shot glass. Lux hesitated for a moment, her eyes going to me. Then that look of determination played in her eyes, and she tossed back the tequila before shivering.

"Fine, let's do it," she said resolutely. Jasmine grabbed her hand and dragged her towards the beach. They paused at the shoreline, pulling their clothes off piece by piece while Desmond disappeared long enough to grab everyone's towels off the line, since nobody seemed to be thinking ahead about *after* the dip.

I swallowed hard as Lux bent to pull her pants down. Then her shirt came off, and I had to turn around lest I approach the water with very noticeable excitement.

"Oh-la-la!" Talia called out with appreciation as Lux and

Jasmine ran into the water. I couldn't help but sneak a peek, the moonlight illuminating Lux's perfect pale ass and her smooth back. *That* was enough to give me heart palpitations, I couldn't imagine what the front view was like.

I waited for Desmond to return with the towels, thinking as many unpleasant thoughts as I possibly could before I finally headed toward the water. I started walking, shucking my clothes as I went.

We'd skinny dipped as a group while drunk a thousand times before, but there was something inherently different about doing it with Lux around. Maybe it was that I'd never been attracted to anyone in the group before; and I was immensely attracted to her. Knowing she was naked was ruining me in the best way.

Luckily, the jolt of cold water at my hips was enough to quiet the biological reaction I felt around her. I dove beneath the water, immerging myself fully. The shock of cool water chasing away the drunken haze I'd been in.

When I resurfaced, I was about an arm's length away from Lux. The dark water obscured everything, but the look in her eyes when our gazes connected unveiled the desire brewing between us both.

We were surrounded by other people, but it was like we only had eyes for each other. Zoey and Kai, Rhiannon and Baz were certainly in their own worlds, not that I blamed them. I was having a hell of a time keeping my hands from tugging Lux to me, and she wasn't even mine.

Desmond ran into the water, diving beneath the surface just as quick. I felt a momentarily pang of sympathy for him. This wasn't his first time skinny dipping with someone he had feelings for, yet he made it look easy.

Talia swam beneath the water, grabbing Jasmine's ankle and tugging her beneath the surface. When they resurfaced, laughing, it was game on. Jasmine swam after Talia in retaliation, leaving Lux and me floating somewhat alone.

"You slippery eel!" Jasmine shouted through her laughter. "Des, come help me get her back for that!"

Desmond shook his head at me as he passed, swimming after them both. There wasn't a thing he wouldn't do for Jasmine.

"They're kinda cute together, huh?" Lux remarked, watching after them. "Jas and Desmond, I mean."

"Yeah, they are."

Lux swam a little closer to me, a look of conspiracy in her eyes. "Wanna hear a secret?"

"Yes, of course," I grinned back, moving a little closer to her.

Lux cupped a hand over her lips. "Jas likes him. Like, *likes* him likes him."

"Really? Did she say that?" I asked, and Lux nodded.

"But you didn't hear it from me," she mimed zipping her lips, that gorgeous smile still tipping the corners up. Her eyes went to my shoulders, resting on my collarbone, and she bit down on her bottom lip. "I have another secret."

"Oh, yeah? What is it?" I asked, feeling affected by the heat in her eyes. She moved closer, the water sloshing over her exposed cleavage.

"Jasmine thinks you'd be a good dick-straction—for me."

"A good dick-straction, huh?" I repeated, lifting a brow. We were surrounded by all that water, but my throat was drier than a desert.

She giggled, sinking lower in the water so that it covered up to her chin, then she nodded. Her greyish eyes luminous in the moonlight. "Yeah, but...I've never had a one-night stand."

"Trust me, you wouldn't be a one-night stand," I swam closer to her, our bodies separated by mere inches. I knew I couldn't have her once and be done. Her eyes widened, taking me in, and her lips parted. Lips that I wanted to claim as mine.

"A casual fling, then..." Lux stood up, the water obscuring

my view of what were probably perfectly pink nipples, the same rosy hue as her lips.

"Mmhmm," I murmured, keeping what I wanted to say locked down; that she couldn't be a casual fling, either. She was the girl you kept, not the one you discarded after some fun. "What are you saying?"

"That I...want to try it," she admitted, her eyes locked on mine. It was too dark to tell if she was blushing, but if I had to place a wager on it—I'd say yes. "A casual fling, I mean."

"Is that so?" I was about to move in closer, to put my hand around her waist and tug her towards me so she could feel how into the idea I was, but then her eyes widened with absolute fear, and she let out a strangled screech, all but leaping out of the water and at me. I didn't even have time to register her naked, trembling body in my arms.

"Lux, what the hell?" Jasmine called out, alarmed.

"Something touched the back of my leg, and it felt *slimy!*" she wailed, trying to climb up my body and out of the water. It put her breasts at perfect level with my gaze—not that I was complaining.

"It was probably a fish," I reassured her. Lux's eyes dropped down to my face, and she realized she had climbed halfway up my body to escape the unknown thing that had touched her.

"A fish? Ew, nope, I'm out," she said decidedly, pushing off me and heading back to the shore as quickly as she could.

To my dismay, Lux went to bed not long after the skinny dipping ordeal.

I, on the other hand, wasn't tired at all. I knew sleep would allude me, so I didn't bother trying to rest. Not even when everyone else went to bed for the night. Instead, I brought an extra blanket up with me to the top of the cliffs at our campsite, spreading it out so I could lay down on it and look up at the night sky.

It was nearly 3 a.m., and I was still laying on my back. My arms were folded behind my head, and I stared up at the stars in the quiet solitude, thoughts too tangled and body too affected to fall asleep.

Lux's words from the water kept replaying in my mind on some sort of tortuous loop. The feel of her body against mine as she'd all but climbed up me to get out of the water imprinted against me. It was like every part of my skin that'd meet with hers was on fire and burning for more.

My thoughts were interrupted by rustling at the bottom of the hill, followed by the sound of a zipper punctuating the quiet. A dark figure climbed out of Jasmine and Lux's tent, pausing to close it before flicking on a flashlight, following the pathway west of camp.

Turning my head, I looked back up at the endless sky, letting the quiet sounds of nature move over me. Crickets, the occasional owl, the rustling of the leaves in the trees—followed by the telltale sign of someone returning.

The flashlight paused between the tents before going out, but the person lingered, seeing my shape on the rocks illuminated by the full moon. Intrinsically, I knew it was Lux.

She wore a dark, baggy sweater pulled up over her head, but I could tell it was her in the way she carried herself. Graceful and poised. I turned my head, listening to her footfall as she climbed the rocky hill. She stepped out of the treeline, her red tresses glowing when the moonlight spilled over her.

She stilled, catching the shape of me on the rocks, and waited until her eyes adjusted. "Theo?"

"Hey," I sat up, tugging my hood down so she could better make out my face, and gave her a friendly smile.

"I'm sorry, I didn't realize anyone was still up."

"Don't apologize," I told her. "I couldn't sleep, so I figured I'd watch the stars."

"Mind if I join you?" she asked, somewhat timidly. "I can't sleep anymore, either."

My heart jolted in my chest, but I covered my reaction with an easy smile. "Sure," I said, laying back down and resuming my position staring up at the sky.

Lux sat down beside me, hesitating for a moment before she laid fully down. I turned my head to look at her while she took in the sky, the stars reflecting in her deep irises.

The urge to get to know her was every bit as strong as the urge to reach out and take her hand. It would be so easy; all it would take was moving my hand a couple of inches to the right.

Instead, I forced myself to look at the sky. "Jasmine's been trying to get you to come camping for years. Looks like she finally wore you down. Gotta say, I'm glad she finally succeeded."

"I know," she laughed, following it with a soft sigh. "I'm glad she did, too. I'm actually having a lot of fun." She stole a quick peek at me. Had I not been so focused on her every movement; I would have missed it.

"You sound surprised about that," I said.

"My family never did outdoorsy activities, not like this. My parents' idea of camping is to rent a cottage with all the amenities, including a pool, so, no chance of fish brushing against my leg there. I never pictured myself doing this," she laughed lightly, shaking her head.

I chanced another glance at her. Her complexion appeared crystalline in the moonlight, her red hair a beautiful contrast. Her chin was angled up as she gazed at the stars. She was heart-stirringly stunning, and I couldn't tear my gaze away from her parted lips.

"What changed?"

She turned her head at my question, and blinked, her long

lashes brushing against the tops of her cheeks fleetingly before those luminous eyes focused on me.

"To be honest, I needed to get out of my parents' house for a bit," she admitted. "I moved back in after graduating, it's only temporary, but..." she pulled her gaze away, focusing again on the sky above us.

I chuckled lightly, nodding slowly. I could understand that. "Parents driving you nuts already?"

"I wish," she frowned, turning her head back to look at me. I met her gaze directly, my breath catching in my throat at the emotion reflecting back at me. She smiled, covering the hurt. "My little sister's welcome home gift was to sleep with my boyfriend."

I whistled lowly. "Ouch. Why would she do that?"

"It's a very long story," Lux admitted. "My sister has mental health issues. Although she won't admit it, or get help..." She sighed, glancing up at the stars. She didn't seem judgmental of her sister, just deeply hurt.

"I'm sorry, that's really rough."

She paused, her eyes dropping to my lips before she forced her gaze to meet mine. "It is. I love her, but sometimes I can't help but hate her for everything she's put me through over the years. Then I feel bad, because you shouldn't hate your own family, your own sister. There's something inherently wrong with that."

I felt bad for her. I couldn't imagine having such a toxic relationship with Olivia. No matter the distance, my sister could count on me, and I could count on her.

"I don't think you hate her," I remarked, turning my head to look at her. "I think you hate the pain she causes, and the divide...but not her."

"Yeah, that's it," she looked astonished that I understood, and I couldn't help but feel good about that.

"And no offence, but your boyfriend—"

"Ex-boyfriend," Lux corrected, eyes snapping back to mine.

"Your *ex*-boyfriend is an idiot," I finished, grinning at her.

"I agree," she smiled, her eyes hopeful. "I'm glad though. Now I can go wherever I want, do whatever I want. There's nothing tying me anywhere."

"Where are you planning on going?" I asked, unable to look away from her.

Lux had no issue breaking our gaze. She looked back up at the sky, letting a soft sigh escape. "Wherever. I've applied to jobs in so many different cities. I'll go wherever they hire me. I have no attachments to anywhere in particular."

"Well, that's exciting. Here's to wherever," I said softly, appreciating her for a moment longer before looking straight ahead.

I felt her turn, felt her eyes on my face and saw her smile out of the corner of my eye.

"What about you? Are you happy with your career?"

"Yes, I am."

"I've never met an environmental geoscientist before," she said, a smile playing on her pretty lips. "How'd you get into it, anyway?"

"My grandfather was really into nature, so was my dad. My family did a lot of camping when I was younger." I shrugged. "My dad was a miner, he's retired now, but he always hoped I'd do something...more. I decided to focus on environmental geoscience because it'd give me the opportunity to be in nature, but also have steady work."

"Do you often go out of town for work?"

"Yeah," I nodded. "I leave in three weeks for Peru to run tests on the soil in one of the mines there. I'll be there for at least a week, then I'll come home and work from the office until after Zoey and Kai tie the knot. I'm in town for the wedding, but I'll be on a flight to Vancouver two days after for a couple of days."

She nodded. Her pinky finger found mine, resting on the

rock beside it, and I wondered if her nerve endings sizzled with the contact too. "It sounds exciting, getting to see all those different places."

"It is," I admitted with a grin, my pinky brushing against hers.

We both glanced back up at the sky in time to catch a shooting star falling. Lux let out an audible gasp, reaching for my hand to grip it with excitement. "I've never seen a shooting star before!" she exclaimed with wonder.

"It's said that when you see a shooting star, it's the universe sending you a message, urging you to listen to the whispers of your soul," I said, turning to her, seeing the astonishment in her eyes.

"Is that so?" she murmured, her hand still grasping mine. Her eyes held me captivated, daring me to make a move. "And what message is the universe sending me?"

"To take a chance," I murmured. Rolling over, I pressed my lips to hers.

Kissing Lux was otherworldly. She tasted like the tail of a shooting star, sparks everywhere. I'd never experienced a kiss so filled with electricity that it left me near dizzy, my body vibrating like it had been struck by lightning. It was more miraculous than witnessing the northern lights. More colourful.

Resounding and amorous, the kiss went on and blessedly on until Lux shifted her body, rolling so she was half laying on me and half on the rock beside me.

Breathless, she lifted her head to study me incredulously.

"Do you have a girlfriend?" The question seemed to come out of nowhere, but the fact that she'd stopped the kiss to demand it had me grinning.

"Nope, currently unattached." Except even as I said it, I tasted the untruth in my words—I was forming an attachment, a new one, to this beautiful illuminating woman before me. I wanted to know everything there was to know about her, and I wanted her to find out everything about me too.

And I definitely didn't want to stop kissing her. Not yet, anyway.

Luckily, my answer seemed to be exactly what she needed. Her gaze went to my lips, and then she was kissing me again.

RAINY DAYS

Theo and I made out on the rocks for just under an hour, until the sun started making its ascent. We watched it crest the horizon, the light painting the underside of the thick clouds gathering in the distance. Then we crept off to our own tents to sleep for a bit.

We'd held hands while we walked back, and he'd kissed me when we reached my tent, his hand cupping the side of my neck, his fingers tangling in my hair. There was something about that kiss that told me whatever we'd started here was far from over.

I passed out again as soon as my head hit the pillow, exhaustion from the adventures the day before hitting me hard. When I woke up a few hours later, it was to the sound of raindrops on our tent.

It was darker than it should have been with the sun obscured by the greyish rain clouds overhead. I could hear people moving around outside, voices rising and falling from the bottom of the hill, and what sounded like a tarp flapping.

Jasmine stirred beneath her blankets, letting out a long sigh and stretching. I sat up, reaching for my sweater to tug it on. It was a little colder than it had been yesterday, and there would be no sun to warm me up.

"Where'd you disappear to last night?" Jasmine asked, her voice croaky from sleep. But her shrewd eyes were studying me, not missing a thing.

"I went to the bathroom, then noticed Theo was still up stargazing…so I joined him." I felt no need to lie to my best friend about it.

"Really?!" Jasmine's entire face lit up. "Did you guys do it?"

"No!" I half whispered, half laughed, my face heating. "We kissed a little, but we didn't do anything else."

I'd wanted to, especially after he'd started kissing me and I all but melted into it. I'd *never* had such an intense reaction to a kiss before. Kissing Scott had never made me feel so sexually aroused, but Theo's lips upon mine had made me want to peel back my clothes and submit myself to him completely. Each stroke of his hand over my body had ignited more flames of desire.

I had no doubts that if kissing him was as explosive as it'd been, that actually having him inside me would blow my mind in the best way. Now I wanted it more than ever, but…I had no idea how to be *that girl*, the one that went for the things she wanted without thinking about the consequences. How to be the kind of woman that could separate an amazing sexual experience from their feelings.

Because I knew without a shadow of a doubt now, that I could easily fall for this man. I didn't know if I even had a casual bone in my body, heck, I already felt a lot of dangerous things for him. How could I have a fling with someone I was already feeling things for? There was nothing casual about that.

A pillow smacked me in the face, rousing me from my rumination.

"You're thinking too loud," Jasmine complained, frowning at me.

"Oh, I'm sorry," I said sarcastically, rolling my eyes and tossing her pillow back at her. "I'll try to keep it down."

"I'm just saying, Lux. Don't overthink it. Let whatever happens, happen. What are you so afraid of, anyway? That you'll actually have an orgasm?"

"Very funny," I frowned. "No, I'm afraid that I'll get attached, and this is doomed to go nowhere."

"Who says it's doomed to go nowhere?" Jasmine said through a yawn, stretching her arms over her head. "You're two consenting adults, you can decide what things look like after. It doesn't have to be one or the other."

"He lives in Sudbury, I don't. He travels for work, I don't even know where I'm going to be in three months. The only thing we can decide on is here and now."

"So, decide on it then. And whatever happens in the future, happens. You have to let yourself be okay with whatever it is." Jasmine stood up, hunting around the tent for her sweater. She tugged it on when she found it, then she peered out the tent window. "Looks like he's already up, constructing a rain shelter with Desmond and Baz."

I couldn't deny it; knowing Theo was down there had me wanting to hurry up and join everyone.

"Is it going to rain all day?" I asked, regretting that I hadn't packed a raincoat.

"Pretty much, but don't worry. I got you," Jasmine replied, turning back to her bag and rooting through it. She pulled out two plastic packages and tossed one at me. It was a clear rain poncho. "This will keep you relatively dry."

"Thanks." I stood up, opening the package. "Wait, how are we supposed to cook food if it's raining?" The site had two fire pits, one on the rocks and one on the beach, but both were exposed to the rain.

"We brought some propane stoves, it'll be okay," she assured me as she unzipped the tent.

Jasmine and I left, zipping the tent up behind us. We headed to the thunderbox first before walking down to join the others who were awake.

Baz, Theo and Desmond had constructed a rather large rain shelter halfway up the hill, tying tarps to trees with ropes. All our chairs were arranged under the shelter, and someone had dragged up the coolers from the beach.

Jasmine gestured to where Desmond had set the propane stoves up along the wooden table built into the circle of trees. It was big enough to hold two camping stoves and not much else. Theo was across from him in front of one with the percolator, brewing coffee, while Desmond heated up breakfast on the other stove.

Theo's eyes met mine as we walked past, his lips kicking up in a smile that had the butterflies swooping low in my belly. I smiled back shyly, letting my hair fall over my shoulder and obscure my face.

"Coffee?" he offered, cocking his brow.

"Please," Jasmine answered for the both of us, and Theo poured the coffee into two tin mugs. His fingers brushed over mine when he passed me the tin mug, his smile deepening. My cheeks heated, remembering how his lips had moved against mine last night—and how those hands had felt on my body.

"Thanks," I murmured, breaking contact and following Jasmine to his cooler to grab the creamer.

"Everyone cool with egg burritos?" Desmond asked, glancing at us. "They're cooked, just have to warm them up."

"Sounds delicious," Jasmine replied, and Desmond grinned at her before he resumed pulling tinfoil-wrapped burritos out of the cooler beside him. "Can we help with anything?"

"Nope, we've got it. Sit back and relax," Desmond said, tossing her another easy grin. Jasmine nodded, tugging my hand and leading me towards our camp chairs. They were a little damp, but not soaked. Someone must have brought them up right when the rain started.

My poncho worked to keep me dry from the dampness, and I was thankful Jasmine had thought to bring an extra one for me. We sipped our coffees quietly, watching Theo and Desmond work the stoves and chat amongst themselves while Baz inspected the rain shelter to make sure it was holding up okay.

A few moments later, Desmond walked over with two breakfast burritos, holding them with paper towels. "They're a little hot, so you might want to let them cool," he said, his gaze resting on Jasmine for a moment.

"Thanks, Des! We'll handle clean up," she promised, sending him a bright smile.

"Don't worry about it, there's not much to clean," he winked before walking back to the camp stove to put more on. We continued sipping our coffees, letting the egg burritos cool a little longer.

When the burritos had cooled enough to eat, I unwrapped mine and took a bite, moaning from how delicious it was. Scrambled eggs with red and green peppers, onion and cheese. I hadn't realized how hungry I was until I started eating, but it hit the spot.

Normally, I wasn't much of a breakfast girl. But there was something about being outside in nature, with all the fresh air, that made me ravenous.

The others weren't up yet, but they started stirring when the scent of egg burritos and coffee reached them. One by one, Zoey, Kai and Talia emerged from their tents, Talia carrying her floaty. It was looking more than a little deflated now.

They came down to join us, Talia blowing her floaty back up as she walked. Her eyes still half-closed.

Baz went back up to his tent to fetch Rhiannon and Moose. The moment he unzipped the tent, Moose barrelled out and headed straight to us, tail wagging. It took Rhiannon and Baz a little longer to come down.

Rhiannon was moving gingerly, as if she was stiff and sore. Baz walked behind her, with his hand on the small of her back. He had a thick blanket in his other arm, and once he brought her over to her chair, he wrapped the blanket around her and helped her get settled.

He planted a quick kiss on her lips before heading over to grab coffee.

"Is it going to rain all day?" Talia asked, dropping her re-inflated floaty onto the ground before wiping the sleep from her eyes.

"Until later this afternoon," Rhiannon replied, accepting the mug of coffee Baz brought her with an appreciative smile. He also brought her a breakfast burrito, which he tucked into her chair's cupholder to cool.

"Ah, sorry Rhi," Zoey said, sending her a sympathetic look, sitting in the chair beside her.

"It's all good, I took some meds. Later I'll get into the cold water, that'll help with the aching joints."

"We could all use a rest day after yesterday," Kai said, stretching near the coffee station. "My muscles are pissed."

"What muscles, bean pole?" Talia teased, knocking him with her hip as she approached Theo with her empty mug.

Zoey snickered, stopping when Kai sent her a wounded look. "You've got muscles, babe," she assured him.

"Wanna arm wrestle?" Talia asked, flexing her bicep. I had to admit, it was muscular—even more muscular than Theo's, and *he* had impressive muscles. It was clear that Talia worked out.

"Maybe later, once I've hit the whiskey," Kai grinned.

"You're right. You'd have to be drunk to not feel the pain and the shame of losing to me again!" Talia snorted, holding her mug out for Theo to fill. He poured the rest of the coffee in, then immediately set to making more.

Jasmine leaned over to whisper something in my ear. I met her halfway. "Talia is a three-time winner of the Canadian Professional Arm Wrestling Championship," she explained. "The guys always challenge her when drunk, but she dominates every time."

"I believe it," I said with a laugh.

Desmond finished cooking up the rest of the burritos, and once everyone was fed, he grabbed one for himself and joined us. Theo waited until he'd finished brewing more coffee before walking over with the percolator. He filled a tin mug for himself and paused in front of Jasmine and me.

"Want a top up?" he asked us.

"If everyone's already had some?" I asked. I was feeling more than a little tired from yesterday's…adventures.

"I can always make more," he grinned, topping my tin mug up before moving to Jasmine's. Once everyone had a top up, he set the percolator down on the stove and joined us.

Jasmine and I sipped our coffee while the rest of the group focused on eating. Everyone seemed as tired as I was, but there was a sense of peace over the camp.

I tried not to stare at Theo, opting to glance over my shoulder toward the beach, watching the raindrops hit the water steadily. The sound of the droplets hitting the leaves around me mixed with the smell of rain and forest was oddly calming.

I had to admit, I was loving this trip. Being outdoors like this felt *healing*. I wasn't stressing about my future, I wasn't thinking about my sister, or holding the ache of what she'd done so closely to me. Yeah, it still stung when I thought about it, but that sting was distant.

When my gaze moved forward again, I caught Theo watching me with a reverent smile.

"It's nice, huh? Even when it's raining."

"It really is," I nodded, feeling that same hope blooming in my chest. Jasmine's words from up at the tent echoed in my mind, but my earlier fears about falling for him and ending up hurt seemed to evaporate with his green eyes on me.

11

FLOATING

IT CONTINUED to rain for the rest of the morning. We hung out under the makeshift shelter, and Zoey brought out a deck of cards. We played a few rounds of friendly poker before lunch.

Time seemed to be passing slowly, but I didn't mind in the slightest. It gave me the opportunity to keep sneaking glances at Lux, taking in her shy smile and the subtle blush that coloured her cheeks each time I caught her gaze.

We had lunch—cold sandwiches and pasta salad, prepped by Jasmine and handed out by Lux. Once we'd eaten and cleaned up from that, the temperature had warmed up enough to go swimming, even though the rain was still coming down.

Everyone changed into their swimsuits. Zoey and Jasmine collected everyone's life jackets so we could float carefree in the river, dropping them in a pile near the pathway while Kai carried a cooler with beer.

One by one, we picked up our life jackets and carefully

walked the lower pathway on the side of the cliff. We wouldn't risk trying to cliff jump today, not with the rocks as slick as they were, so we made our way to the lower ledge.

Talia was the first to jump in. She wore her life jacket like a diaper and bobbed up the second she went under. "Toss me a cold one!" she called out, and Kai threw her a beer.

I tossed my life jacket in and dove in after it, the shock of the temperature zapping my senses awake. I broke the surface, pushing my soaked hair back and wiping the water from my eyes.

It was cold but refreshing. I felt more awake than I had all morning. I'd been in a bit of a fog after not getting much sleep the night before. My inability to shut my brain off had been a factor, but then I got a taste of Lux's lips, awakening the hunger I felt for her. Sleep was futile after that, though I'd tried.

I think I might have gotten about two hours of scattered sleep total before giving up and getting up for the day. I was going to crash eventually, but I didn't want to miss a second of time with this woman.

Talia was already busting my chops about it. She hadn't said anything yet, but I could tell from how she was watching me and Lux at breakfast that she *knew* something had transpired between us.

Zoey and Kai jumped in. Zoey adjusted her life jacket so that she was sitting on it, and Kai rested his upper body over his like I was doing. He reached out, putting his hands on her thighs, and smiled at her. Zoey let out a giggle, trying to stop Kai's fingers creeping up her thigh.

Another splash of someone jumping in sounded behind me, water droplets hitting the back of my head and I turned, giving them privacy, and glanced back towards the ledge to see who'd jumped.

Lux and Jasmine were the only ones still standing on the ledge. Desmond had jumped in while my back was turned, and he was still beneath the water. He popped up a moment later, shaking the water from his hair and beard before swimming back to the ledge and reaching into the cooler that he'd left there to help himself to a beer. He grabbed one for me too, making eye contact with me and nodding before he tossed it.

I caught it one handed and grinned my thanks at him before opening it and taking a deep sip, my eyes once again going back to the woman that had captivated my attention with her kind heart and her newly awakened sense of adventure. She was wearing her black bikini again. It was just as tantalizing as her white one. I'd never wanted to be a scrap of material before, and yet I found myself envious of the way the bikini bottoms hugged her hips.

Lux hesitantly dipped her toe in and pulled her foot back as if the water had electrocuted her. "It's freezing!" she said to Jasmine.

"It'll feel warmer once you're in it, promise," Jasmine assured her, jumping in. Lux deliberated for another moment, holding her life jacket closer to her body like it could keep her warm. The rain was coming down a little harder now, so either way she was getting wet. Her hair was down and damp, curling around the ends.

Lux looked so exquisite, the epitome of a natural beauty. She took my breath away more effectively than the shock of cold water had. Her grey eyes met mine, her cheeks pinkening beneath my gaze. I wonder if she felt the desire rolling off me in waves. I couldn't help but smile wider, lifting my chin, daring her to jump.

She drew in a lungful of air, preparing herself before tossing her life jacket in. Then she jumped. She disappeared beneath the dark surface before coming up, teeth already chattering.

"Nope, it's still freezing!" she exclaimed, grabbing for her life jacket, and Jasmine laughed.

Jasmine floated over to the ledge, grabbing beers for herself and Lux. "Want one Zoey? Kai? Theo?"

"Sure!" Zoey called out, and Jasmine tossed the beers over to us while Lux got situated in her life jacket, sitting on it the way Zoey and Jasmine were.

Talia was still wearing hers like a giant diaper, both legs in the arm holes and the strap around her waist.

Baz and Rhiannon were still up at the camp, taking their time, but they'd be along shortly. I knew from previous camping experiences with the two of them that damp, rainy weather was hard on Rhiannon's body, and Baz did everything he could to make sure she didn't suffer too greatly.

Rhiannon didn't complain outwardly, but we could always tell if she was in pain. She'd be quieter, move slower, her joints stiff and unyielding. Most of her pain came from the spinal surgery she'd had as a child to put rods in her back and straighten it. She dealt with more pain than the average person and typically didn't let it slow her down too much. She was tough as hell, and busy running her own photography business.

During her free time, she and Baz loved camping. They went more than any of us combined. Slowing down completely wasn't in Rhiannon's vocabulary, and she'd once confessed to me that she'd be in pain whether she took it easy at home or went camping—and that she'd much rather have the adventure than the regrets.

Rhiannon and Baz appeared at the top of the pathway, Moose running in front of them. The dog had his life jacket on too, so that Baz wouldn't have to worry about him getting tired while we lazed about in the river.

Baz helped Rhiannon down the pathway, holding her hand and supporting her weight. She said something to him and he smiled, shaking his head. Once they'd made it to the ledge, Rhiannon pulled her hand away and tucked her blonde hair behind her ear, her eyes going to the river.

"Is it cold?" she asked us, sliding her legs into the arm holes of her life jacket like Talia had done. According to the two of them it was the comfiest way to sit on the life jacket, even if it looked like they were wearing giant orange diapers.

"Freezing!" Lux chattered. She was about five feet away from me, floating near Jasmine.

I wanted to bridge the gap but also didn't want to appear over eager, so I stayed where I was, keeping my distance and my gaze off her, but I was still painfully aware of her every move. It was as if each movement that made a ripple in the water made a ripple through me, too.

Rhiannon smiled and shrugged before jumping in. She resurfaced, letting out a sigh of contentment. "It feels good though," she murmured, dipping her head back and letting the rain fall over her face.

Moose jumped in too, swimming over to Rhiannon like he couldn't bear to be apart from her. He sniffed at her, checking that she was okay, then swam after the stick Baz had tossed in for him.

Baz jumped in, and once he resurfaced, he swam to the ledge to grab beers for himself and Rhiannon. "Anyone need a refill?" he asked over his shoulder.

"Me!" Talia called out, paddling a little closer to the ledge so she could toss her crushed empty on it. We'd pile the empties there and bring them up after we were done soaking in the river.

One of the best things about camping with this group is that they were serious about leaving no trace behind. We brought back everything we couldn't burn, and we often did a clean sweep before we left to ensure we got everything people before us had left. I'd been camping with others who hadn't cared as much, and that was always frustrating.

Baz tossed her a fresh beer, and she caught it with a grin. "Thanks!"

The rain was beginning to let up, though if the dark grey clouds in the distance were any indicator, the storm was far from over.

Lux leaned back and looked up at the sky, her red hair fanning out in the river behind her. She was gently moving her legs, propelling herself backwards as she kept her chin tilted towards the sky, her eyelids closed against the raindrops.

She floated until she bumped into my shoulder. I knew it'd happen and hadn't bothered moving because I'd *wanted* her to bump into me. It gave me the perfect excuse to talk to her.

"Oops, sorry!" she exclaimed, her eyelids popping open she turned her head to look at me.

"I'm not," I grinned, loving how her cheeks heated. She bit her lower lip, her eyes dropping down to my lips, and I knew she was thinking about last night too. I couldn't resist touching her a little, so I reached out and gently tugged on her leg, turning her so that she was facing me, and then I left my hand there, stroking along the underside of her knee.

"Oh," she murmured, her breath caught on an exhale. She blinked at me, her eyes—so much like the grey in the sky above—darkening with desire.

"Still…enjoying yourself?" I asked, cocking a brow as my hand worked her calf muscle beneath the water and hoping like hell she didn't regret our kiss.

"Despite the rain? Yes, actually," she replied, a knowing smile gracing her lips. It was as if she was thinking of the night before too. She bit her lip again, her gaze dropping to my mouth, and I knew without her saying so that she had zero regrets.

I moved on to her other leg, massaging her calf and letting my hand travel above her knee. Not enough to be completely inappropriate, but enough to make her lids flutter with wanton need.

"It's supposed to stop soon," I replied, lifting my chin to look up. I pushed my hair back from my eyes with my free hand so it wouldn't obscure my vision. It was still raining, but not as much as before. The water droplets were smaller and less frequent, and in the distance, I could see a slice of the blue sky. "We should be able to have a fire tonight."

"Won't the wood be soaked from the rain?" she asked, drawing my attention back to her.

"No, Desmond covered our firewood with a tarp last night, so it'll be dry," I answered.

"He thinks of everything," she grinned, glancing over at Desmond. He was floating near Jasmine, and they were talking.

"He does, he's a good guy." I remarked.

"I wish Jasmine would follow her own advice and take a chance," Lux murmured, watching the two of them together.

"She gave you advice to take a chance, huh?" I inquired, bringing her attention back to me. Her gaze settled on me, her cheeks heating at my proximity.

"Sort of," she shrugged, trying to act nonchalant. For some inexplicable reason, the fact that she'd been talking about me made my heart soar.

"Personally, I love taking chances," I told her, my gaze falling to her lips. I wanted to kiss her again, wanted to feel her body against mine.

"Well, here's to taking chances, then," Lux said, lifting her beer in a toast. We clicked our cans together and both took a sip at the same time.

12

OPTIONS

ux

WE FLOATED in the river for the rest of the afternoon. I was practically a prune when we finally got out to dry off. By the time we all emerged from our tents, the rain had stopped, and the grey clouds had broken up, revealing the blue sky and the timid sun.

Desmond said there wasn't a whole lot of dry firewood, enough for a fire later but not enough to cook dinner, so we used the propane stoves to heat up the chicken stir-fry Zoey had prepped.

Once everyone had finished eating and we'd cleaned up, the sun had begun to make its descent. We moved our chairs back down to the beach, placing them around the fire pit while Theo and Desmond worked on getting the fire started. It took a few tries and fifteen minutes before they got the flames to take, but I got to enjoy the process of watching Theo's muscles in his arms work.

"I think we're going to have to make a run to the marina for more ice tomorrow," Talia declared, returning with another bottle of whiskey and her speaker ball. "Levels are getting pretty low."

"I could go," Desmond offered. "I should turn my truck over." Desmond's truck was fifteen years old and didn't like sitting for long without use. As it was, we'd have to jump the battery before we could leave here in a couple of days.

"I can go with you, if Talia or Theo let me borrow one of their kayaks," Jasmine offered. "Kayaks move quicker through the water," she informed me when she noticed my questioning look.

"You can borrow mine," Theo offered with a grin.

"It's settled then, we'll go tomorrow morning." Jasmine told Desmond, and he gave her a smile that felt like it was just for her. I turned, hiding a smile of my own, and Jasmine knocked her elbow into my arm. "What?!" she whispered incredulously.

"Oh, nothing at all," I replied easily, my gaze catching Theo's across the new flames he and Desmond had finally coaxed. He had an amused glint in his eyes too, reminding me about our conversation in the water. I hoped this meant Jasmine was considering taking a chance with Desmond, but I didn't want to say anything to spook her.

Talia connected her speaker to her phone and started playing music. "Heck yes! She's charged baby!" she declared, plunking down on her inflatable. "I love the twenty-first century, charging banks are an incredible invention!" she sighed happily, turning the volume to the perfect level.

"I don't know. I mean, don't get me wrong, charging banks are convenient. But I sort of envy our grandparents and parents. They didn't have to worry about social media or staying connected all the time," Rhiannon remarked thoughtfully, frowning at her phone.

"Fair enough," Talia amended. "I barely use social media; life is better without it for sure."

"I need to use it for work, unfortunately there's no getting around it. I've had *five* inquiries about future weddings, and a few of the brides have already sent follow up emails. I announced on my business page I was out of town camping and wouldn't have reliable reception, and they still expect to hear from me." She sighed, letting her phone fall onto her lap.

Rhiannon's worries made my fingers twitch a little, and I wondered if I'd gotten any emails about job prospects. I didn't care about whatever I was missing on social media, but hearing back from prospective employers was important—especially if I wanted to get out of my parents' house.

"Hey Des, have you rented out the spare room in our place yet?" Jasmine asked Desmond. I shot her a look, and she returned it with one of her own.

"Not yet," Desmond answered, poking at the fire with the long stick that was dubbed the designated fire poker.

"Well, hold off. We might have found a new roommate," Jasmine declared, putting her arm around my shoulders.

"Jas," I cautioned, laughing awkwardly. "I have no clue what I'm doing yet."

"I think it's a great idea, and I'm not saying that because you're my best friend and I want you to be my roommate," Jasmine grinned at me. "There are *a lot* of medical clinics and even a hospital in Sudbury that you could apply at, and while you wait for something more permanent, there are plenty of restaurants and stores to work at."

Desmond—and Theo—were watching with interest.

"I don't know," I sighed. I wasn't opposed to the idea of going further north for work, but I didn't want to potentially take a room off a college student, especially if I couldn't find a job in my field.

"My sister works at the hospital in Sudbury, I could see if

there are any openings coming up, and I'm sure she'll put a good word in for you," Baz said. I was touched at his offer.

"Are you sure your sister would be okay with that? She doesn't know me."

"She trusts my judge of character," Baz replied confidently. "I think you're alright," he winked.

"It's settled then!" Jasmine declared happily.

"Not really," I frowned. But if I was being perfectly honest with myself, Jasmine's idea didn't sound half bad.

"Don't you want to get the hell out of Dodge?" Jasmine asked lowly, arching a brow.

"Well, yeah. But moving twice sounds like a lot of work, and what if I don't find a job?"

"With your grades and the glowing recommendations you have from your professors, you will. I have complete faith in you," Jasmine assured me.

"You're welcome to come check it out," Desmond interjected. "If you want it, it'll save me having to find another renter."

"I thought you rented out to college students?"

"We do, or we used to, but it's exhausting vetting people that frequently, and with Theo gone as much as he is, it usually falls to me. I wouldn't mind getting more stable tenants in."

"We don't really care, so long as the rent's paid," Theo winked.

"You're the other owner?" I asked, surprised.

He nodded. "Yeah, but I'm hardly around. Desmond works a lot too, so you don't have to worry about landlords intruding all the time." His smile put me at ease. "However, we are just next door, so if there's any issues, we're on top of it, so to speak."

"Not that there will be any issues, we've done a lot of renovations on the place and pretty much everything is new and up to code," Desmond added reassuringly.

"I approve, you'd make a great addition, Princess. College

students were fun when *we* were college students. Now, well. That season of time is over, and I don't think a college student will jibe with us as well as you do," Talia interjected with a grin. I'd forgotten she was Jasmine's roommate too, but I felt touched she seemed as into the idea as Jas.

"We could make a pit stop in Sudbury on our way home so you could check out the place and see for yourself," Jasmine said.

They were all dangling a huge, juicy carrot in front of my face. I had to admit, it'd be a great opportunity to get out of my parents' house and away from Brinley, *and* to spend more time with Jas. This trip had made me realize how much I missed having her as a constant in my life.

"Alright, fine. We'll check it out and I'll think about it," I said. Talia and Jasmine immediately let out a cheer, and I shook my head, trying to hide the grin.

As pathetic as it was, it felt good to be *wanted*. I mean, I knew my parents loved me and enjoyed having me around, but they were consumed with their own lives and Brinley's antics—and Brinley certainly didn't like having me around, unless she was actively tormenting me. Then I supposed I served some purpose for her, but that wasn't something I wanted.

I wanted an environment that felt like home; an environment I could be myself in. One that I wouldn't be walking on eggshells, constantly wondering when the next hit would come.

Of course, Theo being one of the landlords complicated things a little. It made me hesitate to want to start anything physical with him. Would that be blurring the lines too much? I knew he worked a lot, and was often out of town for work. But I didn't want him to think I was moving to Sudbury to chase whatever this thing between us was.

"You don't have to make any decisions right now, Lux. It's an option to have, and I'd say it's a damn good one. Call me biased all you want," Jasmine said quietly, grinning at me.

I shook my head, lifting my apple cider to my lips for a sip. "I do think being roommates with you would be fun, but..." my gaze cut to Theo, who was involved in a conversation with Desmond, Kai and Baz about fishing, and not paying attention to us. "I think it complicates things."

"No, it doesn't," Jasmine batted away my concerns with a wave of her hand. "It makes it more accessible."

"Exactly, I don't want him to think I'm considering it because he'll be there. I'm not following him," I whispered.

"Believe me, he knows that. Theo is *not* Scott; he doesn't believe everything revolves around him."

"Who's Scott?" Talia asked, picking up on a little of our conversation.

"My ex," I frowned, shooting Jasmine a look that told her to knock it off. The last thing I wanted was for Theo to overhear us talking about him and our...situationship, if that's what it even was. Could a few epic kisses be considered a situationship?

"Sounds like a tosser," Talia said.

"Oh, he is," Jasmine snorted. "The biggest tosser I've ever met, and I've met a fair amount of them."

"Can I ask what he did to earn The Ex title?" Talia asked, loud enough to garner the attention of Rhiannon and Zoey. Maybe it was the amount of alcohol in my system—we'd been drinking since our dip in the river—or the fact that I felt comfortable enough with this group to reveal a little more, but I found myself answering.

"He slept with my little sister," I replied curtly, taking another sip of my drink. "She sent me a Snap of them together in bed."

"Holy shit," Talia leaned forward, her eyes so wide they were comical. "What a *bastard*. The both of them, really."

"It's okay, I'm over him. I eventually would have broken up with him anyway. He didn't have any aspirations or goals and seemed annoyed by mine." I shrugged.

"Yeah, but…*your sister*? That's next-level shitty," Talia shook her head. "I mean, I've had some pretty bad breakups over the years, but that takes the cake."

"Yeah, that's exponentially worse than having a boyfriend cheat on you," Rhiannon said sympathetically. "What an asshole."

"The biggest, floppiest of assholes," Zoey chimed in, looking enraged on my behalf. "I'm so sorry that happened to you."

Now I was beginning to get uncomfortable, especially because the guys had looked over to see what we were bonding over.

"It's okay, I'm fine. Totally fine," I said, smiling to show how fine I was. "Honestly, the only thing that sucks is the knowledge that my sister will always do shit like this to me, and that I'll have to keep her at a distance to keep that harm away."

Zoey's expression softened, like she knew or could really sympathize with that. "I'm sorry, that's really rough. Not all family deserves the title. Blood isn't always thicker than water. Sometimes, that blood is poisoned."

The way she spoke and the heavy knowingness in her eyes had me thinking she'd been through something with her own family, but I wasn't about to ask. I nodded in agreement.

"Sometimes, your real family is the one you choose for yourself," Talia added, taking a shot before holding out her whiskey bottle to me with an encouraging smile. I took it from her, thinking *what the hell*, and took a shot directly from the bottle before passing it to Jasmine.

"Hear! Hear!" Jasmine said, taking a shot herself before passing it to Rhiannon. Rhiannon took a shot and passed it on to Zoey, who tilted the bottle back for her own shot.

"What, we're already getting into the hard stuff?" Kai asked, his voice full of amusement as he stepped over to Zoey's side. She offered him the bottle and he took it with a grin. "I'm not one to miss out on a good time!" he took a double shot before passing it to Theo.

13

METEORS IN HER EYES

 *Theo*

THE WHISKEY BOTTLE was passed around the fire again, but Lux held up her hand and shook her head. "Oh no, I'm already feeling no pain. I don't want to end up puking in the bush," she giggled.

When it came back around to me, I refused it too. I wasn't looking to get drunk off my face. Instead, I continued nursing the beer I'd been working on since dinner. It was warm now, but that didn't matter. It was still something to drink and keep my hands busy.

The restless energy was building in me. The need to fix what was broken; to repair the damage done to this woman was overwhelming. I was afraid if I drank anymore, I wouldn't be able to prevent myself from showing her all the reasons why she should forget her bastard of an ex.

I knew the girls had been talking about him earlier—I'd overheard his name a few times, which is why Talia started passing the whiskey around. I was glad that Lux was finally feeling comfortable enough to open up to the others. I got the sense she didn't do that often: didn't trust people enough to let them in on what was going on in her life.

I still couldn't believe how dumb her ex was, but his careless loss could be my gain—if I played my cards right. I hoped like hell Jasmine would sell her on moving to Sudbury, and I figured bonding with the others would help make that move a reality for us both.

I'd only known Lux for a matter of days, and yet I wanted to rearrange things so I could see more of her. If she moved to Sudbury, it'd be easier to do that.

I'd never felt that way before. I couldn't explain it, but I didn't mind it. It felt…right. Kissing her and touching her had only solidified that for me, that what we had between us was something special—something to hold on to. She'd risen to every challenge and experience with determination and open- ness. She might have been from a different world than mine, but she somehow fit here.

But I knew she'd just come out of a relationship, and had suffered a deeply painful betrayal. While she'd said she was over him, I knew the scars of that experience were still fresh. I was afraid to push her too much or too quickly, so I played it cool, keeping my distance across the fire. Letting her get to know the others when all I wanted to do was get to know her more myself.

Around eleven, Kai got the idea in his head that he could beat Talia at arm wrestling. Desmond tried to talk him out of it, but he wouldn't hear it. "No, I've got this, man! Watch me!"

Kai and Talia positioned themselves in front of the cooking stump and locked arms, the group gathering around them to watch. I found myself standing next to Lux, Jasmine beside her, and Desmond on my left.

Desmond let out a sigh, like a tired parent dealing with a bunch of wayward toddlers.

"You sure about this, pretty boy?" Talia asked, giving him another out. But Kai was too drunk to listen.

"Damn right! Let's do this!" Kai grinned. Zoey shook her head, standing off to the side behind Kai.

"Go easy on him," she mouthed to Talia, and Talia nodded, winking at her. We all watched Kai struggle to move Talia's arm, but she held it in place with barely any effort. She brought her other hand up to examine her nails, bored, while Kai struggled harder, his face going red with effort.

I wasn't surprised—Talia was a professional arm-wrestler, even I couldn't best her—and believe me, I'd tried. Kai had also tried, and lost, many times before. I don't know what had him thinking this time would be different—it was probably the whiskey.

Talia seemed to be toying with him, enjoying that Jasmine and Lux were rooting for her while Zoey cheered for Kai, knowing full well he'd lose the second Talia got bored of playing with him. Baz felt bad for him too, and tried to hype him up, but we all knew it was pointless. Talia had won three arm-wrestling championships; she knew what she was doing.

About two minutes later, Talia slammed Kai's arm down and claimed victory. "Better luck next time, muffin," she said, blowing him a kiss before standing up.

Kai pouted like he'd really thought he stood a chance at beating her and was genuinely disappointed he hadn't. He stood up too, swaying slightly. Zoey touched his elbow, steadying him. "I'll get you next time!" he promised, his words slurring slightly. Talia threw back her head and laughed, unperturbed.

"Sure you will," she patted him on the shoulder, then went back to her floaty and flopped on it with a deep sigh of contentment. "Ahh, look at those stars," she pointed up at the sky, where thousands upon thousands of twinkling lights shone brightly in the night sky.

"Perfect evening for a midnight paddle," I said, low enough for Lux to hear me. She glanced up at me, surprised. "Care to join me?"

Lux looked back at Jasmine, seeking permission.

"Go on, midnight paddles are the best!" Jasmine said, giving her an encouraging smile and nudging her with her arm. "I'm going to head to bed anyway, I'm beat. Des and I have to get up early tomorrow."

"Okay," Lux glanced back at me, her expression a mixture of nervousness and beautiful intrigue.

"Awesome, let me get some supplies, then we'll head out." I couldn't contain my smile as I jogged up to my tent to grab a blanket. I folded it, tucking it beneath my arm, and grabbed a flashlight.

As I was leaving my tent, I passed Jasmine on the way up to hers.

She paused, giving me a knowing smile. "She likes you, you know," she told me. I didn't exactly need the confirmation, but it was nice to hear anyway.

"I like her too," I replied.

Jasmine put her hand on my arm. "Take care of my girl, she's had enough shitty dick in her life. Be a good dick, okay?"

"I'll try my best," I laughed, shaking my head. Jasmine was definitely feeling no pain. She nodded, satisfied with my answer, and continued on her quest to her tent.

When I returned to the beach, Lux was waiting by the dying embers. Zoey was wrangling a drunken Kai back to their tent, leaving Rhiannon, Baz, Talia and Desmond around the fire.

"Practice safe sex out there, kids!" Talia called from her floaty. Lux's cheeks heated with embarrassment, and I shot Talia a glare.

"You can't have sex in a canoe, Talia," Rhiannon scoffed. "Believe me, we've tried. You end up capsizing the damn thing."

"Is that why you and Baz came back soaked that one time?" Talia cackled. "You know what, don't answer that."

"Well, shall we?" I asked Lux lowly, ignoring my friends. She nodded, tucking a strand of hair behind her ear.

I grabbed a couple of water bottles, tucking them under my arm before we walked to Jasmine's canoe. I placed the blanket, water bottles, and flashlight in before turning to Lux.

"Ready?"

"Ready," she confirmed.

I pushed Jasmine's canoe into the water, holding it steady while Lux climbed in, settling in the front. I climbed in after her, taking a seat in the back of the canoe. We both picked up the paddles and I guided the way.

The moon was high enough in the sky to light up our path on the water. We paddled for ten minutes, heading downstream.

Paddling at night was an entirely different experience than doing so during the day; you could feel the magic of the night all around you. It spoke promises of endless possibilities, and I hoped Lux was feeling the same way.

"Wow, the stars are breathtaking out here," Lux remarked, her head tilted back as she gazed up at the sky.

"They really are," I agreed, unable to stop looking at her, at the way the moonlight illuminated her. "Wait until we see the meteor shower."

"We're going to be able to see a meteor shower?" Lux asked, glancing over her shoulder at me, her pretty little mouth agape.

"Yeah, the Perseid meteor shower. It's caused by debris from the comet Swift-Tuttle, last seen in 1992. It takes one-hundred and thirty-three years for the comet to orbit the sun, so it won't be seen again until 2125, but this meteor show is pretty reliable each year. It's a good, clear night for it." I replied, looking up at the sky for a beat.

We paddled to the point we could see only from the top furthest point of the cliffy rocks of our campsite, then continued paddling around the bend until our campsite was out of view and we'd reached another rocky point.

"We won't go too far tonight, but this is one of my favourite spots on the river. We'll have the best view," I said, grabbing the rope and tying the boat off to a branch of a tree that grew out from the rocky point. I climbed out and held the canoe steady with one hand, offering my other to help Lux climb out.

Once she was out, I grabbed the blanket, water bottles, and the flashlight, taking her hand in mind and leading her up the pathway to the top of the cliff. This cliff was at a higher altitude than the cliff at our campground, and it felt like we were closer to the sky.

We reached the top and Lux exhaled, taking in the view over the cliff. She peered into the distance, squinting to see better. "I think I can see the cliff at our site," she pointed with her free hand.

"Yup, you can." I spread out the blanket and put the water bottles beside it, before laying down on my back. "Gonna join me?" I asked, shooting a daring grin as I looked up at her.

Lux smiled back, settling on the blanket. She cozied up beside me and let out a sigh of contentment, her eyes on the sky above us.

"It's so beautiful," she murmured, still in awe. "I can't believe I've never done this before."

"Done what? Stargaze?"

She nodded, her head moving against my arm.

"Well, you've done it two nights in a row now."

"Yeah, thanks to you," she giggled. "I've been spending more time outside than I have in the last six years combined."

"So, what kept you from it?" I asked, curious.

Lux lifted her shoulder in a delicate shrug. "I don't know. Like I said, my family was never really big on nature, and I guess that wore off on me. I never really took the time to appreciate the stars before. I knew they were there, obviously, but I never really stopped to look at them. I was so focused on school..." she frowned.

"It's okay to be focused on something, Lux. Look at what you have to show for it," I told her. "According to Jas, you graduated top of your class with some killer references. That's going to land you a great job in your field."

"I know, I wish I'd...I don't know, let myself experience things a little more. I let my focus keep me from appreciating the moment, you know?" she said, lost in thought, her eyes still on the expansive sky above us. "I look at Jasmine, and I can't help but feel a little disappointed in myself. She has this zest for life, and all these amazing memories of college that go far beyond getting good grades. She's had all these incredible adventures and made a bunch of awesome friends."

"Yeah, we are pretty awesome," I grinned.

She laughed, turning her head to look at me.

"It's not too late for you to make new friends or have your own adventures, you know."

"You're right," she said softly, her gaze dropping down to my lips. Something about the pull in her eyes had me moving closer, desperate for another taste of her.

I kissed her the way I'd wanted to kiss her all day long, my lips moving over hers. Soft and searching at first, then we both gave into our hunger. She tugged on my bottom lip gently with her teeth, rolling her tongue over it to soothe it.

A low growl rumbled deep in my throat, my hand coming up to frame the side of her face as I matched her passion with mine. She tasted like the crisp air after a rainstorm; like apples and cider and everything I didn't know I hungered for.

Lux's hand went to my abdomen, resting against the waistband of my sweatpants. She slipped her fingers under my sweater, resting them against my abdomen, her fingertips pressing against my skin. She kept toying with the skin and trail of hair above my waistband, never quite crossing that boundary, but teasing the shit out of me.

I was as hard as the rock beneath us in a matter of seconds, my erection straining against my pants, searching for relief—searching for her. I shifted my body, moving so that I was half on top of her. "This okay?" I asked, pausing long enough for her to nod her assent before my lips found hers again.

We made out, our lips and tongues moving together in erotic harmony. Lux's hands tugged at my sweater, pulling me more on her. I laughed against her mouth, breaking the kiss again to speak. I lifted my head. "I don't want to crush you," I warned her.

"What if I want you to crush me?" she grinned. I took a moment to really look at her. At her pinkish cheeks, at the desire flickering in her irises. The moonlight made her glow with an ethereal quality.

I went to kiss her again, but she let out a gasp, her eyes widening as she looked beyond me at the sky. "Oh my god!" she exclaimed with astonishment, her hands fisting in my sweater.

I turned my head, following her gaze, catching the beautiful meteor shower that had captured her attention.

"It's starting," I said as I rolled off her, bringing her closer to me so we could both watch the incandescent show.

"I've never seen anything so miraculous," Lux exclaimed, taking it all in.

"It's pretty incredible," I agreed, looking at her and watching the meteors reflected in her irises. She was breathtaking. More stunning than the sky above us.

14

WARM WHISPERS

WE STAYED up on the cliff watching the meteor shower for a couple of hours, until the time between meteors had slowed and I'd nearly fallen asleep in Theo's arms. He gently roused me, and we made our way back down the pathway to the canoe.

When we got back to our campsite, nobody was awake. Soft snores came from every tent. Theo and I walked hand and hand up the hill. We reached his tent first, and I lingered, turning to face him. I wasn't quite ready to end this moment with him. I dropped his hand, instantly feeling bereft of his touch.

"Thank you for that. I've never experienced anything like it," I told him, my voice in a hushed whisper.

He lifted his hands, framing my face, and planted a gentle kiss on my lips before releasing me and leaning back enough to catch my gaze. "I'm glad to have been the one to experience it with you. Thanks for coming with me."

Something about the way he was looking at me felt like an invitation. Maybe it was the sleep deprivation, or the fresh air… or the way my skin felt like it was on fire where he'd touched me, but I found myself stepping into him, my arms weaving around the back of his neck. I kissed him again, feeding off that feeling, wanting to fall into it.

His arms wrapped around my lower back, tugging me against his body, his heated kisses igniting that desire into an inferno, making my lower belly coil with wanton need. I could feel his need against me, hard and unyielding.

"Do you want to…" I tilted my head toward his tent. He arched a brow, a smile gracing his plump lips.

"I mean, if you want to… I'm more than down for that," he said, his voice low, driving the point home by pushing his heavy erection against my lower belly.

"Yes, I definitely want to," I grinned back, and he took my hand, leading me into his tent.

Theo had a two-person tent. It was smaller and cozier than Jasmine's tent, but it smelt exactly like him. Like his heady, unique scent, a woodsy essence that made my mouth water, and my hormones kick into overdrive.

While he was turned around zipping up the tent shut behind us, I pulled my sweater and t-shirt off, letting it fall to the ground beside me. I wasn't giving my insecurities or doubt any room to infiltrate this moment. I was letting my basic needs and desires drive the bus, focusing on the way he ignited my body and soul instead of worrying about the inevitable crash of the tomorrows I couldn't control.

Theo turned and straightened slowly, his eyes on me like I was the miraculous meteor show we'd spent hours watching.

"God damn, you're gorgeous, Lux," he murmured, stepping toward me, his hands going to my hips. He lowered his head, capturing my lips in another searing kiss.

I was desperate to feel his skin against mine. I tugged on his sweater, trying to tug it over him while we still kissed. He laughed, pausing long enough to drag it and his t-shirt over his head before resuming the onslaught of kisses.

Theo's body felt chiselled from stone, muscular and smooth and hard in all the right places. His abs tightened beneath my inquisitive touch. I felt like I could melt beneath the weight of my desire, my need to experience this perfect man in every sense. His kiss and his touch chased away everything negative, leaving behind a candescent warmth in the core of my very being.

His hands worked together as they explored my body reverently—one running up the small of my back to unhook my bra, while the other worked in conjunction to remove the straps from my shoulder—all the while never breaking the kiss.

Once my bra fell to the tent floor, Theo's hands came up to cup my breasts, his thumbs working over my pebbled nipples. I moaned against his mouth, and he smiled. Then he moved his head, his lips trailing a pathway from my mouth to my neck, and slowly moving from there down to my breast, tasting and kissing as he went.

His lips went around one of my nipples, sucking while his teeth teased it. My hands gripped the back of his head, tangling in his hair as I arched against him.

Then he was lowering me to his air mattress, moving with me until he was hovering above me. The way he touched me made me feel like a goddess. It was full of unspoken promise and devotion.

I looked up at him, feeling brave and alluring. I ran my hand down the hard, smooth planes of his sculpted abdomen, slipping it under the waistband of his sweatpants.

Theo let out a tortured hiss as my fingers wrapped around his thick, hard length. My breath caught too when I stroked him, feeling how hard he was for me. My thumb brushed along his engorged tip, spreading the drop of pre-cum. His forehead dropped to mine; his breathing affected as I worked him over.

His hand wrapped around my wrist, slowing my pumps. "Easy, or I'm going to go off like a rocket before we get to the good stuff," he warned with a mischievous smile. "You don't know what you do to me."

"I think I have an idea," I laughed lightly, blushing as I withdrew my hand. Theo kissed me again, his hand moving to explore the softness of my body. He slid his hand down my waistband and under my panties, his fingers gliding over my slit.

"God, you're soaked for me already," he murmured, pumping his thick index finger into me. I arched my back, letting the sensation of his magic fingers bring me closer and closer to the edge.

At first, I was worried that I wouldn't be able to orgasm. Scott had never been able to get me there, certainly not with his fingers. But it turned out that I didn't have to worry, Theo knew *exactly* what he was doing. He seemed to have an uncanny ability to read my body and know what it wanted. He added a second finger, putting the perfect amount of pressure on my clit, and I came hard on his fingers.

He captured my moan with his mouth, swallowing the loud gasp with a kiss.

"Holy hell, Lux. That was hot as fuck," he said, drawing his hand out to lick his glistening fingers. He moaned, as if the taste of me was a delicacy he'd hungered forever for.

"Do you have a condom?" I asked, still panting. I didn't want to stop. I started wriggling out of my sweatpants while Theo rolled over to his bag, searching in one of the pockets.

He found what he was looking for, the foil packet catching the hint of moonlight that filtered in from the open window of his tent. He rolled back over, his eyes catching on my now fully naked body, and swallowed hard, his gaze focusing on the junction between my thighs.

He shoved his sweatpants down over his hips, casting them off, his cock springing free, the tip of it glistening with pre-cum. As far as cocks went, it was magnificent and a little intimidating. I leaned forward, my hair falling over my shoulders as I took him into my mouth, tasting him.

Theo collected my hair in his hands, holding it out of my face while I sucked and explored him, his hips tensing and lifting to meet my mouth.

"Jesus, Lux. You better stop—" he warned, his voice thick with desire.

I obeyed, only because I wanted to feel him inside me.

"We'll revisit that later, then," I promised him, kissing the tip before I fell back onto his air mattress.

Theo watched me, his eyes flickering with desire while he slowly rolled the condom over his impressive length. Then he moved between my thighs, gently nudging my knees open wider to accommodate his body. I brought my hands up to hold his hips, my fingers pressing into his skin a little.

"We don't have to do this, you know," he said, swallowing hard.

I knew if I wanted to change my mind, Theo wouldn't hesitate—nor would he make me feel bad for it. But lucky for him—and me—I did *not* want to change my mind. I brought my arms up to wrap around his neck.

"I need you inside me, Theo," I told him before pressing my lips to his, kissing him.

Theo kissed me back just as passionately, the tip of his cock pushing and sliding against my slick opening. I widened my legs more, and he slid in a few inches, the sensation making both of us let out a sigh of pleasure.

He lifted his head, his eyes locking with mine before he pulled out and thrusted his hips forward, fully sheathing himself inside me. It stung for a brief second, not in a painful way but a delicious way, and he gave me a moment to adjust to him. His lids fluttered when my walls squeezed around him, and he shook his head, smiling.

"You feel incredible, Lux. Just like I knew you would."

To hear he'd thought of this moment too emboldened me. My body relaxed beneath his, and he started moving within me. I met his eager thrusts, lifting my hips as he slammed into me.

Theo pulled out and slammed back into me, gyrating his hips, hitting all the right places. A shiver of pleasure rolled through me, another orgasm cresting as he repeated the movement. My fingers dug into his shoulders—I needed to ground myself from flying.

His lips parted as he took in the expression on my face as I unravelled around him, clenching tight around him.

"Fuck, Lux," he grunted as I clenched around him.

Theo slammed into me a few more times, dropping his head to rest against my neck as he stilled, seated deep inside me. He moaned against my neck as he came.

It was the hottest sexual experience I'd ever had. The sound of his moans, the way he'd filled me and moved within me ignited me in a way I'd never felt before. I wasn't a virgin by any means, but I guess Scott didn't know how to get the responses out of me that Theo inherently knew. I hadn't realized how lacking he was until Theo, that sex could be this explosive and world changing.

"Are you okay?" Theo asked, peering down at me to make sure I was alright.

"Yes," I said, nodding even though I was still unable to catch my breath after my last orgasm had stolen it from my lungs. He pulled out and rolled the condom off, tying it so that it wouldn't make a mess. He set it aside, then rolled over to pull me to his chest.

"I don't even know my name right now," he chuckled, pressing a kiss against my temple. "You are extraordinary."

I could feel my cheeks heating, which was funny—to become bashful over his words when he'd made me come seven ways from Sunday, but I wasn't used to such praise. I curled up against him, my hand going to his chest, feeling his pounding heart beneath my palm.

"I think *you're* the one who's extraordinary. How did you…" I trailed off, my embarrassment growing.

"How did I what?" he asked, amusement colouring his tone.

"How did you know how to…do the things you did? I've never…" I said, pausing again, words failing me and shame trying to creep in. I shouldn't ask him how he learned the skills he had, that was notably unsexy, and I probably wouldn't like the answer. I also didn't want him thinking I was some sad virgin when that wasn't the case. Even if I *had* only been with one other person before, I still had some experience.

Sensing my embarrassment, Theo put a finger to my chin and lifted my face to look at me. "What feels good for you feels good for me, so why wouldn't I want you to feel good?" he asked, arching a brow.

"Makes sense," I murmured, and he kissed me again, slow and deep. The kiss ended all too soon, but before I could say anything else, a yawn escaped.

"Are you tired? It's getting close to four o'clock," Theo said, his voice wistful like he wished that wasn't the case.

"Yeah, I'm tired," I replied, trying to swallow back the lump of emotion in my throat. Part of me wondered if this was him trying to politely dismiss me, so I sat up and searched for my clothes.

"What are you doing?" he asked, leaning up on his elbows.

"Well, I thought I should…go?" I replied, so far from my element I didn't know which way was up.

"I don't want you to go," he grinned. "You can stay and sleep with me if you want."

I debated, looking at how relaxed he was. I didn't want to leave, but the mounting pressure in my bladder told me I couldn't roll over and fall asleep with him. I had to tend to my basic needs. "Alright, I'll be right back, I have to pee."

Theo nodded as I tugged my sweater and pants on. He handed me a flashlight, and I disappeared to the thunderbox to take care of business before returning.

I paused at the pathway, looking between Jasmine and Theo's tents. Was this truly a good idea? What would the others say in the morning when I stumbled out of Theo's tent?

Did I even care what they said?

"You're thinking pretty hard over there," Theo's voice was a low whisper, but I still jumped as if he'd shouted the words. I hadn't expected him to be waiting for me near his tent.

"Having regrets?" he asked, arching a brow at me.

I let out a small laugh, shaking my head at my own ridiculousness, and walked toward him. "No, no regrets. Just wondering how bad of an idea it is to fall asleep in your arms."

He grinned. "I think it's a great idea, personally. But if you don't want to, I understand."

"I want to, but..." I let my words fade, glancing at the other tents. A symphony of snores, soft and deep, surrounded us. Everyone was still asleep, but what if they got up before us in the morning? It was like Theo could sense my train of thought.

"They might tease us a little, but they won't judge," he assured me, holding his hand out to me. I took it, following him back into the warmth of his tent. "Besides, I want to know what it feels like to wake up with you in my arms."

Something about his words and the way he said it made me swoon. Theo zipped the tent up behind us while I got comfortable on his mattress. The temperature had dropped considerably, so I didn't want to take off my pants, but the sweater was too bulky for me to sleep comfortably in. I took it off, my top half naked.

"God damn," Theo murmured, taking in the sight of my breasts and adjusting himself. "You're too irresistible, Lux. I'm not sure how I'm supposed to keep my hands off you for the rest of this trip."

"So don't," I challenged, peering up at him.

15

A REASON

I SLEPT BETTER than I had in years, with Lux tucked into my arms, her soft breath fanning across my chest. The sun had fully risen before I opened my eyes to the sounds of the day. People were up and moving around, talking amongst themselves down at the beach.

I could smell coffee and food being prepped, but I still didn't want to move. Not when Lux was still sleeping peacefully in my arms, her warm breasts pressed against my side.

I could lay like this with her forever and be content to do just that, raging morning wood and all. But Lux started stirring too, stretching beside me, her fingers splaying out across my chest.

"Mmm," she murmured, nestling closer to me. "Good morning."

"Good morning, beautiful," I pressed a kiss to her forehead, and she smiled sleepily at me.

"What time is it?" she asked.

"Probably ten or eleven, judging by the sun," I replied, and Lux's eyes widened as she took in the sounds of the camp.

"Oh," she blushed. "So much for sneaking back to my tent. I need to change and brush the nest out of my hair."

"You could still do that," I assured her.

Neither one of us moved, though.

"Don't worry about the others. Like I said last night, they might tease us a little, but I think we can handle that."

Lux nodded, biting down on her lower lip, her eyes contemplative. "I bet Jasmine's dying to launch an inquisition."

"Oh probably," I chuckled, holding her closer and running my hand along the small of her bare back. "But for the record, I really like you, Lux. A lot. I'd be willing to see where this takes us, if that's what you want. But if you just want a hookup, I'm more than happy to be that, too." It pained me to say it, because I wanted to be more than a rebound hookup for her—but if that's all I was to her, I'd be happy for that tiny slice.

Lux's mouth opened and closed, she was at a total loss for words. She took a minute before responding.

"I like you a lot too, Theo."

"That's all that matters then," I said before kissing her again. Lux's hand travelled from my chest down my stomach until she reached my throbbing cock. She arched her brow, finding me hard.

"What can I say, I loved waking up with you in my arms," I added, unashamed of my body's reaction to her.

"I'd love to help you out, but I have to pee again," she giggled, giving me a squeeze and a pump that made my hips tense and a groan escape me before she withdrew her hand and sat up.

"God damn, you're vicious," I teased as she moved about my tent, collecting her clothes. She put her bra on and sent me a devious smile over her shoulder before she pulled on her t-shirt and sweater.

"Want me to kiss it better?" she asked, eyeing my massive problem. I wrapped my hand around my cock, stroking it, the very idea of having her lips on me made me feel like a hormonal teenager.

"Don't make promises you can't keep, Lux. If you start that, we'll end up fucking again—and I can't promise to go gently on you. You won't be able to keep quiet."

Lux's eyes widened, her cheeks pinkening as her tongue darted out to lick the seam of her lips. "Rain check?" she asked hopefully, and I grinned wider.

"Bet on it," I told her. She shivered with delight before standing up and unzipping my tent, peering outside. When she found the coast was clear, she snuck out, zipping it up behind her.

I could see her shadow walk around my tent, towards her and Jasmine's. I remained in my tent, willing my throbbing erection to calm down so I could leave.

It took me ten minutes of forcing myself to think about unpleasant things before it went away. Then I got dressed and tidied my tent, throwing away the used condom in one of the small empty garbage bags I'd had tucked in my bag for dirty clothes.

I brushed my teeth outside my tent, using the water in my water bottle to rinse my mouth before shoving my toothbrush and toothpaste back in my bag. After putting on some deodorant, I felt presentable enough to join the others.

Rhiannon, Baz, Talia, Zoey and Kai were all gathered around the fire on the beach. Breakfast had been cooked and coffee had been made. Baz saw me approaching and sent a knowing grin my way.

"Morning, sleepyhead," he said.

"Sounds like you had a great night," Talia chimed in. "Not much sleeping at all, huh?"

Lux still hadn't come down from her tent, so I sent them all a no-nonsense look. "Yeah, and I'd appreciate it if you guys could leave her alone about it."

Talia lifted her hands, surrendering. "Easy, cowboy. We won't comment on your ride in front of the missus. Just saying, congrats on finally growing a pair."

I ignored her, fixing myself a coffee. "Where's Des and Jasmine?"

"Still getting ice. They left around eight this morning, so they should be back soon." Baz answered.

I looked up, seeing Lux approaching the group warily. I made her a coffee the way I'd seen her make it the last few days, adding cream and a few scoops of sugar to it. She smiled when I handed it to her and went to sit in her chair.

"Morning, Lux. Hope you slept well last night," Rhiannon said warmly, her smile welcoming.

Lux had been taking a sip of coffee, and choked on it a little. She coughed, her cheeks heating. "Yeah, I slept great," she managed after a moment.

Talia sniggered, but Baz kicked her floaty and when I shot her a glare, she peered up at me innocently.

"Are Jasmine and Desmond still gone?" she asked. I knew she was trying to change the subject.

"Yep," Talia answered. "When they get back, we're planning on doing another day of cliff jumping—if you're up for it."

"That sounds fun," Lux nodded.

"There's some egg hash if you guys are hungry, it's a little cold but it still tastes good," Rhiannon commented, gesturing to the cast iron pan with breakfast in it.

"Thanks," Lux smiled at her, but before she could stand up and fix a plate, I was already grabbing two plates.

"I've got it," I told her, our eyes connecting across the fire. She smiled, her cheeks heating beneath my gaze.

I could tell Rhiannon and Zoey were struggling not to make a big deal of it, and Talia was acting fully absorbed in her playlist. I had to give her credit, the only tell she had was her twitching lips. I knew the second we were alone, she'd razz the hell out of me about it.

I didn't care, though. Lux was worth every moment of razzing from my friends, I didn't want them to make her feel uncomfortable about what had transpired between us, or what would continue to transpire between us on the rest of the trip if I had my way.

After grabbing us something to eat, I moved to sit in Jasmine's empty chair beside Lux, handing her the plate I'd fixed for her. She smiled her thanks, her gaze timid as she accepted the plate from my outstretched hand.

"Gonna be a beaut of a day!" Baz remarked, glancing up at the clear sky with approval.

"Might suck packing up and leaving tomorrow, though," Talia snorted, holding her phone up to show her weather app. "A massive thunderstorm is moving in tonight."

A flash of alarm filtered across Lux's stunning face, her fork freezing halfway to her mouth with a scoop of egg hash on it. "Thunderstorm? Aren't we supposed to not be on the water for that? Or in a tent with metal poles?" she asked, her voice full of concern. She set the fork down without taking a bite.

"How much rain, Tal?" I asked, leaning forward.

"8 millimetres per hour from midnight, and steadily coming down until dusk with scattered thunder and lightning throughout the day."

"That sounds like a lot of rain, and thunder," Lux worried her bottom lip.

"Hmm," Rhiannon said thoughtfully. "Maybe we'll pack it up and head home later this afternoon."

At that moment, Jasmine and Desmond rounded the corner in the canoe, paddling up to the beach.

Jasmine jumped out of the canoe carrying a bag of ice. "Morning, friends! Glad to see you're all awake and functioning," she said, her attention going to Lux and me with a knowing look.

"Yeah, yeah, we slept in. So sue us," I shook my head, watching as Desmond pulled the canoe onto the beach.

"We were debating on whether we should pack up and head home later this afternoon, actually. It's a beautiful day today, but tomorrow's supposed to be a nightmare."

"Yeah, Des and I were talking about that too. I wouldn't mind packing up and canoeing in the rain, but I'm worried about the thunderstorms. That's gonna make getting back to the marina a little sketchy. I guess we could always miss check-out and get charged another night."

"I work Wednesday, so that won't do," Zoey frowned with a sigh.

"Well, we could pack up camp, then go do some cliff jumping, then come back to get our supplies before we head to the marina?" Rhiannon suggested.

"Sounds good to me," Jasmine shrugged, opening the main cooler we were using for food now and dumping the ice in. "What do you think, Lux?"

"Well, I definitely don't want to get caught in a thunderstorm, so I'm down for that." Lux replied. With the issues resolved, she resumed eating the rest of her breakfast.

Desmond and Jasmine grabbed something to eat, and once we'd cleaned up from breakfast, we started packing up camp. Everyone went off to start taking down their tents.

Once all the tents were put away and all our gear piled nicely beneath the shade of the trees, we packed a small cooler of food and drinks and headed to the cliffs.

Lux

. . .

JASMINE and I lagged behind the others, following at a distance enough away that we could talk quietly.

"So, you didn't come back to the tent last night," she said.

I glanced over my shoulder, and she wiggled her eyebrows at me.

"You're right, I didn't…I uh, crashed with Theo," I replied, turning my head to face forward again. My gaze went forward to where Theo and Desmond were cutting through the water ahead of us.

"Mmhmm, and how was *crashing* with Theo?"

"Amazing, actually," I answered, smiling to myself. "He was incredible." I shook my head, trying to find the adequate words to describe how I felt and coming up short.

But Jasmine didn't seem to need me to elaborate. "That's great, Lux! I knew you guys would be amazing together."

"How did you know that?" I frowned, glancing back at her.

She lifted a shoulder in a delicate shrug. "Call it intuition, but I've been wanting to introduce you to Theo for years. You kept dodging my attempts to get you to come visit."

"Hmm," I murmured, returning my gaze to the front. Jasmine was right. I had dodged her invites to visit her in Sudbury or join her on camping trips. "Well, I don't know what's going to happen tomorrow—or in the future, for that matter."

"Did he say anything?"

"He said he really likes me, and that he's willing to see where this goes…" I shrugged.

"That's awesome! All the more reason for you to move to Sudbury and be my roomie."

"Jas, I don't want to move for a guy." I sent her a look over my shoulder.

"I know, and you're not. You're moving to get away from your toxic sister and your enabling parents," Jasmine replied.

I stopped scowling, she had a point there.

After a few days of clarity, I could honestly say I didn't *want* to go back to that environment. I loved my parents dearly—hell, I even loved my sister, despite the pain she caused—but I knew I couldn't stay in that situation. It was breaking me apart bit by bit. I knew if I stayed there, my confidence would continue to take hit after hit as these wounds festered in the toxicity.

"I could get you a job at the Burger Bar," Jasmine added. She'd worked at a bar that served burgers and other grilled foods part-time for the past four years to bring in some extra cash while she was in school.

"We'll see," I said. I wasn't against the idea, but I was still holding out hope for a position in my field. I reminded myself that it might take time, and a job would be a job, regardless of its description. Plenty of post-graduates had to find filler jobs while looking for positions in their new fields, Jasmine included. She still worked at the Burger Bar.

We joined the others. Talia had been the first to arrive, and she'd already tied her kayak off and was helping Theo and Desmond with the canoes.

Talia held Rhiannon and Baz's canoe steady so Moose and Rhiannon could climb out. Baz handed Talia the cooler, and she took it, setting it down on the rocky platform.

Once Baz was out on the platform, Theo swam the rope, tugging their canoe along behind him to tie it off with the others.

Then it was our turn.

"The way you guys work together is impressive," I remarked, taking Talia's hand while she tugged me out. She grinned.

"Lots of practice, Princess," she told me, winking.

Jasmine threw her pack out onto the ledge, then tossed the rope to Theo in the water. She took Desmond's hand, pulling herself out. Her foot caught the edge of the rocky platform and she tripped, falling into him. Desmond caught her with ease and smiled down at her. I couldn't help but giggle; that same pesky edge had gotten me the other day.

Jasmine wasn't usually a blusher, but her cheeks flushed. She stepped back abruptly, busying herself by picking up her pack from the ledge while Theo swam our canoe over to the others and tied it off.

"Let's get this party started!" Talia rubbed her hands together gleefully. We all started walking up the pathway, and I ended up walking in front of Theo and behind Jasmine and Desmond. I could feel Theo's eyes on me, and I tripped on the uneven ground.

His hands came out to steady my hips, his fingers gentle but firm. His steady touch reminded me of how his hands had felt on me last night, and my body heated in response.

I looked back at him over my shoulder, and his lips curved into a dazzling smile. "Are you okay?" he asked.

"Yeah, I'm fine," I replied, tucking my hair behind my ear as he released me. We continued walking up the incline.

By the time we reached the top of the cliffs, Talia, Kai, and Zoey had already set their packs down and headed to the edge of the cliff. We'd barely made it to the campfire area before the three of them launched themselves off the cliff, wasting no time getting to the business of cliff jumping.

Rhiannon was relaxing in the chair Baz had carried up for her, a paperback on her lap and her big sunglasses on. She wouldn't be jumping but said she'd wanted to catch some sun and rest a little before our journey back to the marina. Moose was curled up at her feet, chewing on a stick he'd found along the trail up. Baz clipped Moose's leash to his collar.

"You good?" he asked, handing Rhiannon the leash. She took it, wrapping it around her hand once.

"Yup, peachy!" she replied, tilting her head to kiss Baz when he leaned over.

Though they'd mainly kept him off leash for the duration of

the camping trip, he was tied up now to prevent him from launching off the cliff after Baz.

Once Baz was sure they were situated, he saluted us and walked over to the edge of the cliff, peering down to make sure nobody was in his way.

"Are you coming, Lux?" Jasmine asked me.

"Not yet, I'll chill here for a bit." My thighs were burning from the exertion of climbing the steep cliff pathway, and my legs felt a little weak. I was tired; I needed a moment to catch my breath, and a bottle of water to rehydrate. It was hot with the sun overhead.

"I'll hang with you," Theo offered, reaching into his bag for a couple of water bottles. "Want a water, Rhi?"

"I'm good," Rhiannon answered, holding up her giant water bottle. Theo nodded, his hand going to the small of my back as he guided me over to one of the large rocks nearby.

I sat down, sliding my backpack off my shoulders and letting it fall to the ground beside me. Theo held out one of the water bottles to me, and I took it with a grateful smile, twisting the cap and holding it up to my lips. Taking a long pull, I watched as Baz, Jasmine and Desmond all leaped from the edge of the cliff.

"They have so much energy, where do they get it from?" I commented, feeling weary down to my bones. This trip had exhausted me as much as it exhilarated and awakened me.

"They weren't up all night," Theo reminded me with a subtle wink. Rhiannon snorted with amusement from behind her paperback, and my cheeks heated with embarrassment.

It was strange having so many people know our business, but I suppose we couldn't have been more obvious about what we were doing. It was easy to put two and two together.

Instead of replying, I avoided Theo's gaze and continued sipping my water. He sat down beside me, his thigh pressed against mine.

"So, what did you think of your first camping trip? Is it something you'd do again?" he asked a few moments later.

"Yeah, actually. I would totally do it again," I surprised myself by answering.

If I'd been asked a few days ago, I would have had a different answer. But now that camp was packed up and we were on our last little adventure before heading back...I was already missing it.

And already dreading having to face the drama I'd left behind.

Theo's smile lit me up, and I couldn't help but grin back. The drama felt miles away when he looked at me like that.

"It's a lot of work, but it's worth it for these views, huh?" Rhiannon remarked, gazing around with contentment.

"It really is stunning," I nodded, taking in the landscape. My phone was in my bag, so I reached over to grab it. I hadn't checked it nearly as many times as I thought I would, nor had I taken many pictures, but I wanted to take one of this view from the top of the cliffs. I turned my phone sideways and took a landscape shot, hoping I captured at least half of the beauty I was witnessing.

Once I'd taken a few photos, I shoved the phone back in my bag, not bothering to check my emails. I still had no reception, so nothing was loading anyway. I was thankful for the silence, though.

I knew it was a temporary respite from what awaited me back home. Jasmine's idea of renting a room off Desmond and Theo fluttered around in my brain. I had to admit, that idea was sounding more and more appealing the closer time got to when I'd have to face my sister—and parents—again.

16

SUDBURY SECLUSION

I KEPT Rhiannon company on the top of the cliffs while the others jumped several more times, Theo included. It was a good opportunity to get to know her a little more, and I found I really enjoyed her company and her outlook on life.

"I'm from Scarborough, originally. I grew up there and then went to school in Guelph."

"How'd you end up in Sudbury?" I asked, teasing a little. It was a far cry from Guelph. Rhiannon seemed to be a few years younger than me, and she had her whole life figured out—her business was thriving and so was she, and she fit in as perfectly as everyone else, despite growing up in the city, too.

"Once I graduated from my photography program, I started getting some wedding jobs here and there. One of those jobs led me to Baz's sister, and I ended up doing the photography for their wedding in Parry Sound and fell in love with the area. And Baz," Rhiannon explained, giggling. "I moved to Sudbury to be with him, mainly. But there's something magical about northern Ontario. The terrain is gorgeous, but the sunsets and sunrises are next level."

"They really are," I nodded my head in agreement, gazing back out over the top of the cliff.

"I didn't really start camping until I met Baz," Rhiannon admitted. "It's not something my family did with me when I was a kid. Probably because they worried that I'd get injured. They were a little overprotective of me growing up." She let out a rueful chuckle, shaking her head.

"How are they now?"

"They've come to terms with it," Rhiannon replied, grinning. "They had no choice, really. I'm an adult and can live my own life on my terms, but it helps that they adore Baz and trust him to keep me safe."

"You guys are really great together," I told her.

Rhiannon seemed to light up from within. "I agree! I wasn't sure of him at first," she admitted, laughing a little. "He's like a golden retriever. Definitely not the kind of guy I usually go for, but I'm glad I gave him a chance. He's changed my whole world for the better."

"What kind of guy did you usually go for?"

"The bad ones, the boys with commitment issues and anger problems. The ones that wouldn't take care of me if I dislocated something." Rhiannon wrinkled her nose with disdain.

I nodded slowly, thinking about how uninvolved and disinterested Scott had been throughout our relationship. We always had to do what he wanted, or he'd get sulky and mad and punish me with silence. I was so glad that relationship was behind me forever, and now that I'd gotten away from it I could see how problematic it had been for years.

She'd done me a favour, in a twisted roundabout way.

A chorus of voices interrupted our chat, the group rejoining us on the top of the cliffs. Baz came over to check on Rhiannon, pressing a devout kiss to her lips and dripping water all over her.

"Arg!" she laughed, trying to move her paperback out of the way.

Theo sat down beside me; he was just as wet as Baz but kept the droplets as much to himself as he could.

Zoey and Desmond passed around hot dogs in buns that had been cooked up before we'd left. They were cold, but they hit the spot. I washed mine down with the rest of my water.

"Want to join me on a little hike before we go?" Theo asked, his green eyes smouldering with intent. I knew he wanted to get me alone for a minute, and I didn't mind in the slightest. I nodded, standing up and following him.

There was a pathway halfway down the cliff that led to a rocky enclave that provided shade from the bright overhead sun. It was perfectly secluded, too.

Once we reached the enclave, Theo splayed his palms against the smooth rock on either side of my head. Our chests were touching, my nipples hardening against the heat of his bare chest, pressing against the thin material of my onyx bikini top. His eyes bore into mine, darkening with need—need that I mirrored, that I felt stronger than anything I'd ever felt before.

Desire rolled through me like a monsoon, and I thought of nothing as my hands reached to wrap around his neck, pulling him against me. I shivered while I burned for him.

He lowered his head, his lips brushing across mine. Savouring me as if I were a delicacy, Theo let his hand drop gently to my neck, and he held me, his fingers tangling in my hair. The intoxicating scent of him encircled me, making me feel dizzy with potential.

I moaned when his tongue brushed against mine. He smiled and deepened the kiss. I dropped my hands so I could tug the waistband of his swim trunks. He got the hint and moved toward me, using his knee to separate my legs before he pressed harder against me, driving his hard length against my lower belly, pressing my back flat against the rocky enclave.

His kisses seared me in the best way possible, and I felt like I was freefalling into something wonderful.

It was akin to the way I had felt when I jumped off the cliff. It was utterly terrifying; a moment that stole the very breath from my lungs, and yet I'd never wanted to fall into anything more.

Theo pulled away, and the look in his eyes was like the way I felt. Struck.

"I don't think I'd ever tire of kissing you," he murmured, his eyes lighting me on fire. The words spilled from his lips with reverence, like a prayer.

I smiled, my heart thundering in my chest, and a small laugh escaped. I looked down at our feet, feeling a thousand different things. I wanted to tell him I wouldn't get tired of kissing him either, and I knew in my heart I wouldn't, but before I could get the words out, Theo brought his lips to mine again, tasting me ardently.

And then I felt it. That horrifying sensation of an insect with far too many legs crawling against bare skin. I looked at my shoulder and let out a terrified screech, seeing an ugly dark brown spider the width of a beer can crawling over my shoulder. Before I could run screaming back down the pathway, Theo was carefully scooping it up into his hands.

"Don't like spiders?" he asked, releasing it on the ground. It scurried away, eager to get away from us. The feeling was mutual, and I shivered, this time in disgust.

"No," I wheezed, my chest still heaving with adrenaline.

"It's a striped fishing spider, he won't harm you. They eat tadpoles, fish and insects."

"Lovely," I said, my voice an octave higher than a squeak. I cleared my throat, my eyes landing back on his.

His eyes danced with amusement, and he went right back to

kissing me, his lips making me forget all about the silly, not-so-little spider. The goosebumps that broke out over my skin came for an entirely different reason, and I couldn't help but rub brazenly against him.

"Lovely indeed," Talia whooped, and we both turned to look at her. She stood before the pathway we'd used to climb up the cliff.

"How long have you been standing there?" Theo asked, equal parts amused and irritated. He made no move to step away from me, and I found I didn't want him to.

"Long enough to have witnessed some serious tonsil hockey," she responded with an arched brow. "I heard a scream and thought you were murdering Lux."

"No murdering is happening," I assured Talia, blushing. "Just a spider."

"Ah, yes. That can evoke the same terror as being murdered," Talia nodded with understanding. "Well, if you don't require a rescue, I'll be on my way."

"Alright, see ya," Theo said without looking over his shoulder, his gaze still on me.

"I think we're packing up to head back now, though. So you might want to wrap up whatever illicit things you're doing here," Talia added before she turned around and headed back to the pathway.

Theo looked back at me, the amusement and irritation gone, replaced with a smouldering intensity. "Guess we should head back," he said, his eyes flitting to my lips again. I felt his erection jump against my thigh, and I sighed.

"You're right."

He tilted his head down, his swollen lips lifting in a sideways smile that made the butterflies explode low in my belly.

"Feel like jumping off the cliffs again before we leave?"

I thought about it for a moment, then nodded. "Okay. But

are you sure jumping with that is safe?" I asked, looking pointedly at the erection he was still sporting.

"I'm sure it'll go away before we reach the top of the cliffs. But stop staring at it, you're not helping," Theo joked, adjusting himself before taking my hand. I laughed as we started back up the pathway to the top of the cliff.

Rhiannon and Baz were collecting their things. Jasmine and Desmond had come up to help carry things down, and Jasmine offered to carry down our bags so I could jump with Theo.

She was encouraging me to get time alone with him, I could tell by her delighted smile when she saw us walking up the pathway hand in hand.

Theo was still holding my hand. He squeezed it, drawing my attention to him.

"Ready?" he asked me, cocking a brow. I nodded and took a deep breath, pulling oxygen into my lungs before we made a running start.

This time, I let out a screech as we fell. Theo held my hand the whole way down and tugged me to the surface after we hit the water. The cool water was exactly what my heated skin needed.

"That was amazing," I laughed breathlessly.

Once I'd caught my breath, Theo tugged me closer to him and kissed me again, only stopping when someone started catcalling us.

"Time to go, lovers!" Talia shouted. "Unless you wanna paddle back to the marina in the dark!"

17

HOMEWARD

WE PADDLED BACK to the campsite to grab our gear before heading to the marina. It didn't take us long before our canoes and kayaks were all loaded up.

Before we left the campsite, we walked around to make sure we hadn't left behind any garbage or recyclables. Once satisfied we'd be leaving the campsite in a better condition than we found it, we left.

Our group was a little more reserved on the way back, our energy mellow. It sucked that we'd had to call it early, but nobody wanted to get stuck in tomorrow's thunderstorms.

Luckily, Jasmine had managed to convince Lux to come back to Sudbury with us to check out the duplex. From the sounds of it, Jasmine was working on getting Lux to be her and Talia's roommate. I had zero complaints about that idea; in fact, I hoped like hell Lux said yes—and not only for the purely selfish reason that I'd get to see more of her.

She'd told me about what awaited her back home with her sister, and I thought it'd do her good to get away from that situation. I had a younger sister, Olivia, and while we weren't super close, I couldn't imagine having her hurt me in such a manner. I'd always watched out for her and protected her, and I knew she'd always have my back too.

Lux moving in with Jasmine and Talia really would save Desmond and me the headache of trying to find a college student to rent that room. It might have been easier back when we only rented to college students, but now that we had two semi-permanent renters, it was a little harder to fill that spot.

We really had to vet potential renters and make sure they got along well with Jasmine and Talia, which wasn't impossible as they were both pretty laid-back people, but our last renter wasn't exactly a good fit, although she'd seemed to check all the boxes. It turned out she wasn't comfortable with "Talia's lifestyle" and was standoffish with Jasmine. She didn't exactly cause problems, but I knew both Jasmine and Talia felt like they had to walk on eggshells and were relieved when the renter's term was up.

It'd be nice to avoid another situation like that by finding someone that already got along with both Jasmine and Talia.

It took our group just under two hours to get back to the marina. We made it within minutes before the general store closed, giving us enough time to let the owners know we'd be heading out tonight instead of tomorrow.

We unpacked our canoes and kayaks as dusk fell, working together as a group to get everything loaded up. The good thing about that was that we were the only people in the parking lot getting ready to leave.

I'd hitched a ride with Desmond in his old truck, and once we jumped the damn battery again, we kept it on to recharge it and used his headlights to finish loading everyone's gear.

We packed Zoey and Kai first so they could head out, Kai

wasn't feeling the best and Zoey was worried he was going to have a seizure. He'd been on top of his meds but sometimes that didn't matter, especially if he was overtired and overstimulated.

Once they'd left, we helped Baz get their canoe on the top of his Jetta while Rhiannon and the other girls helped load their supplies. They took off too, honking as they left the parking lot.

Then it was just Talia, Jasmine, Lux, Desmond, and me. Desmond and I put Talia's kayak and Jasmine's canoe on top of her CRV while the girls finished loading their gear. Talia had driven in with Baz and Rhiannon, but she'd be returning with Jasmine and Lux since they were going to the duplex.

"Alright, see you guys back at the house!" I said, grinning at Lux in particular. She smiled back, a little uncertain. The girls piled into Jasmine's CRV, Talia squishing into the backseat while Lux rode shotgun.

Desmond and I climbed into his truck and he put it into gear, following Jasmine out of the marina. It was only a forty-seven-minute drive back to Sudbury, but I itched to hold Lux already.

"Well, that was a good trip. Sucks we had to cut it short," I commented, sitting back in my seat and casting a glance at Desmond. "Did you have fun?"

"Yeah, it was great," Desmond replied. There was something about his tone.

"What happened?" I demanded, eyeing him warily.

"Nothing," he sighed, running his hand over his face. "Nothing happened at all."

"You know, a little bird told me that a certain someone has feelings for you," I told him, trying to hide my grin.

He shot me a look, his brow furrowing. "What little bird?"

I sent him a look in reply, knowing he knew exactly who I was referring to.

He grunted, turning his attention back to the road. "I don't know about that. I think you and the little bird have your hopes up."

"We'll see," I lifted a shoulder in a casual shrug.

Lux seemed serious when she'd told me Jasmine had feelings for Desmond that night, plus I'd been observing the two of them for a while now. There was something there, something that they were both fighting.

But Desmond wasn't in a talkative mood, and he put on the radio to drown out my attempts at conversation. I chuckled, unperturbed, and ended up falling asleep after fifteen minutes. The late nights and little sleep I'd gotten over the last few days had caught up with me.

ABOUT AN HOUR LATER, we pulled into the driveway of our duplex. Jasmine's car was already parked, the canoe and kayak still on the roof rack, although the girls weren't in it. I could see the lights on in their house.

We unloaded the truck, carrying everything into our place. The two coolers, our sleeping bags and our duffle bags went inside, while we carried our tents and air mattresses around back to the storage shed.

Once that task was completed, we took down our kayaks and hung them up at the side of the shed. Then we returned and unloaded Jasmine's canoe and Talia's kayak, hanging them up on the other side of the shed.

When that was done and we were about to head inside, an unfamiliar car pulled up with a few boxes of pizza. Jasmine stepped out to pay for it and caught sight of us. "Hey guys! Come in for some pizza, I ordered enough for all of us."

"Sounds good," I grinned, taking the pizza boxes off the delivery guy while Jasmine handed him a wad of cash. She grabbed the bag of pops and dips, and the three of us walked inside.

Lux was sitting at the small round kitchen table, her hair damp from a shower she must have recently taken. She smiled timidly at me when I walked in and set the pizza down on the table in front of her.

"So, what do you think of the place?" Desmond asked Lux, glancing around with pride. Jasmine and Talia always kept it clean, and I know that made Desmond happy, especially after the amount of money we'd sunk into renovating it.

"It's very nice," Lux told him, smiling. "I'm not opposed to the idea; I don't know if I can commit. I need to find a job first."

Desmond nodded. "Well, consider it yours, if you want it. If you don't, just let me know before the end of August. I'd really hate to have to find another student renter, but I can if it doesn't work out. I think Jas and Talia would prefer having you as a roommate."

"Definitely!" Talia shouted, peeking her damp head out from the bathroom down the hall. "Like, I beg of you. I'll even pay your rent for the first few months until you get a job."

"Hell, I will too!" Jasmine offered, her eyes wide and pleading. "Student renters were great when we were students, but the last one was a nightmare. Please say you will, Lux! I want you to be our roomie so bad!"

"I don't think that'd be necessary," Lux blushed beneath their attention. "I have some savings I could dip into."

"So, it's settled then?" Jasmine asked hopefully, her eyes going from Lux to me and Desmond again.

Lux bit her bottom lip, deliberating. I could tell a lot of thoughts were racing through her mind at that moment.

"If it doesn't work out long term, that's alright. There will be no hard feelings. You're welcome to give it a trial run if you'd like," I chimed in. I held her gaze, hoping she could see how much I wanted her to say yes, too. Not that I wanted to pressure her.

"Fine," Lux's lips twitched as she tried to suppress a smile.

Talia let out an excited whoop as she came into the kitchen, high-fiving Jasmine and then holding her hand up for Lux. Lux tentatively high-fived her, the smile on her face widening.

"You guys are ridiculous," she laughed, shaking her head.

"Oh, you'll learn," Talia joked, diving into the first box of pizza.

Lux

THE FIVE OF us ate pizza and hung out on the back deck overlooking the yard, sheltered from the rain beneath a gazebo. It was still a warm evening, despite the rain, but I much preferred the shelter of the gazebo and the nearby house to the tent and a tarp.

I couldn't believe I actually said yes to them, that I'd be their new roomie and move to Sudbury. But on the drive up, I'd loaded my emails and I had no responses from any of the places I'd applied at.

I did have several messages on the Gram from people back home sending me Brinley's latest antics. Brinley even sent a few herself, of her and Scott out on a boat somewhere sharing a disgustingly vulgar kiss. Brinley had never sent me her videos before this conquest of hers, and I knew she was doing it to rub it in.

Apparently, while I'd been camping, she'd scored herself an invite on someone's fancy yacht and brought Scott along with her for the ride. The resulting social media posts were excessive.

I was surprised that it didn't hurt as bad as it would have a few days ago. It irritated me, yes, but it didn't sting. If anything, it made me more resolved to move out as quickly as possible.

And I really *did* like the house. The front door opened into a small foyer with a front hall closet, then led into a rather large living room with high ceilings and beautiful exposed wood beams.

The kitchen was at the back of the house, it was cute and updated with fresh white cabinets and black hardware. It had a beautiful marble white and black countertop and a deep matte black sink and tap. The appliances were all relatively new from the looks of them, and there was even a dishwasher. A sliding door led to a large porch and a spacious shared backyard.

To the left of the kitchen was a hallway that led to the three bedrooms and bathrooms. Jasmine, having lived there the longest, scored the master bedroom and ensuite bathroom, but the other two bedrooms were still large. The main bathroom was newly updated too; Talia and I would share that one.

There were beautiful dark hardwood floors throughout, and the paint colours were light and modern. Jasmine had told me while giving me the tour that Desmond and Theo purchased this duplex for super cheap, and that it'd been in dire need of a gutting and full renovation on both sides. But the end result was remarkable.

She said Desmond and Theo's side was more masculine but had the same layout, only in reverse. They also didn't have another roommate. After Baz moved out, they didn't bother renting out the third bedroom.

Once we'd eaten the pizza, Talia suggested we play a few rounds of Yahtzee. I'd never played it before. Theo was sitting beside me, so he showed me how to, his arm around the back of my chair as he whispered instructions.

By the end of the thirteen rounds, I'd mostly gotten the hang of it, and somehow managed to win.

"Should we play again, see if that was beginner's luck?" Talia asked with a wicked grin. She seemed to be hoping my win would inspire me to play another round, but I was a firm believer in quitting while I was ahead—that, and everyone else wasn't into the idea.

Jasmine yawned, stretching her arms above her head. "I'm out. Damn, I'm so tired. The rain is making me sleepy."

"Don't forget all the paddling we did," I pointed out, smiling a little. My arms were aching from the exertion, and I was a little tired too. But I was also wound up. The heat radiating off Theo's arm over the back of my chair against the nape of my neck wasn't helping.

My thoughts kept going back to our night together—to the feel of his body against mine. I desperately wanted a repeat, but the opportunity hadn't arisen. Not that Theo was keeping his distance, he'd touched me subtly every chance he could. His arm across the back of my chair, his knee brushing against mine. The glances he kept stealing suggested his thoughts were very much in the same place as mine.

"Yeah, I might call it a night," Jasmine said, yawning again. "You can bunk with me if you want, or you're welcome to sleep on the couch." The other bedroom was currently empty, awaiting furniture and a new roommate—which was me, I guess. Before I could respond, Talia interrupted.

"Or…" Talia said, looking at Theo with a smug smile. "You could sleep with Theo. I'm sure he wouldn't be against that idea."

My face heated at her suggestion, but Theo's fingers toyed with the hair over my shoulder, and he smiled at me.

"I don't mind at all," Theo said, his eyes practically smouldering as they held my gaze. "I've got a spacious and rather comfortable bed."

Desmond hid a smile behind his beer, shaking his head slightly, and Jasmine smiled with delight. "It's settled then. Lux can crash with you tonight."

"I—" I started, then stopped. I wasn't opposed to this idea, in fact it gave me an opportunity to spend more time alone with Theo, exploring his body the way I wanted to. It was embarrassing that everyone else knew we were hooking up. Not that I was ashamed of it, I wasn't used to so many people knowing my business.

"Yeah, I guess that's okay."

TO BE HELD

Theo waited for me in the living room while I had a quick pee and then grabbed my bag from Jasmine's room.

"Enjoy your night," she said, wriggling her eyebrows at me.

"We will, I guess," I said, trying to hide a smile.

Jasmine blew me a kiss before disappearing into her ensuite bathroom.

I could hear him talking to Talia while he waited. When I emerged with my bag, Talia sent me a knowing grin and waved goodbye, disappearing down the hall to her own room.

I found it slightly amusing how everyone kept trying to push us together. I would have found it irritating if I wasn't so attracted to Theo. If he weren't so easy to be around. Instead, I was thankful Jasmine and Talia—and Desmond, in his own way—were giving me the push I clearly needed.

He stole a peek at me as we walked over to his side of the duplex. It was exactly as Jasmine had described: a masculine, opposite version to her side—soon to be *our side*. Giddiness welled up inside me at the thought. Theo took my hand, leading me through the main part of the house.

My stomach was a little twisted with nerves over the idea of going home and dealing with that situation, but the fact that I had an escape plan made me feel like I could handle it.

I didn't think my parents would be thrilled with my decision to move without even having a job lined up, but I had a huge chunk of savings from the inheritance my grandmother left me when she passed. I didn't really want to dip into it, but I would if I had to. I could keep looking and applying for jobs in Sudbury. I knew I'd find something, even if it was temporary.

Even if I ended up serving tables at Burger Bar with Jasmine, the respite of being far away from my sister's antics would make it all worthwhile. People had moved to new cities and countries even with less of a plan.

Desmond had already retired to his room for the night, so we were quiet as we moved through the house, still holding hands. Theo opened the door to his room and flicked on the light, leading me inside with a cheeky grin.

The moment the door closed, Theo moved toward me, his hands framing my head before his lips descended. He kissed me deeply and passionately, igniting flames of desire up my spine. I dropped my bag, letting it fall to the ground behind me, returning his kiss with as much enthusiasm.

He pulled away long enough to speak, his green eyes sparkling. "I've been wanting to do that all night." His thumb traced along my cheekbone.

"Good, because I've wanted you to do that all night," I smiled, standing on my tiptoes and kissing him again.

I could feel him getting excited, his thick length hardening against my lower abdomen. He let out a low curse, pulling away again with a rueful grin. "I need to shower first, but then we're doing this. Make yourself comfortable, I'll be a few minutes."

Laughing quietly, I stepped aside so he could leave. Theo glanced at me over his shoulder, biting his bottom lip like the last thing he wanted to do was leave me. He shook his head, pulling the door closed behind him.

I could hear the pipes as he turned on the shower. With nothing else to do, I glanced around Theo's bedroom, taking it all in.

The walls were painted a light grey. His furniture all matched and was a beautiful, dark walnut finish. His dresser was on one side of the room, a television on top of it. His desk was on the other side beneath the window, and other than the laptop and a stack of papers piled beside it, it was otherwise organized and clean.

He also had a small bookshelf the same height as his desk that was full of books, and there was a paperback on one of the end tables beside his bed with a bookmark in it. Theo was a reader. That knowledge made me swoon internally.

His king-size bed really did look comfortable, especially after the last few days of sleeping on the ground. His bedding was a masculine pattern of dark grey and black. His bed was made, and the room had a fresh and clean scent to it. Heck, I couldn't even see a speck of dust along the furniture.

It was the opposite to Scott's messy, disgusting room. I used to hate hanging out in Scott's room. It smelt like unwashed gym socks and stale pizza. He *never* washed his sheets, not unless his mom came up to do it for him. Any surface in his room was guaranteed to be sticky, either from spilt drinks or God knows what else.

I shivered in disgust at the memory, then listened. Hearing that the shower was still on, I walked over to the end of Theo's bed and sat down. It was so soft, like sitting on a cloud. I let myself fall back on it, and a waft of freshly laundered sheets welcomed me.

It was official: Theo was my dream guy. Organized, clean,

motivated, *kind*. The list was endless, and it seemed like at every turn, he was checking off another trait I hadn't realized I desperately wanted in a partner. The fact that he was outdoorsy and adventurous wasn't something I'd previously considered needing, but now...I couldn't imagine going back to dating a guy who only wanted to hang out in his basement playing video games.

The shower turned off, and a few moments later, I heard the bathroom door open and Theo's footsteps along the hall. I sat up in time for him to open his bedroom door. He stepped inside, his gaze immediately finding me and his eyes heating with desire when he saw that I was sitting on his bed.

A thick black towel was wrapped around his waist. His abdomen was glistening with water droplets, like he hadn't properly dried off yet. Closing the door and shaking his head to rouse himself from whatever thoughts he'd had, he stalked toward me. "I could get used to that sight."

"What sight?" I asked, my voice sounding as breathless as I felt.

"You, in my bed," Theo's voice was almost a growl, and the evidence of his arousal was already apparent. My hands went up to his pecs, feeling his muscles contract beneath my palm. I slid them over his still damp body, exploring all the ridges and dips with precision.

The towel around his waist fell loose, but Theo made no move to grab it. His erection jutted out proudly, hard, and thick and glistening at the tip. The sight of it made my mouth water. My hands slid down his abdomen, wrapping around his cock. I brought it into my mouth, sucking him the way I'd started earlier that day in the tent.

Theo's head fell back, his Adam's apple moving in his throat as he swallowed hard. It was hot, watching him react to the feel of my mouth. I loved how he tasted—he was shower clean, but I could taste his pre-cum, a heady, salty flavour that danced on my tongue. I worked him over for a few minutes, enjoying the low sounds coming from the back of his throat.

"You've got to stop, or I'm going to embarrass myself," Theo laughed, drawing out of my mouth with a wet pop. Before I could think of a reply, he bent over me to capture my lips in a kiss, his hands running up my exposed thighs to toy with the hemline of my shorts.

My hands went around the back of his neck as he moved over top of me, still kissing me as he laid me down on his bed. My legs were still dangling over the edge of his bed, so Theo scooped me up with one arm, tugging me up towards the pillows, never breaking the kiss.

He stopped kissing me long enough to tug the blankets from under me, pulling them down beneath us both with one strong arm before he hovered over me. I could feel his hard length between us, and I arched my hips—desperate to feel that contact.

He went back to kissing me; relishing in me. I could get lost in this man's kisses, and in the way he touched me. I'd never felt so desired, or so much desire, before; I didn't know what to do with it all. The feelings he evoked were so strong and right, it left me confused at how someone I'd known for such a short time could affect me like this so profoundly.

He pulled back enough to look down at me. "Let's get you undressed," he said, shooting me a mischievous grin.

"Okay," I murmured.

His fingers went to the button of my jean shorts. I was practically panting beneath him. He unbuttoned them effortlessly while his lips lavished kisses on the side of my neck. He tugged them down my thighs slowly, the rub of denim on my skin as he pulled them off working in perfect tandem to drive me deeper into arousal. I knew my panties were soaked with desire for him.

He left my underwear on and started removing my tank top,

until I was in my matching red lace bra and panty set. Theo brought his fist up to his mouth, biting his knuckle as he looked down at me.

"Fuck, you're absolutely gorgeous, Lux."

It was hard to feel insecure with the way he looked at me, and how reverently he spoke my name. I didn't know what to say, words completely escaped me. I wasn't used to the amount of affection he was showing me with each touch and glance.

But in that moment, I didn't dare question it. Theo looked at me with appreciation for another minute, shaking his head like he couldn't quite believe his luck. Then he unhooked my bra, tugging it away from my heavy breasts, and lowered his mouth to my right nipple while his hand toyed with the other. He sucked on it, tugging his teeth gently over the puckered peak. I moaned, my back arching in response.

My body was so sensitive and responsive to his touch, and I felt him smile around my nipple as if this delighted him. His hand moved from my nipple, sliding down my stomach to my mound over my panties, his fingers brushing against my covered slit.

"I can already feel how wet you are for me," Theo moaned, his voice sounding tortured as his fingers rubbed along my covered lips.

I was officially panting now, and I couldn't be bothered to care.

"Yeah, well. Can you blame me? Somehow, you know exactly how to get me there..." I whispered as he lowered himself down my body, nestling between my thighs. He peered at me with a devious grin before his tongue lapped over my covered sex.

The feeling of the lace and his tongue against me had me twisting on the mattress with anticipation. Theo tugged my panties aside with his index finger, making sure to run it along the seam of my lips. My hips bucked, desperate for more, which he all too happily gave me a moment later when he lowered his mouth to me.

Theo licked and sucked and kissed me, eating me like I was a five-course meal and he'd been starved of food for far too long. Each pass of his tongue had my hips trembling, and when he added a finger I nearly bucked off the mattress. He had to hold me down with his other hand.

"Theo!" I moaned, dripping around his tongue as I exploded. But he didn't stop, he kept going, lapping up my orgasm, drawing it out. When he was satisfied, he pulled away, taking my soaked panties with him.

He leaned over, opening his end table, and rooting through it. A frown marred his handsome face, his hand still moving things in there. "Shit," he swore, running a hand through his already-tousled hair. "I don't have any condoms."

"I have some in my bag." I replied, still panting. "In the front pocket."

Theo smiled at me with relief, hopping out of his bed to grab them. The box was a little crushed, but he didn't seem to mind. He tore open the box, grabbing a handful of condoms, and tossed the mangled box aside on his desk before stalking back to the bed. He stood beside it, opening a foil packet, and rolling it on his thick length as he looked down at me.

He didn't say anything, but the heady look he gave me made me squirm in anticipation. Once he was sheathed, he climbed over top of me, gently moving my knees apart to make room for his body.

All too eagerly, I spread my legs. Theo lined himself up with my entrance, rubbing his tip through my wetness, coating himself in it. We locked eyes as he sank deep inside of me, filling me to the hilt. He exhaled, his warm breath fanning across my lips.

"You feel incredible, like you were made for me," he said gruffly, moving his hips and dragging out of me only to slam back into me a moment later. I let my thighs fall open more, my hands scraping along his lower back as I tried to drag him deeper into me.

"You feel pretty amazing yourself," I managed, feeling myself tighten around him. Theo's eyelids fluttered, and he pulled almost all the way out before thrusting again.

I let out a satisfied groan, tilting my head back on the pillow, exposing my throat to him. He kissed my neck, his speed increasing as he slammed home harder and harder, spurred on by my body's response to him. I could feel the orgasm building, each thrust making me wetter and wetter, propelling me to the point of unraveling.

Theo could feel I was close, his body so in tune with mine. He slammed into me hard, gyrating his hips, the tip of him hitting that sensitive spot inside of me, making me erupt. He kept thrusting, drawing my orgasm out until my eyes practically rolled in the back of my head. He drove into me again and tensed, letting out a low moan as he came, too.

Our hearts were pounding in sync, and Theo didn't move for several minutes as he tried to catch his breath. When he finally did pull out of me, I felt bereaved by the loss. Theo removed the condom and stood, tying it off before he deposited it in the wastebasket by his desk before he rejoined me in his bed.

My hair was a tangled mess, and he brushed it tenderly from my face as he gazed at me.

"I really love doing that with you," he grinned.

I turned toward him, covering my breasts with my arm. "Well, I love doing that with you, too."

"Can I be honest?" he asked, and I nodded, biting down on my lower lip. "I'm glad you're moving here, especially if it means we'll get to do more of that."

"Yeah, I'm glad I'm moving here too. And that's an additional bonus. Is it included in the rent, or do I have to pay extra for it?" I teased.

He laughed, the sound of it rich to my ears. "Consider it a free perk." He smiled, and I grinned back at him. "Seriously, though. Jasmine and Talia are stoked about this arrangement."

"I honestly can't wait to live with them. Jasmine and I used to talk about being roommates when we were in high school, but then our program choices pulled us in different directions. I'm a little nervous about moving without a job though." I admitted.

"There's a lot of local places you could find work at, and Baz's sister works at the hospital, so you have that in."

"I can't see someone who doesn't even know me vouching for me, though it's nice of Baz to offer."

"She'll vouch for you, I have a feeling you guys will get along great. You'll meet her soon; she lives in Sudbury with her husband, and they often go to Baz and Rhiannon's gatherings."

"Do they have a lot of gatherings?"

"Oh yeah. They put on a wicked Halloween party every year. Baz and Rhiannon have enough property that people can just toss up tents and camp out."

"Sounds like fun," I said, yawning. I was exhausted, the last few days of camping and late nights finally catching up on me.

"It really is," Theo pulled me closer, and I nestled into his embrace.

My eyes felt heavy, and my body felt sated. I drifted off to a comfortable, relaxed sleep in his arms, feeling at home in his embrace.

LOOSE ENDS

Theo

THE NEXT MORNING, I awoke feeling like I'd had the best sleep of my life for a second night in a row. I couldn't help but wonder if it had anything to do with a certain redheaded beauty tucked into the crook of my arm.

Her hair fanned out over my pillows and her palm splayed across my chest sent a visceral reaction through me; it made me want to experience it as frequently as I could.

Lux started to stir a few moments later, the shifting of her body against mine doing little to help the hard on I'd woken up with. My desire for her only grew with each moment that passed.

She blinked sleepily, drawing in a slow breath as she looked around and took in her surroundings. Lux gave me a drowsy smile when our eyes connected. "Morning."

"Morning, gorgeous," I replied, returning her smile. "How'd you sleep?"

"Amazing," she murmured, stretching beside me. "What time is it?"

I turned my head, glancing at the alarm clock on my bedside table. "Nine o'clock." I answered. With no sun slipping in through the cracks in my blinds, it felt earlier than it was. I could hear the rain hitting my window and the distant clashing of thunder, promising the stormy day we'd packed up early to avoid.

"We should get up, then," Lux sighed, though she made no effort to move. I was in no rush either, though I let out a sigh of contentment in response. I could lay there with her all day and be happy just holding her, but a buzzing from my dresser interrupted our peace.

"That's probably Jasmine."

"Probably," I grumbled, a little annoyed at the interruption. If I had it my way, we'd be staying in my bed all day exploring each other's bodies.

Lux got up, searching for her clothes I'd peeled off and tossed haphazardly around my room. She put on her underwear, bra, and shorts—her shirt still missing in action—before she grabbed the phone and opened it. Her lips twitched into a smile as she read.

"Yup, Jasmine's wondering if our epic boning session is over yet. She wants to go for breakfast."

My stomach growled. "I could go for breakfast. Are you hungry?"

"Ravenous," she replied, eyeing me as if I was the meal. The sheet covered my lower half, but it did little to hide the effect she had on me, not that I wanted to hide it.

I grinned, tossing the sheets off, and climbing out of bed, my cock standing at attention. Lux's gaze dropped down, her eyes widening as she took me in. She licked her lips, making my cock jump as the blood surged.

"When do you have to go home?"

"I was supposed to go this afternoon, but technically, I don't have a curfew," Lux managed, finally lifting her eyes to mine. She had a devious twinkle in her eyes, like she was thinking the same thing I was.

Still stark naked, I moved towards her, my palms going to the smooth skin of her waist. Lux's eyes dropped down to my length, and her hand reached out to grip it. She fisted it, pumping slowly as she ran her thumb across the tip. I closed my eyes, letting my forehead drop against hers. I couldn't help but thrust into her hand a little.

"When we get back..." I paused, opening my eyes and arching a brow suggestively. Lux pumped me again, her smile growing, but before she could respond a knock sounded against my door.

"We're heading out to breakfast in ten minutes, if you guys want to join." Desmond said, his voice muffled through the thick door.

"Better get dressed, Theo," Lux teased, releasing me and stepping away. She picked up her shirt, pulled it on, and rooted through her backpack for her toiletry bag. She opened the door a crack, checking to make sure the coast was clear before sending me a smile over her shoulder and leaving my room.

I dressed quickly in a pair of clean cargo shorts and a black t-shirt. I put on some deodorant and ran my hands through my hair to tame it before hiding it beneath my cap.

Lux was leaving the bathroom when I stepped out into the hallway. She'd brushed her hair and washed her face. She had forgone makeup and still, she looked radiant.

"God damn, you're gorgeous," I put my hand on the doorframe over her head, leaning in to capture her lips in a chaste kiss. I'd have delved into her mouth like the starved man I was, but the fear of my own morning breath held me back. I could taste the hint of mint on her lips, though.

Lux smiled at me prettily when I pulled away. "They're going to leave without us if we don't hurry."

"She's right, you know!" Desmond called from the kitchen area. I nodded, moving around Lux to brush my teeth quickly and take a piss.

When I finished in the bathroom, I found Desmond and Lux talking quietly and waiting in the front hall with their shoes on. I took one look at Lux in her shorts and thin t-shirt, then turned around. I went back to my room, opening the closet door and grabbing my Trent University sweater.

I returned, handing it to her, and she took it from me with a curious look on her face. "It's going to be cold at the restaurant."

"That's so thoughtful of you," Lux smiled, tugging it on over her head.

The three of us made our way outside to see that Talia and Jasmine were already waiting on the front porch. Jasmine's car was still loaded up with camping gear, and Desmond's truck was only a three-seater, so we took my car. I drove a Volkswagen Golf R. It wasn't my dream car, but it got me around well enough.

Lux, Jasmine, and Talia slipped into the backseat and Desmond climbed into the passenger seat. I got behind the wheel, and we headed to our favourite restaurant on Lasalle.

Weekends and evenings were usually packed at Rudy's. Everyone in town knew it was the best place to go for burgers. Their breakfast menu was great too, and the service was unbeatable, even when it was busy. Since it was a weekday and it was storming, there wasn't much of a lineup.

When we walked in, a group was leaving so we scored a booth. Talia, Jasmine, and Lux squeezed into one side of the booth while Desmond and I sat across from them. I had the gorgeous view of Lux across from me, and she smiled when she caught me perusing her, tucking her hair behind her ear.

A moment later the waitress came by with a cloth to wipe

the table down, five menus tucked under her arm, and a steaming pot of coffee. While she wiped down the table, another waitress arrived with five clean coffee mugs and a bowl of creamers, setting them down with a smile before scooting off to her next task.

"Well, if it isn't some of my favourite regulars," the waitress, who's name tag read Bonnie, grinned, looking at us all. "And a fresh face! Welcome to Rudy's!" she added, her welcoming gaze going to Lux.

"Thank you," Lux murmured, her cheeks heating at the attention.

"Can I get you some coffee to start?" Bonnie asked her kindly. She was in her early sixties and had worked at Rudy's for as long as I could remember. Bonnie had curly dark brown hair, always tossed up in a messy bun. She'd been serving us for years now and knew our order well, so while she waited for Lux to reply, she filled up four of the mugs with coffee.

"That sounds good," Lux replied with a nod.

Bonnie poured her a mug too, then sent a cheeky smile to our group. "Let me guess, a Hangover special for Miss Talia, Western with Bacon for Miss. Jasmine, Lumberjacks for Mr. Theo and Mr. Desmond?"

"Are we that predictable?" Talia teased as Bonnie wrote down our orders on her notepad.

"Not predictable, just reliable. At least when it comes to your breakfasts," Bonnie laughed, her gaze going back to Lux. "What about you, sweetheart?"

"Uhh," Lux scanned the menu quickly. "The two egg special sounds good, with bacon and the home fries."

"How do you want your eggs?"

"Sunny side up would be great," Lux answered, smiling warmly. I lapped up this new tidbit of information about her eagerly.

Bonnie jotted it down with a nod, then collected the menus.

"We'll get that right out to yous," She said, heading to the kitchen to put the order in.

"So, do you still want a ride home this afternoon?" Jasmine asked, turning her head to look at Lux beside her. "Because I work tomorrow, unfortunately."

"Uh…" Lux's eyes went to me briefly before she looked back at Jasmine. "I guess so. I should get back and start making arrangements if I'm going to be moving in next month."

I wasn't ready for her to go. "You're welcome to hang out with me. I could drive you back whenever. I don't have to be back at work until Monday." The offer spilled from my lips before I could call it back, not that I wanted to.

Lux looked back at me, debating. "That might create more problems for me," she admitted. "To have an unfamiliar guy drop me off and then announce I'm moving would make my parents question my choices even more than I know they already will."

"I'm not unfamiliar," I winked at her, referring to all the ways we've gotten to know each other in the last few days, making her lips twitch in a repressed smile. "But I understand."

"I could drive you back Friday. My parents are hosting Camellia's birthday dinner this weekend," Jasmine chimed in. "What arrangements do you have to make?"

"I need to go buy a car so I can get around, and I'll have to pack my things up. Plus, I need to…deal with some family stuff." Lux said.

"Ah, yes. The evil sister," Talia nodded sagely. "You don't *have* to deal with that right away, though. You could kick around for a few extra days, put our poor Theo out of his misery."

I frowned at Talia, not liking that she was calling me out. I wouldn't be *miserable* if Lux left, but I wouldn't say no to spending a few more days with her before I had to head back to work.

"You'll need furniture, right? You could get Theo to take you to the furniture surplus store in town and pick something out, so it'll be delivered before you move," Jasmine added helpfully, her eyes bright with excitement. She was stoked that Lux had agreed to be their roommate.

Desmond shook his head, trying to hide his grin behind his coffee mug. The way the girls were working hard to convince Lux to stay a little longer had me internally laughing.

"I don't mind taking you to the furniture store," I told her.

Lux glanced at me, considering my offer. But before she could reply, Bonnie returned with three heaping plates, and the other waitress from earlier who carried the other two.

"Breakfast is served," she said with a flourish, setting our plates down. "Anybody need a refill on coffee?"

"I will," Desmond held his empty mug up. "Thanks, Bonnie."

Bonnie and the other waitress left us to our food, with Bonnie returning briefly to top up coffee for us before making the rounds at other tables to do the same.

Conversation lulled into a comfortable silence while we all dived into our breakfasts.

Lux

AFTER BREAKFAST, we returned to the duplex and Jasmine insisted on stealing me for a couple of hours. "Don't worry, Theo. we'll have her back by dinner," Jasmine teased, tugging me toward the door.

I still hadn't decided on if I wanted to stay a few more days, and I could tell Jasmine wanted to talk about that *and* about my night with Theo. Plus, she had some clothes I could borrow. I was a little sick of the few outfits I'd brought, and I desperately needed to do a load of laundry if I was going to stay.

"Alright, spill. Why are you hesitating on staying a few extra days? Are you second-guessing your decision to move here, because if so I'm going to be really sad," Jasmine demanded the moment the door closed behind us. Talia was watching, her expression a mixture of amusement and curiosity—like she was invested in my answer and entertained by the entire situation.

"I'm not second-guessing *that* decision," I assured her, rolling my eyes at her dramatics. "I mean, I know my parents aren't going to be thrilled with the idea, but they'll have to get used to it. I can't remain in that house much longer. There's nothing there for me."

"Yeah, I know. I saw the posts," Jasmine made a face, dragging me to the living room and flopping down on the couch.

"What posts?" Talia asked, taking a seat too.

I joined them, figuring there was no escaping the girl chat session.

"Lux's sister is rubbing it in that she's currently dating Lux's ex. It's weird, and gross," Jasmine shivered. "I could not do that, be with someone my sister had been with. Ick."

"Yeah, that's next level," Talia wrinkled her nose. "What do your parents think about the whole thing?"

"They don't know yet," I replied, shrugging. "I'm sure they won't be happy about it. They never really liked Scott, either. They were relieved to hear we'd broken up. My mom said it was about time when I told her."

"So, you're going to tell them the whole truth when you get home, right?" Jasmine prodded.

"Feels a little like tattling on her. I'm sure they'll find out on their own eventually. I'm going to tell them I'm going to be your new roommate and that there are plenty of job opportunities out this way."

"I think you should totally rat her out. Your parents need to know what psychological warfare she's been unleashing on you. It's amped up since high school."

I shrugged again, uncomfortable. "I don't want to cause

more friction. Who knows how long this fasciation of hers with him will even last? Brinley loses interest in guys so quickly."

"Yeah, but the intent to hurt you is concerning." Talia chimed in, siding with Jasmine. "I don't know your sister at all, obviously but… that whole situation is twisted. I'm thankful I'm an only child."

"I have sisters, and none of them would ever do something so vile to me. Brinley needs to be checked," Jasmine shook her head. I didn't disagree. I was so used to our parents sweeping Brinley's concerning behaviours under the rug. It would shatter my heart if they did it again.

"Did you post any photos from the trip yet?" Talia asked, a wicked grin on her face.

"Not yet."

"Oh yes, let's definitely do that," Jasmine held out her hand for my phone and I gave it to her. She selected several photos from my gallery and typed out something before passing me my phone back for approval.

The caption read "Jumping into new adventures", and the photos were the ones Jasmine took of me jumping off the cliff with Theo. The way he looked at me in the photos caused butterflies to riot. I bit my lip and posted them.

"So, tell me again why you're hesitating about staying a couple more days?"

"I don't want Theo to think I'm like, obsessed with him or something."

"I think Theo would *love it* if you were obsessed with him," Talia commented with a grin. "I've never seen him so interested in someone before."

"I second that, he's already obsessed with you. I'm sure he won't mind a little return-obsession. Besides, you can hang out for a few more days and really get some of that good dick therapy."

"Dick therapy, I like it," Talia cackled, doubling over. "Although I'd prefer a different type of therapy myself…"

"Speaking of, did Eliza call you back?" Jasmine asked. I had no clue who Eliza was, but judging by the smitten look on Talia's face she was someone Talia was interested in.

"Yeah, she did. We're going out for dinner, then going back to her place for the night. So, I won't be home," she grinned.

"Oh, pity, I'll have the whole house to myself, since Lux will be shacking up with Theo again."

"I can hang out with you, if you want," I said quickly, feeling my face heat up with embarrassment.

"Don't be silly, we'll be roommates soon enough. You get that good dick girl, you deserve it," Jasmine teased, her eyes sparkling.

I tossed a throw pillow at her, and she caught it, laughing. "I mean, it *is* really good," I admitted, biting my lower lip in contemplation. It was hard *not* to be obsessed with him, with the way he made me feel.

I didn't have much to compare it to, but I knew the connection Theo and I shared was something special, that our chemistry was intense.

"So, again, why the hesitation?" Jasmine circled back, arching a brow at me.

I sighed, rubbing my temple. "I don't want Theo to think that I'm expecting a full-fledged relationship. We haven't defined what we're doing and I'm already moving in." We'd touched lightly upon things the night before, but the most we'd clarified was that we enjoyed being around each other and having sex.

"You're moving in with *us*, not Theo," Talia corrected, easing my mind a little. "And do you need a definition?"

"No, not right now," I rushed to explain. "I don't want him thinking I have a bunch of expectations for things. Having him take me to a furniture store seems really couple-y."

"You're not picking out furniture together, you're going to pick out furniture for your own room *here*."

"True, I guess. But isn't it weird that I'm having sex with my about-to-be-landlord?" I frowned.

"So long as you aren't getting a deal on rent because of it, we don't care," Talia laughed.

"Actually, if you could get *us* a deal on rent too, I wouldn't be mad," Jasmine teased, setting off another round of giggles.

Once they subsided, Talia looked at me with a deep understanding. "I think you're worrying too much about everything. Let the chips fall where they may and enjoy life as it's happening. Do something spontaneous for the sake of spontaneity."

"Can you do that, Lux?" Jasmine challenged.

She knew me better than most, and she knew I had a hard time letting go of my meticulous need for control. My tendency to over-analyze everything was often more of a fault than a perk. Sure, it meant I was pretty organized and thorough with schoolwork, but it didn't exactly translate to a peaceful mindset in the rest of my life.

"I can try," I managed, finding a timid smile for her.

DINNER GUESTS

It was hard to let Lux walk away, especially when all I wanted to do was carry her like a Neanderthal back to my bed. I was in uncharted waters, already craving more of her time and attention than I should.

Desmond watched me watch Lux disappear with a bemused smile. He shook his head, opening our door and disappearing inside.

"What was that look for?" I demanded, following in after him.

"Nothing," Desmond raised his hands innocently.

"That was *not* the look of nothing. That was the look of you having an opinion."

"Not an opinion, just a thought." Desmond corrected, putting his shoes in the front hall closet and standing.

"What thought?"

"That it's refreshing to see you this interested in someone. Usually *I'm* the one pining."

"I'm not pining, I'm—I don't know," I let out a heavy sigh, flopping down on the living room couch. Desmond disappeared in the kitchen, grabbing two pops for us before joining me in the living room. "I wasn't expecting her, and now…I don't know what to do with her. It's crazy, I know, but I'm already so into her."

"And why wouldn't you be?" Desmond asked, popping the tab. "She seems great. Jasmine has always spoken highly of her."

"Yeah, I know," I nodded. "I don't want to freak her out with how much I'm into her. I've only known her for a few days, and she's agreed to be our new tenant. This could get messy."

"It will only get messy if you don't communicate. Be honest with each other, and you'll avoid any messes. Did you tell her you were into her?"

"In more or less words," I lifted a shoulder and took a heady sip of beer. "I mean, I haven't officially asked her out on a date or to be my steady girlfriend or anything. I told her I liked spending time with her and being with her."

I'd wanted to make things official between us, but I didn't want to rush her into anything. I figured there would be plenty of time for that when she moved to Sudbury.

I was worried that I might need to tone it down a little, let her have her space to think over everything before I frightened her away. She'd just gotten out of a long-term relationship, and while she seemed like a relationship girl, she needed a little space to breathe and figure things out for herself. *Especially* with the mess she was dealing with back home.

I was reluctant to be a rebound, too. I felt in over my head with this girl—but what if I *was* just a rebound, a good time after a shitty relationship? Already, I wanted to mean more to her than that, and that could be dangerous if she wasn't on the same page as me.

So, I let her have her space. I didn't bother her for the rest of the afternoon, which she spent next door, hanging out with Jasmine and Talia. I could hear music pumping through the shared wall and laughter.

Desmond and I hung out for a bit, then he went to his room for a power nap. I unpacked the camping gear and got caught up on laundry. Then I cleaned a little, not that the house needed it, Desmond was a neat freak and I hadn't been home much in weeks. But the near empty status of our refrigerator suggested we would need to go to a grocery store soon.

When I was trying to figure out what to make for dinner around five o'clock, my cell phone chimed.

Jasmine: Tell Des you guys can come over for dinner. Be here around six-thirty.

I still had an hour and a half to kill, so I decided to grab a shower.

Twenty-minutes later, and I was feeling refreshed. I dressed in a pair of dark denim jeans and a grey Henley, then knocked on Desmond's door. A moment later, it swung open.

"Yeah?" he asked, wiping the sleep from his eyes. He had to be back at work tomorrow night. I felt bad for waking him up, but knew he had to eat something—and would be pissed as hell to miss the invite next door.

No matter how tired Desmond was, he never turned down an opportunity to be around Jasmine.

"Jas invited us over for dinner tonight," I told him.

"Cool. What time?"

"Six-thirty?"

"Alright, great. I've still got time for a shower." Desmond had the master bedroom with the ensuite bathroom. He hadn't wanted to take it at first, but I figured it made more sense for him to have the private bathroom with him working nights a lot of the time.

While I waited for six-thirty to roll around, I stopped off in my room and made my bed. I'd been in a hurry this morning and had left it a rumpled mess. I normally kept my spaces clean and tidy. It was a habit instilled in me from my days living with my parents. Coming home at the end of a long workday to a mess wasn't exactly relaxing, so my younger sister and I had a list of chores we'd had to accomplish each day before my parents got home.

I wasn't sure if Lux was going to want to come back and spend another night in my bed, but if she did I wanted to welcome her to a clean room.

The minutes seemed to trickle by, but finally it was six-thirty and Desmond and I were stepping out onto the back porch and walking over to tap on the sliding door. We could see Lux and Jasmine in the kitchen, drinking glasses of white wine and dishing food out.

Lux heard us knocking and looked over, surprised to see us at the back sliding door. But that was usually how we called on each other, especially when invited over. Game nights were a semi-regular occurrence when both Desmond and I were home. Usually, we'd have dinner and then play cards or a board game.

Jasmine gestured at us to come in, and Desmond opened the door. "Good evening, ladies."

"Hey guys, hope you're hungry. Lux's been cooking up a storm; tomato-cream pasta with sautéed mushrooms and grilled chicken."

"It smells incredible, thank you for inviting us over" my voice sounded way too formal, but I couldn't help it. It was a miracle I'd even managed to string words together at all.

Lux looked like a freakin' domesticated vision, standing in the kitchen serving the meal she'd made. Her red hair was pulled back in a high ponytail and she was wearing a pair of form-fitting denim jeans that made her ass look even more delicious than the incredible dinner she plated for us.

Normally, seeing an attractive woman in a kitchen didn't do much for me—I wasn't one to buy into that traditional stuff. Gender roles weren't something my parents had focused on while bringing us up. Olivia and I were both expected to learn how to cook and do our own laundry. It was my parents' goal to make sure we were self-sufficient by fourteen.

But Lux...she invited a fantasy into my mind looking like she did. A fantasy that I didn't want to focus too much on, because it was the opposite of taking things slow and easy so as to not overwhelm her.

"Let me help you with that," I said, reaching for the bread-basket in Lux's hand. She smiled, letting me take it, and turned back to the counter to grab two of the plates. We walked over to the small round table.

"Where's Talia?" Desmond asked while Jasmine grabbed the other two plates.

"She's on a hot date with Eliza, so she won't be joining us tonight," Jasmine grinned, setting the plates down on the table.

"Good for her," I commented with a grin. She had been sort of seeing Eliza casually for a while now, but Talia had some reservations about commitment, and Eliza wasn't exactly out of the closet with her family yet. I got the impression Talia wanted more.

I was glad to hear they were figuring it out, though. Talia had brought Eliza to a few bonfires and parties, so we'd met her a couple of times.

"So, what did you guys get up to today?" Lux asked, pulling a chair out and sitting down between Jasmine and me.

"Not too much. I did some stuff around the house and Desmond took a nap." I answered.

"I'm back on midnights tomorrow," Desmond explained.

"That must be tough," Lux said sympathetically, her eyes softening.

"It can be, but the pay's great," Desmond shrugged before taking a bite of pasta. "Damn, this is delicious, Lux."

I took a bite too, the flavours exploding on my tongue. It wasn't just homecooked good, it was restaurant-level good. The sauce was creamy and rich, the mushrooms were sauteed to perfection, and the grilled chicken was flavourful and not at all dry. "It really is, where'd you learn to cook like this?"

"Mainly boredom," Lux admitted with a shy smile. "My mom's not much of a cook and my dad's the chief of Cardiovascular Surgery, he's usually really busy. We have a chef, Maria, that comes over and prepares a bunch of meals. I learned how to make a few dishes from her."

"A chef, huh? That's pretty fancy," I commented with a grin. I knew Jasmine came from a higher tax bracket, what with her family being in politics. I guess it made sense that Lux came from money, too, especially if her father was the chief of Cardiovascular Surgery.

"Yeah, I guess," Lux's gaze dropped as she shifted uncomfortably in her seat and took a bite of her pasta. I could tell the topic of her family was a sore one for Lux. If her sister's actions were any indication, Lux's family had a complicated dynamic.

"Maria's an excellent chef, I used to love going over to Lux's for dinner. It was like eating at a five-star restaurant, but at someone's house," Jasmine grinned. "Does she still work for your parents?"

"Every Monday, she comes over with a ton of groceries and preps enough meals for the week." Lux confirmed. "I definitely missed her cooking when I was at college. Cafeteria food didn't hit the same, and our dorms didn't exactly have kitchens to cook in. There was a hot plate, a microwave, and a refrigerator."

"Well, this is delicious. You could have been a chef yourself," I told her, already halfway through the pasta. Lux gifted me with a smile that reached her eyes.

With everyone eating, we fell into a comfortable silence.

Once the food was consumed, Desmond and I offered to tidy up the kitchen. There wasn't much to do, the cookware Lux had used to prepare the meal was already soaking in the sink. Less than ten minutes of effort, and everything was spotless.

Once the dishwasher was loaded, the four of us made our way into the living room, the girls carrying a bottle of white wine while Desmond and I cracked open some beers.

"Anyone want to play a game?" Jasmine held up a black box that said *Answer This* on it.

"How do you play it?" Desmond asked, mildly curious.

"You answer questions about your friends. The first to answer ten questions correctly wins the game."

"Sounds interesting," Lux said, her lips twitching.

Jasmine looked at the three of us with hopeful eyes.

"We could play one round," Desmond managed, unable to tell her no even though I knew he detested games like this— games that could force him to tell a lie to avoid potentially exposing his true feelings.

Jasmine clapped her hands, delighted. "Okay, great," she wiggled into a more comfortable position on the couch and opened the box, grabbing four of the dry-erase boards and markers and passing them out. Then she shuffled the cards inside before handing them out. "You'll have to show your answers on the dry-erase board, and if your answer matches the answer of the person who asked the question, you get a point. The first to get ten points wins."

"I don't really know everybody here all that well, Jas," Lux said, worrying her bottom lip.

"It's okay," Jasmine assured her. "You can take wild guesses and it'll still be fun, plus you'll hear the answers at the end so you'll get to know these guys pretty well."

There was no talking Jasmine out of an idea once she had it, and Lux knew this. She nodded, relenting, and settled onto the couch cross-legged with her dry-erase board on her lap.

The game started with Jasmine going first to show us how it was done.

"Which public figure annoys me the most?" Lux and Desmond scribbled quickly on their boards. I was less sure, jotting down *Killian Barker* after remembering a heated rant Jasmine went on recently about the American punk-rock singer and songwriter.

"It's Dudley Wadsworth, although Killian is a close second!" Jasmine laughed. Lux and Desmond had answered the question correctly, both earning a point.

Then Lux went. "When is my birthday?"

I wish I could say I guessed right, but that honour went to Jasmine. "July 15th!"

So she was a Cancer; it checked out. Lux had an emotional depth to her and was highly empathetic. I couldn't help but absorb each new detail she revealed about herself like rain on dirt after a drought.

We kept playing, getting through several rounds with Jasmine and Desmond neck and neck before Desmond ended up accumulating ten points and winning the game.

"Well, that was fun." He stood up, quitting while he was ahead. "Thanks for dinner, ladies. I need to get back and force myself to sleep for a bit," he added, sounding like it was the last thing he wanted to do. He sent a covert look at Jasmine, but I don't think she caught it as she was putting the game away.

"Oh, bye Des. See you later," Jasmine said, looking up at him with a smile. Desmond nodded, then headed to the back door.

"What now?" I grinned, looking between them.

It was nearly nine o'clock, still early, but I was no longer interested in playing board games. Lux and I had kept stealing glances at each other as the game had worn on, and the desire between us was palpable. I was eager to get her alone; eager to claim her lips and her body again.

"Are you still crashing next door tonight?" Jasmine asked

Lux, her question rousing me from the inappropriate turn my thoughts had taken.

"Well, all my stuff is still over there. Is that okay with you?" Lux looked at me uncertainly.

"Absolutely. I was hoping you would," I replied easily.

"We won't keep Desmond up?"

"He could sleep through a hurricane," I assured her. Our eyes locked on one another, the heat between us ready to boil over. It'd been simmering all night, rolling off us both in waves. I knew Jasmine could sense it.

"Well, you two crazy kids have at it. I'm going to have a shower then turn in too. Work tomorrow. Blech," Jasmine wrinkled her nose with disdain. "But I'll see you after work, Lux? We'll watch a movie or something?"

"Sounds good," Lux said, smiling at Jasmine. I stood up, offering my hand to Lux to help her off the couch.

I couldn't get her back to my place quick enough. Desmond had left the kitchen pot lights on, but the rest of the house was dark. "So, what do you want to do? Your choice. We could watch something out in the living room, or..."

"Or?" Lux arched a brow at me, her lips curling in a seductive smile. My hands went to her hips, stroking the sliver of skin between the hem of her shirt and her jeans.

"We could hang out in my room. Put something on the television in there and get even more acquainted with each other."

"Hmm," she pondered. "I like that second option." Lux rose on her tiptoes to capture my lips in a slow kiss. It was all the permission I needed. I deepened the kiss, pulling her towards me by her hips. I let out a tortured moan as her tongue danced with mine, my erection driving into her lower stomach, the friction making us both wild with want.

We parted a few moments later, our breaths frantic. "Let's go, before I end up taking you on the kitchen counter."

Lux's eyes widened with surprise, and intrigue—like the idea entranced her. I let out a low growl, the idea appealing to me so much that I'd have done it if Desmond wasn't home. Sure, he could be down for the night sleeping, but I didn't want to run the risk of him walking in on that.

I grabbed Lux's hand, tugging her down the hallway to my bedroom. I turned to face her, about to lower my mouth to hers again when she placed her finger on my lips.

"Hold on, I need to freshen up first."

"Okay, yeah. Sure. Did you want something to sleep in?" The words tumbled from my mouth, and she smiled.

"That would be great," she bit her lip, waiting while I grabbed a pair of gym shorts and a baggy t-shirt from my dresser, handing them to her. She grabbed her toiletry bag and disappeared down the hall into the bathroom.

While she was gone, I tugged off my t-shirt and turned on the 36-inch TV on my dresser, putting on a random show for background noise, then turned down the blankets in my bed. She returned a few moments later, looking ravenous in my gym shorts and t-shirt.

"You're so god damn gorgeous, Lux," I said, my voice a low rumbling in my throat. She blushed prettily, dipping her chin like she didn't quite believe what I was saying. I stepped toward her, tilting her chin up to force her to meet my eyes. "You truly are a vision. If I was a painter, I'd spend hours painting your beauty, and never come close to encompassing it."

"You flatter me," Lux accused, biting her lip. I moved my hand, using my thumb to gently free her lower lip from its trap. That this woman could think less of herself had me reeling.

"No, I'm telling you the truth. Seeing you in my clothes...it does something to me," I admitted before I finally let myself kiss her.

Our kisses quickly turned passionate, Lux's hands roaming over my bare chest and abdomen, sending waves of desire licking across my skin. I touched her reverently, like she was a gift I wanted to take my time unwrapping. I lifted the t-shirt, pulling it over her head before dropping to my knees in front of her.

I peered up at her, my hands gripping the waistband of the shorts and tugging down slightly, revealing that she'd gone commando. I swallowed hard, so affected by that as I slowly pulled them down over her thighs.

When she was bared to me, I leaned forward, kissing her pretty mound. Her honey sweet scent made my mouth water, and I didn't hesitate before sampling a taste.

I'd never been a selfish lover, except for my first time ever at sixteen. I'd been clumsy and hurried, unsure of how to move and what to do. Since then, I've taken the time to know my partners' likes and dislikes, to read their bodies and bring them as much pleasure as I possibly could. It wasn't about my pleasure because I knew my pleasure would come with my partner's pleasure.

Lux, though, I wanted each and every time with her to be beyond what I'd given other partners. I wanted her to feel my intent, feel my desire for her on that spiritual level, and I was not a spiritual person.

I wanted to leave her legs shaking and her heart and body fulfilled.

I was salivating for the taste of her. I pressed my mouth to her, licking and sucking, lapping up every drop I pulled from her body like a greedy man. Her moans and sighs were music to my ear. The way her fingers tangled in my hair, holding me to her, drove me mad with the desire to consume her. I had to force myself to pull away when her legs started to tremble from the effort of standing after she came on my tongue.

Standing up, I licked her essence from my lips before kissing her. I knew she could taste herself on my tongue, and that made me throb with an unrelenting ache. I picked her up and carried her to my mattress, easing her down on it before crawling over top of her.

We still had two condoms left, and I made quick work of rolling one on. Lux peered up at me with trusting eyes, her thighs spreading to welcome me home.

I positioned myself between her legs, holding myself up with one arm while I rubbed my throbbing erection against her lower lips, coating myself in her arousal. Lux's eyelids fluttered at the sensation. She arched her back when I pushed all the way in, her walls squeezing my shaft deliriously tight.

I rolled my hips, pulling out before thrusting forward and filling her to the hilt again. I lowered my mouth to hers, kissing her while I fucked her, our tongues and lips matching the crazed hunger we both felt.

Each thrust brought her closer and closer to the pinnacle, and when I felt her walls tighten before a rush of warmth and wetness surrounded me, I nearly came along with her. I stilled, throbbing inside her as I caught my breath and forced myself to slow down.

"Can we try something?"

"What?" she was breathless, her cheeks flushed.

"I want to take you from behind," I admitted. I wanted to take her every way she'd let me, but I especially wanted her ass up in the air while I pounded her from behind.

Lux bit her lip. "Okay," she nodded after a moment of thought.

I pulled out, hating leaving the warm tightness of her but knowing I'd be back inside moments later.

Lux moved into position, her perfect ass on display for me. I nudged her legs open wider, spreading her, and got myself situated behind her. The tip of my cock brushed against her back entrance, and she let out a surprised gasp.

"Sorry," I chuckled, leaning down to press a kiss to her shoulder blade before sliding back into her warmth.

She moaned, her hands fisting my sheets as I filled her. At this angle, I could go so much deeper. Her slick walls clamped down on me, and I knew I wasn't going to last long like this.

I drew in a breath, preparing myself, my hands going to her hips, my thumbs pressing into the sweet dimples on her pale back. I held her in place while I thrusted, and she pushed back on me, moaning.

I kept the pace, our bodies frantic with need, her orgasm building and cresting until she came around me, my name escaping her lips on a gasp, calling my own release.

"Jesus, Lux," I swore, my balls tightening before I spilled into the condom in hot spurts.

PLANE OF EXISTENCE

I FELT like my body had been taken to an entirely different plane of existence. My thighs trembled from the aftershocks, my core wringing out every drop of Theo's release.

His hands still gripped my hips, his thumbs still pressing into the small of my back as he drew in a shaky breath and pulled out. I practically collapsed, rolling over onto my back and watching as he removed the condom and disposed of it in the trash can before shaking his head and flopping down beside me.

We were both out of breath, our bodies still reeling from the exertion.

"God damn, that was incredible, Lux."

"You sound surprised," I teased.

He shook his head again. "I'm not, I should have known it'd be like this with you. You're my dream girl, after all." he chuckled.

My breath caught in my lungs, my heart skipping a beat in its chest. When Theo said stuff like that, my heart couldn't help but to feel hopeful—and that was dangerous.

I was trying desperately to keep my head on straight, to not free fall into another relationship so soon after escaping my last. But Theo made me want to do that. He made me want to say *screw it*, and dive into this beautiful connection we seemed to have.

He'd called me his dream girl, and I'd thought of him as my dream guy. I couldn't have imagined a better match. That made me doubt it all though. Made me feel like it was all too good to be true.

"What's wrong?" Theo's smile slipped, like he sensed my inner discord.

"Nothing," I tried to assure him, but he wasn't buying it.

"Something's wrong. Did I hurt you?"

"No, not at all!" I rushed to say, my eyes never wavering from his. "That was beyond anything I've ever experienced before. I'm—I don't know. Worried."

"About what?" he asked me, his green eyes taking in every emotion that filtered across my face.

It was my turn to shake my head as I deliberated on how honest to be with him. Jasmine, Talia, and I had spent most of the day talking about my reservations over trusting my feelings, but I was no clearer on the matter.

I'd expressed my fears, but Jasmine shot them down. *"You aren't moving up here to be closer to Theo, you're moving up here to be closer to me, and to see what opportunities await you here."* She'd insisted, and she was right. Theo was a bonus, for sure, but he wasn't even one of the top three reasons. Not yet, anyway.

But I was still scared.

"Everything. I'm scared to make this move, especially without a job. I feel like I haven't really thought things over."

Escaping Brinley's bullshit and getting to be roommates

with Jasmine were great reasons, but what if I couldn't find a job?

"We could see how things work on a month-to-month basis, for now. If you end up hating it here, or you find a really great job somewhere else you can always move out with no penalty. Desmond and I know your situation and want to help you out, and it happens that helping you out helps us out, too."

"Okay, that takes a bit of the pressure off," I admitted, biting my lower lip. It was a relief to hear that I wouldn't be locked in a rental agreement I couldn't get out of, especially if this living arrangement turned out to not be the best thing for me.

But I think what scared me the most was that in my heart of hearts, I knew it *was* the best thing for me. Moving to a new town and getting some distance from Brinley was the best thing I could do for myself. Being around Jasmine would be healing, she was more of a sister than my own flesh and blood.

As for Theo, I knew it was soon, but I also knew that the things I felt for him surpassed anything I'd felt for Scott, and that had to mean something.

Theo placed his hand on my hip, peering at me with those green eyes that felt like magic and forest. "I know you're moving here for a fresh start, not for me, but I'm not going to lie to you, I'm looking forward to getting to spend more time with you—with whatever label you want to slap on us."

"I'm not sure about labels right now," I admitted quietly, hoping my honesty didn't hurt him.

He smiled, not a trace of pain in his expression. Just under-standing and empathy.

"That's perfectly fine. I can wait to label things, so long as you know that I really am into you. This thing we're doing, it means something to me." Theo brushed his finger along my hip, making my skin erupt in goosebumps.

"It means something to me too, even if I'm not ready to label it. I recently got out of a long-term relationship, and I want to be certain that what I'm feeling is the real deal," I whispered, worried my words were too candid for the moment.

But Theo's smile didn't waver, and his eyes were warm with understanding. "I get it," he said before he pressed his lips to mine, kissing me softly.

I FELL INTO A DEEP, peaceful sleep with Theo's arms wrapped around me, holding me against his hard body.

When I awoke, I felt more solid with my decisions, and more excited about the prospect of moving.

At the very least, I was doing something spontaneous. I was stepping into the unknown without a solid game plan, which was something far outside my comfort level.

"Morning, sleepyhead," Theo's gravelly voice stirred the arousal that had been dormant while I slept.

"Morning," I replied, smiling. I stretched, the sheets sliding off my breasts, gifting Theo with a few of my pebbling nipples. He licked his lips hungrily.

"We're going to have to pick up more condoms when we go out today," he remarked before lowering his mouth to my nipple. He sucked on it, his tongue rolling across the pebbled peak.

I arched my back, bringing my breast closer to his mouth. "Don't we have one left?"

"Yeah," Theo lifted his head long enough to shoot me a mischievous grin before returning his attention to my breasts.

"Better use it up, then," I challenged.

He wasted no time, crawling over top of me.

I TOSSED a load of laundry into the washer before we left to run errands. First, Theo drove me to the furniture surplus store, where I took my time picking out a furniture set for my new room.

I found a bedroom set in a soft wood grain design with clean lines, a sleek contemporary frame, and subtle aluminum accents that gave a modern aesthetic. It came with a queen-size bed, a six-drawer dresser, a drawer chest, a night table, and a desk.

I also ordered a pillow-top mattress next, arranging for it all to be delivered in two weeks' time. It made my decision to move more real and more definite. I hadn't told my parents yet, but I had furniture ordered.

After we finished at the furniture store, Theo took me out for a late breakfast, insisting that we had to eat something before hitting up the grocery store. He'd pointed out how dangerous it was to go grocery shopping on empty stomachs, and I knew he was right. We went to Rudy's again, and Bonnie seemed excited to see us walk into her section.

Once we had eaten breakfast, we went to the grocery store.

It should have felt strange, running all these domestic errands with Theo, but it felt right. Theo made sure to toss in an extra-large box of condoms to our cart with a cheeky grin.

It was quiet when we returned home. Desmond was still sleeping, trying to get as much rest as he could before his midnight shift, and Jasmine was gone to work for the day.

I helped Theo unload the groceries, then switched my laundry over. Everything I'd brought was enough to fit into one load.

Jasmine had returned from work by the time my laundry was in the dryer. I felt a little guilty, ditching Theo, but he seemed unbothered by the prospect.

"If anything, I owe Jasmine an apology for occupying most of your time," he insisted, seeing me off with a kiss. "I promise,

I'll survive until later. The back door will be unlocked, come in whenever you're ready for bed."

"I'm ready for bed now," I said, my hands running over his bulge with intent.

"And I'll hold you to that, later," Theo grinned back. "Go hang with Jas, I'll see you in a bit."

I nodded, forcing myself to walk away from him, even though my hands itched to slip into his pants.

Jasmine was waiting next door in the living room with takeout boxes from her favourite Thai restaurant set up on the coffee table. "Oh good, I thought you were going to ditch me, and I'd have to eat all this Thai food alone."

"Where's Talia?"

"Not back from Eliza's yet," she replied with a coy smile. "Did you find furniture?"

"I did," I pulled my phone out of the pocket of my jeans before I sat down beside Jasmine, opening up my gallery to show her the photos I'd taken.

"Ooh, fancy!" Jasmine said with approval. "When does it get delivered?"

"Two weeks," I put my phone down on the coffee table and reached for a box. Jasmine had ordered my favourite, Thai fried rice.

She nodded, chewing on her chicken pad Thai. She finished chewing and swallowed before speaking. "So, that means you're looking at moving here in two weeks?"

"About that," I answered. "Unless…well, unless things get even more unbearable at home."

And I had a sinking suspicion that they would. Something told me my leaving would cause more drama in the house. Brinley thought she had more time to torment me, and me leaving would be like removing her favourite toy.

"Of course. You can seriously move in tomorrow, I'm sure Talia wouldn't mind. You could crash on the couch until your furniture arrives, or get them to deliver it sooner. Or keep staying with Theo." She winked at that last part, and I flushed with embarrassment. "How's that going, by the way?"

"Good, I guess. I really enjoy spending time with him."

"So you've said," Jasmine chuckled. "You guys really seem to have hit it off. I was right in thinking you'd be good for each other."

"It's too early to tell," I frowned.

"Not really, he's already made you more adventurous and confident. You might not see it, but I do. You're a different person than the defeated girl I picked up on Friday to drag into the backwoods," she commented, her tone kind. "I was really worried about you. Brinley really did a number on you this time, but I'm so glad your shine has returned."

I couldn't deny it—getting away from the situation back home had been even more healing than I could have imagined when I'd said yes to the camping trip. I felt more like me; a version of me I hadn't seen in so many years. I felt ready to take on new opportunities, to make a life for myself that was completely my own.

"Well, I don't know if *he's* made me more adventurous and confident, or if being here with you has," I lifted a shoulder in a shrug, pausing to take another bite of food. Jasmine's eyes lit up at that, and she grinned. "But we barely know each other."

"You guys have a lot in common. You'll get there," Jasmine said.

"I do think he's awoken something in me, though." I admitted.

"I bet he has," Jasmine snorted. "I told you that good dick therapy would help."

"How did you know Theo had a good dick?" I narrowed my eyes, studying her.

"His ex-girlfriend liked to brag a lot." My friend wrinkled

her nose. "Like, a lot. It was a bit much. I think she did it because she felt threatened by us girls living next door."

"Ex-girlfriend, huh?"

"From like, two years ago or so. They were never really serious, and they broke up after four months or so of dating."

"Why?"

"She was super possessive and a bitch to any other female. Especially Rhiannon."

"Why Rhiannon?! She's so sweet." I exclaimed, not believing it.

"She was always condescending and rude to her and kept making comments about how she didn't know how 'someone like Rhi' scored Baz'," Jasmine's eyes flashed with anger at the memory. "But Theo overheard her one time, and that was it. He sent her packing."

I nodded, absorbing this new information. "I didn't expect Theo to be celibate before me, but hearing he'd had a serious girlfriend makes me feel a little twinge of jealousy," I confessed.

"Don't worry, Lux, it was ages ago. He never looked at her like he looks at you," Jasmine assured me.

It was a relief to know that it'd been a while ago, and he hadn't been heartbroken by her.

"And how does he look at me?"

"Like you're the missing puzzle piece in his life," Jasmine grinned.

"I don't know about that," I laughed, shaking my head.

"You don't feel it? That connection between the two of you? It's pretty noticeable. I know you both, I can see it."

"Oh, I feel the connection," I replied, setting the carton of food on the coffee table and adjusting my position on the couch. "I just…I don't know. It's too soon to think like that."

"They say when you know, you know."

"Is that so?" I challenged, arching a brow. "So then, why are you hesitating over your feelings about Desmond?"

"That's more complicated," Jasmine argued, her lips pinching as she set her own carton down and swiveled to face me. "We've been friends too long. There's a shared history there, and it's hard to untangle my feelings for him. I care about him a lot as a friend, and if it's not right between us, we'll never be able to go back to just being friends."

"Maybe you won't need to go back to being friends." I shrugged. "Maybe he's your forever."

"But if he isn't? I don't want to lose him as a friend, Lux. I'm not ready to take that risk, his friendship is too important to me. And honestly, I don't know if I'll ever be ready to risk it."

JASMINE and I agreed to disagree on the Desmond front, and sensing a topic change was for the best, we put on a movie and fell silent. Halfway through, Talia came home and joined us for the ending, snacking on the leftover Thai food Jasmine and I hadn't finished. She confirmed that I could move in as soon as I wanted, and then spilled the details on how her time with Eliza went.

After the movie ended, I returned to Theo's place. He was sitting on the couch in the living room, reading. He glanced at me when I walked in, his muscular arm slung over the back of the couch, the picture of relaxation with his book on his lap.

"How was it?" he asked, closing his book and setting it aside.

"Good. We had Thai food and talked, then watched a movie," I smiled, sitting beside him.

"That sounds fun," he murmured, moving closer and placing his hand on my knee.

"It was. It's been so long since we hung out like that. What'd you end up having for dinner?"

"A grilled cheese sandwich and soup," he answered with a smile.

"That doesn't sound like much," I frowned.

"Don't worry about me, I'm hungry for something else now." His eyes were sparkling with intent. "Desmond's at work."

"Meaning?"

"We have the entire house to ourselves, and I can finally spread you out on the counter. Been thinking about it for days now," he admitted, biting down on his lip and looking at me through hooded eyes.

My blood simmered in my veins at his suggestion—and at the slow slide of his hand on my thigh.

Theo

LUX'S EYES widened at my suggestion, and she swallowed hard as my hand continued to slide up her thigh, my fingers coming to a rest at the junction between her legs.

"I—I don't know about that," she said breathlessly, her cheeks pinkening. "I've never really done anything so out in the open before." She cast a worried glance to the back door.

"If you're uncomfortable with the idea, that's okay, but we do have the house to ourselves until tomorrow morning."

Lux's tongue darted out to wet her lips, drawing my gaze to them. I couldn't resist leaning forward and capturing her mouth in a kiss. Our lips met in a slow kiss, and before I could deepen it, Lux was crawling over top of me to straddle my lap, her hands sliding into my hair.

She kissed me deeply and moved her hips, grinding her pelvis against me. This girl made me harder than hell, and I knew I'd never get enough of her. Not even if I got to have her like this every night for the rest of our lives.

She pulled away and tugged her t-shirt off, letting it fall to the ground behind her, her eyes heated with rolling desire, making them appear like liquid metal.

I picked her up effortlessly, flipping her so that she was laying on her back on the couch, then I moved over top of her, settling between her legs. I kissed her again, our tongues meeting and dancing in slow reverence. Each slide of her tongue on mine made the blood surge to my erection, which I couldn't help but thrust against her.

Breaking the kiss, I moved my hand to the waistline of her jeans. "You're still wearing entirely too many clothes," I complained, sliding the zipper down.

"Let's fix that, shall we?" she challenged, lifting her hips so I could tug her jeans off. I threw them over my shoulder, hearing them land somewhere behind me, leaving her in her lacy black bra and matching panties. I took in the sight of her, at a loss for words.

"You are exquisite," I told her, bringing my mouth back to hers.

She moaned, arching up into me, grinding against my cock, her hands tugging on my shirt to remove it.

I'd take her then and there, but Desmond and I had an unspoken rule about furniture in the common areas of the house. Especially the couch.

Regretfully, I pulled away from her, leaving her pouting until I scooped her up in my arms and carried her into the kitchen. I set her down on the counter and she giggled, her cheeks still flushed and her eyes a little wild.

I had no qualms about the counter. It could be cleaned up if we made a mess, and nobody would be any the wiser.

"Just one taste," I promised, licking my lips as I tugged the lacy material aside and brought my mouth to the sweet junction between her thighs.

I should have known one taste wouldn't be enough. I couldn't stop with one pass of my tongue against her slick folds, with one hint of her taste. Growling with impatience, I tugged her panties off, then brought my mouth back to her, my hands massaging her legs and thighs to relax the tension from her.

It was a dream, having Lux spread out on the counter in front of me, mine for the taking. I feasted on her like she was a five-course meal, gently tugging at her clit with my lips and not letting up until she was trembling from her second orgasm and begging for me.

"I need you, Theo," she pleaded, my name sounding like a melody coming from her lips. Her hands slid into my grey sweatpants, wrapping around my hard cock. I hadn't bothered with boxers, figuring once she got back from Jasmine's, we wouldn't be dressed for long.

"Now." Her eyes were full of impatience and desire.

"Condoms are in my room," I grunted, closing my eyes against the feel of her hand wrapped around me. She stroked me, making my body tense with wanton need.

"I have an IUD and I've been tested recently. I'm good, if you are?" she peered at me, her eyes full of trust and explicit need, her hand moving against me again, urging me closer.

"I'm good," I assured her. I'd always used condoms, but despite that I still got regular testing after being intimate. I trusted Lux irrevocably, but I still needed to make sure she was sure.

"Are you sure?"

Lux bit her lip, nodding with determination. "I'm sure," she whispered, her hand still wrapped around me, working me at a torturous pace. I was gone for her; I'd do whatever she wanted without question.

"Well, if you're absolutely sure..." I said, letting my voice trail off as she reached behind her and unclipped her bra, letting it fall to the ground, her eyes taking me in. I couldn't stop staring at her; she was so beautiful, sitting naked before me.

She reached for my hard cock again, guiding me, and I

moved with her, pressing my engorged tip against her soaked entrance. I rubbed against her, not yet entering, reveling in the feel of her slick arousal and heat while she expertly worked my sweatpants down my legs with her feet. I stepped out of them, kicking them aside, and moved back to capture her lips in a claiming kiss, our bodies so close that I was notching against her.

I knew there would be no going back, not after I had her without barriers. Hell, there was already no going back, but this would solidify things.

My thoughts were confirmed when I slipped inside, slowly pushing my way into her slick heat. Her legs parted more, and she arched her pelvis, taking me deeper, her breath escaping on a pleasured sigh.

She felt so incredible that I couldn't hold back the groan that pulled from the back of my throat. "God damnit, Lux—you feel amazing," I grunted, pulling out only to slam back in.

Her head fell back and she moaned, her breasts pushing out toward me as she arched more. I took a nipple in my mouth, sucking on it, my tongue swirling around the hardened point, my hips driving forward in a pace that made my entire body thrum and tingle.

There wasn't a chance I'd be able to last long, not with the no-barrier feel of her heated walls squeezing me with each thrust, but I forced myself to hold back until I coaxed another orgasm out of her.

It didn't take me long, not with the punishing pace of my thrusts. When I brought my hand down to rub against her clit, she went off, her body trembling with release.

The feel of her coming had my balls tightening up, the base of my spine tingling as my own release followed. I pulled out in time, my cum splashing against her belly and thighs in a delectable mess.

Lux's chest heaved with her heavy breaths as she looked down at the mess I'd made of her.

"Sorry, I wasn't sure if you wanted me to come in you." I reached over and grabbed a paper towel, running it under the tap for a minute to dampen it before I cleaned her up.

"You could have, but that was surprisingly hot. I've never had someone finish on me like that." Lux bit her lip, her cheeks heating with embarrassment at her confession.

"You're so fucking hot, Lux, I couldn't help myself." I told her, my forehead resting against hers. "And I'm not going to lie, I'm glad to hear I was the first to do that to you."

If I had it my way I'd be the first and the last: the only one.

She smiled in response to my words, her eyes sparkling.

DAY DATE

THE NEXT MORNING, I awoke to an empty bed. Voices drifted down the hall, along with the scent of bacon and eggs. I dressed in a pair of gym shorts and a t-shirt, leaving my room to find Lux in the kitchen with Desmond.

From the looks of it, Desmond had gotten home to find Lux making breakfast in our kitchen. If he was irritated by her presence, he didn't show it. Not that he had any reason to be irritated. From the looks of it, she'd made enough breakfast for him, too.

Lux's hair was pulled back in a loose ponytail, and she was wearing my old university sweater over her denim shorts. Seeing her in my sweater made me feel a sense of possessiveness.

"Hey," Desmond said, lifting his chin in greeting when I walked into the kitchen. Lux glanced at me over her shoulder and smiled.

"Good morning," she grinned.

"Morning," I said, walking up behind Lux and wrapping my arms around her waist. "Mmm, that smells amazing."

"Figured I'd earn my keep a little," Lux replied, lifting a shoulder in a delicate shrug. "I feel bad that I'm crashing here."

I glanced at Desmond, arching a brow, silently asking if he'd said anything to make her feel that way.

"I've got no complaints, she made egg sandwiches with bacon," Desmond grinned, holding up the half he still had left of his.

"You don't need to feel bad for crashing here, we're happy to have you."

"Especially if you keep cooking for us," Desmond added. "Keep doing that, and we might not let you move in with Jasmine and just keep you over here."

Lux laughed, her cheeks heating under the attention. The toaster popped with four slices of bread, and she casually moved out of my embrace so she could make two more egg sandwiches. "I think Jasmine would have something to say about that."

"Oh, probably," Desmond grinned, taking another bite of his sandwich.

"How was work?" I asked him. He was still covered in grime from his shift. Usually, when Desmond got home after working a night shift, he stayed up long enough to eat something before showering and crashing.

"Same old," he replied, shrugging. "Wish I'd had the foresight to book extra days off. I'm still beat from camping."

"Yeah," I chuckled. I hadn't had a vacation in so long. Sure, I'd travelled for work, but those trips weren't exactly restful, so I'd decided to take the full two weeks off. I certainly wasn't regretting it now, since it gave me the opportunity to spend more time with Lux.

"Got any exciting plans for today?" Desmond asked us both as Lux handed me a plate.

"No," Lux replied at the same time I said "Maybe," and looked at her. Her curious gaze shot to me. "I figured I'd see how you felt about going on a day date."

"Where?"

"To Science North. I feel the pressing urge to take you to a few of Sudbury's finest attractions." I grinned.

"You don't have to woo me on the idea of Sudbury, I've already decided that I'm moving here," she reminded me with a smile.

"I know, but if you're going to be a resident of Sudbury, you're going to have to check out the attractions."

"Hmm, well. I suppose you're right," Lux smiled.

"Well, I'll leave you guys to it then. I'm beat," Desmond said, yawning. "Thanks again for breakfast, Lux."

"My pleasure," she smiled. Desmond headed down the hall to his room, leaving us alone with our breakfast. We ate, then took turns showering and getting ready for the day.

It was all very domestic, and I loved it. It'd been a while since I'd last had a serious relationship, but I couldn't remember ever feeling this…ease. Although I'd only known Lux for a short while, being with her felt right.

After we were both dressed and ready, we headed out to my car to go to Science North.

"This is one of my favourite places," I admitted to her on the drive over. "My grandpa used to take my sister and me all the time."

"Does your sister still live nearby?"

"No, actually. She moved to Alberta a couple of years ago," I replied. "She still comes home for Christmas, but she's the manager of parks and recreation in Bonnyville."

"Oh, so she has a diploma in nature too," Lux teased.

I let out a chuckle, shaking my head. "I guess you could say that."

"Do your parents still live in Sudbury?" she asked, twisting in her seat so she was facing me. The wind from the open car windows lifted her long locks, blowing her hair around her face. She tried to tuck it behind her ears.

"Yeah, they do. They still live in the house I grew up in. Both are too stubborn to retire, but they take more vacations now. Usually to see Olivia."

"Olivia…that's your sister's name?" I nodded. "It's pretty. Are you guys close?"

"We're not super close, she's four years younger than me. We don't really confide in one another, but we get along well. She's great. Adventurous, and fiercely independent."

Lux let out a wistful sigh, the sound of it pulling my eyes from the road to her for a moment. "I'm always so envious of other peoples' easy-going sibling relationships, I've yet to meet anyone who has as many issues with their siblings as I do."

I didn't know what to say. Keeping my left hand on the steering wheel, I reached over to place my hand on Lux's thigh and gave her a gentle squeeze. "Maybe Brinley will grow up one day, and you two could repair your relationship."

"Maybe," Lux hedged, her expression uncertain, like she didn't believe it.

Before I could say anything else, the Science North facility came into view. I put on my turn signal and waited for a break in traffic to pull into the parking lot. We found a spot and headed in.

"Have you ever been to the Science Centre in Toronto?" I asked as we waited in line to pay for our entrance, my hand resting on the small of her back.

"Yeah, a few times for school field trips. Haven't been since I was in public school, though," Lux replied, glancing at me. "Have you been?"

"Once, back when I was a kid. My grandpa used to watch us during the summers, and he'd take us on all kinds of adventures. Usually local, but a few times, he took us to Toronto. We also went to Ontario Place once."

"Oh, Ontario Place! I forgot about that. The amusement park and waterpark were my favourite growing up. Have you ever been to the Exhibition?"

"No, my grandpa didn't like crowds. He'd rather take us camping in the backwoods than deal with the amount of traffic The Ex gets," I chuckled, missing the old man. He'd passed away six years ago. "Ontario Place was busy enough for him."

Lux smiled sympathetically. "I get it. I hated the crowds whenever we'd go to The Ex, but it's a lot of fun."

"We'll have to go. You could show me around your favourite local places back home sometime," I grinned down at her, making her smile grow.

"I think we could arrange that…" she said, noticing it was our turn to pay. I'd already pulled my wallet out and quickly slid my card out to cover our charges.

We spent the next several hours walking around the different exhibits and talking about everything and everything. Lux smiled the whole time, her eyes light and happy. I made any excuse I could to touch her—subtly, of course. I was aware of the children and families around us.

We stopped off at the gift shop before we left. When she was distracted buying rock candy suckers, I couldn't resist picking out an agate butterfly for her. It reminded me of how she'd fluttered into my life with her natural beauty and captivated me.

"Aww, thank you, Theo. You didn't have to do that!" she exclaimed when I handed it to her.

"I wanted to," I told her, watching as she studied it.

"It's so pretty! I love it," she replied, turning it over in her hand.

"So are you, which I guess is why it made me think of you," I scratched at the back of my neck, cringing. "I know, that's pretty damn cheesy—but it's the truth."

She glanced back at me with bewilderment. "Well, thank you. For this and for the day date."

"Oh, we're not done yet. I still have to take you to see the Big Nickel," I grinned.

"Stop! I forgot that was a thing," Lux laughed, her nose wrinkling and eyes sparkling with amusement. "Why is it a tourist attraction again?"

"Well," I said with flourish, taking her hand and heading toward the exit, explaining while we walked to the parking lot. "It commemorates the two hundredth anniversary of the isolation of metallic nickel by a Swedish mineralogist and chemist, Baron Axel Frederic Cronstedt. It also pays homage to the ingenuity of chemist Ludwig Mond, who developed the first commercial process to produce pure nickel."

"Okay…" Lux said, still not getting it.

"Since the Sudbury area is rich in nickel-bearing ore and has a history of supplying it to the world, it's *kind of* a big deal for us locals. And tourists love it. Pretty much everyone who comes here ends up with a picture in front of it. I think Jasmine even has one."

"Yeah, she does. She took it when she first moved here and sent it to me. I didn't get the hype," Lux admitted with a grin as I unlocked my car.

"You still won't get it after you see it, but it's a requirement." I opened the door for her, holding it while she climbed in.

"At least you're honest," she laughed.

The drive to the Big Nickel wasn't far, only ten minutes. We grabbed some lunch and then took our time exploring the educational mine before making the Big Nickel our last stop. Lux stared up at the three-storey high coin, tilting her head, trying to figure it out.

"Huh. It's cool and all, but rather anticlimactic."

"I'm still going to take your picture in front of it, so go stand there and look impressed," I teased. Lux crunched up her nose and laughed as I pulled out my phone.

"Are you going to make me do one of those 'holding it' pictures?"

"I wasn't, but now that you mention it…" I said, waggling my eyebrows. "Move forward and put your hand up, like you're holding it."

"You're ridiculous," Lux was blushing, but she did as I asked, the megawatt smile on her face. I snapped a few photos with my phone of her appearing to hold the nickel between her index finger and thumb.

Then I asked someone else to take one of us together with the nickel off to the side. "Gotta commemorate this moment," I told her, putting my arm around her. She glanced up at me, and I looked down at her, smiling.

It was nearly five by the time we were done at the Big Nickel, and although we'd grabbed lunch earlier I wasn't ready to end our date day. I couldn't remember the last time I'd had so much fun on a date.

Tomorrow, Lux would be heading back to Guelph. Sure, it was only for a couple of weeks until she officially made the move, but I knew I'd miss having easy access to her.

"Feel like grabbing dinner out before we head back to the house?"

She glanced at me. "I could eat."

Lux

MY MIND WAS WHIRLING from an incredible day spent with Theo. I knew we were sexually compatible, but I wasn't expecting being with him to feel so easy and right.

When Theo had suggested a day date earlier, I'd been skeptical. It'd been a *long* time since I'd gone on a date, and I wasn't sure what to expect from it. But Theo made it all feel so effortless and smooth.

I honestly couldn't remember the last time I had that much fun. Even when Theo insisted on making me take ridiculous photos with the Big Nickel, something I normally wouldn't have done, I was laughing and had felt lighter than I had in years.

He pulled something out of me, something good. Something I *liked*.

Theo drove us to a beautiful bistro for dinner, where we ate authentic Indian food. The romantic atmosphere made me feel a little underdressed, but the waitstaff was incredible at making us feel welcome. I ordered the butter chicken and nearly had an orgasm right there, from the taste of it.

The way I'd moaned around my fork had Theo's eyes darkening with heat, but he kept it together long enough for us to finish our meal and walk back to his car. Then he pulled me in for a kiss—a kiss that seared me straight to my core. It was brief, but full of promise and more than enough to get me primed.

When we finally got back to his place, it was nearly seven. Jasmine's car was in the driveway, so she was back from work. She'd texted me earlier, wondering where we were and what we were doing. When I told her Theo took me on a day date, she sent a series of excited emojis and told me to enjoy it.

Theo turned off his car, and I faced him. "Thank you for today, I had an amazing time."

"Me too," he grinned at me. "Thanks for letting me nerd-out about minerals."

"Anytime, you're adorable when you're in the middle of a tangent."

"Ah, yes. *Adorable*, the word every guy hopes to hear from their date," Theo teased, his eyes sparkling with mirth.

"Better than boring, or mediocre," I pointed out, joking

along with him. Theo was neither boring nor mediocre. He was anchored, smart, and always seemed to know exactly what to say and how to act.

"You're right, I'll take adorable over boring or mediocre any day," Theo chuckled. He lifted his hand, cupping the side of my face. I leaned into his touch, my eyes raising to meet his. "I hope you'll say yes to another date with me in the future."

"I think the odds are definitely in your favour for that," I told him, smiling.

Theo grinned back, then leaned forward to kiss me. His lips were soft at first, and it was me who urged him for more with the teasing swipe of my tongue.

The kiss deepened, and then we were making out in his car, the heat between us steaming up the windows. We made out for nearly ten minutes, until my hand dropped down to his lap, rubbing against the strained erection in his Chino shorts.

He broke the kiss, resting his forehead on mine and chuckling a little. "We should get inside, unless you'd rather visit with Jasmine tonight?"

I glanced over at the house, biting my lip, my hand still running over his erection. I'd had more sex in the past few days than I'd had in all the years I'd been with Scott, and yet I still wanted more. I craved Theo's touch, the feel of his hands and his mouth on my body.

But I was afraid to be greedy, afraid to crave him as much as I already did. Things between us were so new—and yes, we'd had a wonderful date and intense sexual chemistry, but I didn't want him to grow tired of me.

"I should spend some time with Jasmine." Even as I spoke, my hand was rubbing and gripping Theo's hard length through his shorts, teasing him. His hips lifted toward it, and he let out an affected sigh.

"As much as I want to drag you to my bed and not let you out of it for days, I did get to spend the whole day with you while she had to work. I understand if you want to hang out for a little bit, and we can always pick things up where we left off later, when you come back."

"Bold of you to assume I'd be sleeping over again," I said, turning back to him with a teasing smile.

"All your stuff is still at my place," Theo reminded me. "Plus, my bed is very comfortable."

"That's true. Your bed *is* comfortable. I guess I could spend one more night in it."

My stomach knotted at the thought of leaving tomorrow. *It's only temporary*, I told myself, even though it felt like I was heading to the gallows. I knew the drama waiting for me back home would bring right back to the cold hard ground.

"Alright, so it's decided then. Go hang out with Jasmine for a bit, tell her all about our incredible date and how I rock your world, then come back to me so we can finish what we started here." Theo pressed a kiss to my forehead, the action making me swoon. I never realized the power a tender forehead kiss could have.

SHATTERED PEACE

THE ANXIOUS FEELING in my chest grew the closer Jasmine got to my parents' house. I was having difficulty breathing by the time she pulled into the driveway, but the anxiety released a little when I realized Brinley's car wasn't there. She wasn't home. Neither was my dad, but Mom's car was parked in its regular spot.

My shoulders slumped in relief. At least I wouldn't have to face Brinley immediately. Since I was moving up north, Jasmine convinced me to leave most of my camping gear in the shed there. All I had with me was my bag of clothes and toiletries.

I took a steadying breath, preparing myself for the battle I was sure would ensue.

"Let me know if you want to hitch a ride back with me. I talked to Des, and he said you could move in whenever."

"I appreciate it, but I still have a lot to do here," I reminded her. But I also wasn't about to close myself off to the idea. If

Brinley was unbearable, I'd tie up things quickly and leave sooner.

"Okay, good luck," Jasmine said, reaching across the console and hugging me tight. "I can't wait until we're roomies. In the meantime, try not to let the wicked witch get to you."

I got out of the car and watched Jasmine back out of the driveway before I spurred into action, walking through the expansive house in a quest to find my mom.

She was in the back sunroom, reading a fashion magazine and listening to music. I opened the sliding door and stepped outside, and she lifted her head in surprise.

"Oh, Lux! You're home. How was your trip?" she asked.

"It was really good, actually. I had a lot of fun," I told her, sitting down across from her at the glass patio table.

"Meet anyone worth noting?" she asked, a playful grin on her still youthful lips. Mom's appearance was enhanced by plastic surgery—a little Botox here and there, some lip fillers to plump things up. She didn't shy away from plastic surgery, but she also didn't want it to be a noticeable thing she did.

"Well, I did meet a great guy. All of Jasmine's friends were great, actually—"

"Oh, tell me more about this great guy. What's his name?" Mom was relentless when she got a whiff of interesting information. "I knew you met someone when you extended your stay."

"His name is Theo," I replied. I didn't want to reveal too much to her, that we'd started sort of dating, and I didn't want to let it slip that I'd be living next door to him when I moved in with Jasmine. Instead, I opted to change the subject. I tucked a strand of hair behind my ear, looking toward our manicured backyard. "Has Brinley been home?"

"She's supposed to be back sometime today from her trip with her friends. She's been on a yacht the last few days, lucky girl," Mom replied, smiling and shaking her head ruefully.

"So…you haven't seen much of her?"

"Not lately, why? Is everything okay between you two?" Mom asked, her brows creasing, not that a wrinkle appeared on her perfect brow.

"No, not really," I sighed.

"What's going on?" Mom sat back in her chair, her eyes narrowing with suspicion. My stomach tightened with anxiety, but Jasmine was right. I couldn't keep my parents in the dark about Brinley's latest antics. They'd end up finding out eventually, especially if she continued to carry on the way she was online.

Neither of my parents had social media, but some of their friends did. Sooner or later, it would get back to them. I took a deep breath, preparing myself.

"She's been seeing Scott."

Mom blinked. "I'm sorry, I don't think I heard you right. Scott, as in…your ex-boyfriend Scott?"

"Yeah. Turns out Scott was cheating on me with Brinley. She was kind enough to tell me before I came home for the summer, but she's still seeing him."

Mom's mouth opened and closed several times while she absorbed this information. "Oh, honey…I'm sorry, I had no idea. Why didn't you tell me sooner?"

"It's all over her social media," I looked down at the table. "Everyone knows. I'm surprised it hasn't gotten back to you guys already. Besides, I wasn't sure what telling you would do. Brinley's going to do whatever Brinley wants to do. And what Brinley wants to do is hurt me, however and whenever she can."

Mom put her hand on my forearm. "You know that's not true, your sister loves you, she just—"

"Mom, she willingly slept with my boyfriend, then sent me a picture of herself in bed with him. She sends me regular videos and stories of herself draped over him. If that's Brinley's version of love, I don't want anything to do with it." My voice shook and my hands trembled, my heart cracking with the power behind revealing this aching truth.

Mom looked stricken by my words. I don't know what hurt her more, to hear how Brinley was acting, or to hear me saying I didn't want anything to do with it or with her.

"Let me talk to her, I'm sure I can get to the bottom of this. It's a big misunderstanding. You said you and Scott had drifted apart years ago, so—"

"Seriously?" I interrupted, staring at her in bewilderment. "You're going to tell me it's okay she did that because Scott and I drifted apart?"

"No, that's not what I meant," Mom said, frazzled. "I think there's something more going on behind the scenes for your sister to act this way. She's never done anything like this to you before."

"She's done thousands of microaggressions towards me over the years, Mom, and I'm done. I can't handle it anymore, and I shouldn't have to. If we weren't sisters, if Brinley was some acquaintance or friend from school doing the things she's done to me over the years, your advice would be very different right now. Our familial ties don't mean that I have to forgive her for purposely being toxic and cruel."

Mom listened, her lips trembling a little. "I know you've tried to talk to us in the past about Brinley's.... mental health, and I'm sorry for shutting you down when you did. Over the last few years that you've been at college, I've noticed the things you tried to warn us about. Your sister does have some issues, and as a family we need to help her work through it. I know she's hurt you, but please, don't give up on her yet."

I paused, not expecting that. "I'm not going to give up on her, Mom. But I do need to distance myself. I can't be a target for her aggression anymore. I'm going to be moving out."

Mom looked surprised by my announcement; as surprised as she could look with Botox. "Where are you moving to?"

"Sudbury. Jasmine's looking for a new roommate. I'll be moving in with her," I answered, my eyes meeting hers. "There are some opportunities for me there."

"But you have opportunities here too, Lux. I thought you were going to apply to work with your dad at the hospital."

"I thought about it, but rents are high in Toronto. It's more affordable up north, and there are plenty of hospitals and clinics for me to find work at," I answered, leaving out the main one: I didn't exactly want to work in the same hospital as my father. I'd always wonder if I'd landed the job on my own or if he'd had a hand in things. He had a lot of sway at the hospital, with his position and his seniority. His hospital was the only one in Toronto I *hadn't* even bothered applying at.

Plus, the rents in Toronto really *were* high. They were high everywhere down south, but worse in Toronto. If I stayed, it'd be a long time before I could afford my own apartment. I'd have to live at home until then, and I couldn't fathom doing that.

"Does this boy, Theo, live in the area?" Mom asked.

"He does, but that's not why I'm moving," I replied.

"Mmhmm," Mom tsked with disbelief, giving me a secretive smile. "You know, things moved fast for your father and I, too."

"This isn't about him," I frowned, a little frustrated she was conflating the two things. "This is about me, needing to put distance between me and Brinley, and getting on with my life." My reminder wiped the smile off my mother's face, and she sighed.

"I know," her shoulders slumped. "I'll try to talk to Brinley about it."

A FEW HOURS LATER, I was in my bedroom sitting on my bed, my laptop open in front of me as I searched the job postings in Sudbury. I applied for three: one at the hospital, and two at different clinics. I also applied at a few restaurants to make sure I had something lined up for when I moved.

I could always work temporarily at a restaurant until something came up in my field, but I was optimistic. I had to be. I reminded myself that I had a great resumé and many recommendations from my professors and the place I'd done my co-op at.

Halfway through submitting another application, my bedroom door banged open. I looked up, not at all surprised to see Brinley lingering in the doorway. She was the only one that didn't bother knocking before she burst in. My fingers tightened into a fist at my side, and I tried to control my breathing—keep it even and steady even as I seethed at the sight of her.

Brinley smiled smugly. "Home from your little 'roughing it' trip so soon?" Her tone was sickly sweet, with an undercurrent of poison. "I was hoping you'd get eaten by a bear."

"Sorry to let you down, I guess," I rolled my eyes and shook my head. "Is there a purpose for your disturbance?"

"Is there a purpose for you telling on me?" Brinley retorted, crossing her arms and leaning against the doorframe, her eyes narrowed into slits.

"Oh, was it supposed to be a secret? I couldn't tell, what with the non-stop posting you've been doing on social media."

"Admit it, you're jealous and bitter Scott wanted me over you."

"I don't care about Scott, Brinley. Not even a little bit," I sighed deeply, closing my laptop. "What I care about is how cruel you are to me. We're sisters, we're supposed to have each other's backs and yet you slept with my boyfriend, sent me pictures, and bragged about it everywhere you could."

"*Ex*-boyfriend," Brinley corrected smugly. "He's *my* boyfriend now."

"But he was my boyfriend when you went after him," I reminded her. "And again, this isn't even about Scott, I don't care about him. I cared about you. What sister does that? It was disgusting and beyond cruel."

Brinley's expression changed subtly at my last sentence, but she threw up her walls as quickly as I noticed the change. "Oh, get over yourself, Lux. You were done with him years before he took an interest in me. You just dragged him along because you didn't have anything better waiting for you."

I shook my head, appalled at her reasoning—if it could be called that. "Even if our relationship had run its course, you shouldn't have done what you did. I think deep down, you know that."

"You should be thanking me!" Brinley exclaimed. She laughed darkly before continuing. "If I hadn't forced you to let go, you'd still have your claws in him, and he'd still be miserable with you. I make him happy."

"But do you make yourself happy, Brin?" I asked sadly.

My sister blinked as if she was forcing my question away. "You bored him," she continued with a sneer, stepping into my room. "I don't. And you can't stand that someone prefers me to you—finally."

"I really do hope you find the happiness you so desperately seek, and I hope that one day, you won't tear others down in your quest to find it." I told her.

Brinley scoffed, rolling her eyes again. "Whatever." When she finally stomped out of my room, I closed the door behind her, leaning against it. My heart still felt battered and bruised, more so from her than anything with Scott.

The interaction left me feeling even more like my decision was the right one.

Dinner only solidified things for me. When Mom called us down, Dad was finally home from the hospital. Brinley was the last to join us. She gave me a smug look as she pulled out her chair.

Mom didn't bring up the news I'd dropped on her earlier,

and neither did Brinley. It was like neither one of them wanted to fill Dad in on the Scott thing. Halfway through dinner, I couldn't take the silence anymore.

"Dad, are you able to come with me to the dealership this week? I need to get a car." Even before I'd decided to move to Sudbury, I knew I'd have to go car shopping. Now that I had finished college, I'd need a reliable mode of transportation to get to whatever job I landed.

"Sorry, sweetie. I'm pretty busy the next few weeks with surgeries and clinicals. Could your mother take you?"

I'd read somewhere that car salesmen always tried to swindle women. My mom didn't know much about vehicles, and neither did I. She was also more gullible than my father, and didn't really care about the cost of things the way he did.

"I could take you," Mom smiled at me across the table, but it didn't quite reach her eyes.

"Yeah, I guess that's fine." I'd have to do my research beforehand and make sure I knew what I was going in for and what I was willing to pay.

Brinley rolled her eyes, pushing her food around on her plate and barely eating any of the chicken piccata Maria had prepared in advance for us. It was one of her best dishes, but the tension coating the room made it taste dull.

"I don't know if Mom mentioned it yet, but I'll be moving out at the end of the month," I informed my dad. Brinley's brows furrowed and she shot me a dirty look.

"Oh, did you get a job?" Dad asked, his red brow arching.

"Not exactly, but there are a few opportunities for me up north. I'll be moving in with Jasmine."

"You shouldn't move without a job secured." Dad shook his head, like he was going to tell me no.

"I'm an adult, if I want to move I can. With or without a job. It's not like I'm asking you to foot any of my bills."

"What's *that* supposed to mean?" Brinley demanded, crossing her arms and scowling at me.

Even though it wasn't meant as a dig at my sister, Brinley took it that way because she expected my father to foot all of her bills. She didn't work, outside of her social media influencing. Our father still paid her phone bill, her car payment, and anything else she needed or wanted.

Sometimes, Dad would tell Brinley to get a real job, but the fight that'd follow his suggestion was never worth it. Brinley would accuse him of not supporting her the way he supported me—because Dad had covered the things bursaries and scholarships hadn't for my higher education.

"It means I'm not expecting our parents to cover my expenses, Brin. I can manage them myself."

"Wow," Brinley said, taking my response as a personal insult to her.

"Respectfully, this isn't about you or your feelings." I deadpanned, looking straight at her.

"Now, Lux. That was a little harsh," Mom interjected. She frowned at me, like I was being unnecessarily cruel or causing unmerited drama.

"I don't see how it was. I'm stating facts. If that hurts her feelings, that's on her, not me. I'm not going to apologize for living my life anymore." I felt a tangible sense of relief once the words spilled from my lips.

"Girls, what's going on?" Dad asked, his brow furrowed as he took in the tension. Brinley was shooting daggers at me with her eyes, and Mom was sending me a beseeching look, silently begging me not to involve him further.

The knots in my stomach twisted with anxiety and disappointment. I dropped my eyes to my plate, feeling utterly disparaged. I don't know what I'd hoped to happen after the conversation I had with my mom earlier, but to see that she was still desperately trying to sweep things under the rug stung.

"A lot is going on, Dad, but I'll let Brinley or Mom fill you in. I've lost my appetite. Can I be excused?"

"No, you can't. Not until you girls tell me what's happening here." Dad's voice was full of authority, leaving no room for argument.

"Nothing's going on, Daddy," Brinley said, her eyes wide with innocence. I scoffed, rolling my eyes.

"I think the girls are having some difficulties adjusting to living together again. They'll work it out," Mom said, sending Dad a reassuring smile.

"Really?" I demanded, looking right at my mom. She shook her head, her lips pursed like she was disappointed *in me*. "This right here, this is why I'm moving before I have a job. Because I'd rather start over somewhere new on my own than have to deal with this situation any longer."

"What situation?!" Dad exclaimed, clearly confused.

"Brinley going out of her way to harm me, Mom excusing it and acting like it's a simple misunderstanding. I'm tired of pretending everything is perfect because that's what Mom wants. This family has serious issues and I'm done being the scapegoat."

I pushed my chair out and took my plate to the kitchen, letting it clatter on the counter before retreating to my bedroom. From the stairwell, I could hear my mother working overtime to soothe things over and act like everything was fine.

In my bedroom, I started pacing and pulled my phone out, noticing that I had several missed text messages from both Jasmine and Theo.

Theo: Hey, checking in to make sure you got home safely.

Jasmine: How's it going over there? Need a rescue yet?

I replied to Theo first.

> I've arrived home safe and sound.

Pff, if I could call it that. Then I texted Jasmine, filling her in on the latest.

> Jasmine: You know my family won't mind if you crash Camellia's party. You're practically one of us.

> Me: You know what? You're right. I can't be here anymore, especially after that dinner.

> Jasmine: Be there in fifteen.

While I waited, I packed my large roller luggage bag with all the clothes and essentials I'd need. I'd have to come back at some point for the rest of it, but I made sure to pack enough clothes that I could go a few weeks before I needed to do that. I packed a change of clothes for tomorrow and some pajamas in my overnight bag, attaching it to the bar of my luggage bag.

My eyes burned with unshed tears as I packed, but I refused to cry. I didn't want Brinley to catch me vulnerable.

Tucking my phone charger in the front pocket of my bag, I moved over to my bed to put my laptop away in my laptop bag. I tossed the strap over my shoulder and grabbed the handle of my luggage bag before turning toward the door and leaving.

My phone buzzed with another text from Jasmine, telling me she was waiting in the driveway for me. I descended the stairs with my things.

Dad came out into the foyer when he heard me, his eyes widening with surprise when he saw all my luggage.

"Where are you going, Lux?"

"I'm sorry, Dad. I love you, but I can't be here anymore. I can't handle how toxic Brinley is, or how Mom constantly excuses every shitty thing she's done to me and expects me to act like everything's fine and dandy. I'm done. Jasmine's waiting for me in the driveway, I'll be back in a couple of weeks to get the rest of my things."

I didn't wait for him to say anything else; I opened the door and left.

ONWARD AND UPWARD

ux

"FOR WHAT IT'S WORTH, I'm proud of you, Lux." Jasmine told me as we drove to her parents' house. "That couldn't have been easy, but you did it—you stood up for yourself. You set boundaries."

"Yeah, I know," I wiped the moisture from my cheeks.

The moment I slid into the passenger seat of Jasmine's car, I started sobbing. She hugged me tightly for a moment, then released me to put her car in reverse and get me the heck out of there.

"Are you sure it's okay with your parents that I'm there?"

"Absolutely. You know you're always welcome there," Jasmine assured me. "We'll head back to Sudbury Sunday morning, if that's okay?"

"Yeah that's fine, if you're sure your family doesn't mind me crashing Camellia's birthday dinner."

"They won't mind. Camellia knows what Brinley's been up

to, and she's already filled our mom in on it. Did you know Camellia finally ditched her? Camellia was so disgusted with what Brinley did to you, and how she's been acting since. They're no longer friends."

A wave of guilt rose in me. "Now I feel bad, they've been friends forever—"

But Jasmine cut me off by shooting me a look. "I'm going to stop you right there. Camellia hasn't agreed with a lot of Brinley's behaviour over the years, this was her decision because their morals clearly don't align."

"Brinley will blame me for it, though." I sighed.

"Who cares? Brinley blames you for everything. This is why you set boundaries, remember?"

"I know, you're right." I sighed. "I can't believe my mom tried to sweep this under the rug, too."

"I'm honestly not surprised. Your mom has always tried to live up to this perfect image of what a family should be, and it's always been at your expense. Brinley's too, in a way, not that I'm excusing any of her behaviours, but. Yeah. And your dad, how did he take it?"

"He's confused. None of us really told him what happened. He knew something was going on and tried to get us to tell him, but Mom said we were just having difficulties 'adjusting to living together again' and I...imploded. I didn't have it in me to tell him exactly what happened, I needed to get out of there."

"You never implode. I'm sure he'll get the truth out of your mom soon."

"Not sure that'll change anything, though," I sighed again, glancing out the window. We were in the subdivision Jasmine's parents lived in, less than a minute away from their house.

"It might. Your dad's not a bad person, he's consumed by work and has missed a lot of what's gone on under his roof." Jasmine was completely right about that, too. My best friend had the insight of knowing my whole family for years.

"Yeah, I guess you're right about that, too," I took a deep breath, trying to collect myself as Jasmine pulled into her parents' driveway. The Kade's lived in a beautiful six-bedroom custom-built estate home nestled on a 6.2-acre ravine lot.

I grabbed my overnight bag and my laptop bag, leaving the rest of my things in Jasmine's car.

She led the way inside, pushing open the front door to the grand entrance. We toed off our shoes, tucking them into the front hall closet before peeking into the magnificent great room with twenty-one-foot ceilings where Jasmine's parents were currently sitting, enjoying glasses of brandy in front of the gas fireplace.

"We're back," Jasmine said.

"Lux! It's so wonderful to see you," Mrs. Kade said, rising from her seat and setting her brandy glass down before sauntering over to give me a welcoming hug. "You're looking radiant, dear."

"Thank you," I told her, knowing she was being generous. I looked like I'd been sobbing—because I had. "It's good to see you again too. Thank you for letting me stay here this weekend."

"It's our absolute pleasure!" Mrs. Kade insisted with a sparkling smile.

Iris Kade was a lot like my mother—very put together and beautiful, always dressed to the nines. But despite how formal she was, maternal warmth poured from her very essence.

"You're welcome here any time, Lux. I hope you know that," Mr. Kade said from his chair by the fire.

"We would put you up in the guest room, but Jonathan's parents are coming out for Camellia's birthday dinner tomorrow."

"That's alright, she can bunk with me in my room," Jasmine interjected. "We're going to go get settled. Night Mom, night Dad!"

"Good night," I murmured before following Jasmine up the stairs to the second storey, where the bedrooms were.

I'd always loved everything about this house, from the crown moulding and waffle ceilings to the bespoke cabinetry in the library, kitchens, and even the walk-in closets. Yes, Jasmine's house had a *library*, and it was my favourite room in their entire house.

"It's going to be a little crazy tomorrow, what with the birthday dinner, pretty much all our relatives are coming out and some of Dad's friends and work colleagues," Jasmine warned me, speaking over her shoulder. "But you're used to Kade craziness," she added with a grin.

Two doors opened, almost in sync with one another, revealing the similar faces of Jasmine's two youngest sisters, Azalea and Violet. They were still in high school. Azalea would be going into grade eleven in the fall, and Violet would be entering grade ten.

"Lux! We haven't seen you in forever!" Azalea exclaimed, tackling me with a hug. Violet wrapped her arms around me too, both girls so familiar with me from the amount of time I'd spent with Jasmine over the years, that they treated me like a part of their family.

"Hey girls, how has your summer been so far?"

"Good!" Violet exclaimed. "I had an epic pool party for my birthday. It was so great that people are still talking about it!"

"And I just got back from sleep away camp. Officially finished with my required volunteer hours!" Azalea grinned.

"I thought you finished those a while ago?" Jasmine teased.

"I did. But I wanted more! I now have two thousand and four hundred volunteer hours on my record. That's more than you!"

"You beat me by double," Jasmine chuckled, smiling warmly at her younger sisters. "That'll look great on your university applications."

Azalea seemed to glow from Jasmine's praise. Each of

Jasmine's sisters had always looked up to her, and it was so sweet to see. It reminded me of a simpler time before Brinley decided I was her nemesis.

When we were little, we got along. Mostly because I'd go out of my way to make sure Brinley got *her* way, but still. There was a time when she didn't look at me with seething resentment and hatred; a time when she didn't plot to hurt me.

"Azalea has a boyfriend now, too," Violet reported, earning a glare from Azalea.

"I do not!"

"Then why does that boy keep calling you?" Violet retorted with a sneaky grin.

"Stop spying on me!" Azalea snapped, irritation making her cheeks flushed. "He's not my boyfriend, he's a guy I met at camp. We like talking."

"Oooh, where is he from?" Jasmine pressed, getting in on the razzing.

"North Bay," Azalea answered, her cheeks heating. "But he's not my boyfriend."

"Mmhmm," Jasmine said, sounding like she didn't really believe that.

Azalea let out a growl and stomped back to her room, slamming the door.

"It's not nice to spy on your sisters, Vi," Jasmine lectured, though her smile said she wasn't mad.

"I know, but I'm so bored, it's hard not to! Azalea hardly ever hangs out with me anymore," Violet sighed.

"Well, you're both growing up. Azalea's going to feel the age difference a little more right now, and that's okay. Distract yourself with your friends. Plan another epic end of summer pool party."

"Ooh! Yes! Good idea," Violet grinned.

"You do that. Lux and I are going to go to my room and hang out."

"Can I come?" Violet asked, her eyes hopeful and wide.

"No, we've got important adult things to discuss," Jasmine ruffled her littlest sister's hair, and Violet darted out from under her hand with a scowl.

I felt a little guilty for sending her off, but my heart still felt raw from everything happening with my sister. Seeing their easy bond stung like rubbing salt in the wound, because I didn't have that easy bond with Brinley and likely never would.

"Is Camellia here?" I asked as we made our way into Jasmine's bedroom.

"Not yet, she's still in Ottawa. She's doing a summer internship at the House of Commons, but she took a few days off for her birthday. She'll be arriving tomorrow morning," Jasmine answered, walking into her room. She waited until I entered to close the door. Camellia attended Carleton University in Ottawa, where she was taking Communication and Media Studies.

I set my overnight bag down, taking in Jasmine's room. It hadn't changed since high school—the same photos still decorated her mirror, mostly of us. Her queen-size bed still had the same soft lavender bedspread.

"Have you talked to Theo yet?" Jasmine asked, sitting down on her bed.

"I told him I got here safely...but no, I haven't filled him in on everything that happened in the short eight hours I've been back." In fact, I hadn't really talked to him at all, aside from answering his text message so that he wouldn't worry.

"Why not?"

"I don't want to bombard him with all the drama," I sighed, sitting beside her. "You're not supposed to go into a new relationship with a heaping pile of baggage, and I feel like I'm doing that."

Jasmine nodded thoughtfully, mulling over my words. "Well,

Theo's not one to shy away from baggage. He can handle more than you think."

"He shouldn't have to," I flopped backwards so that I was laying down, staring at her ceiling. "I'll figure it out."

Jasmine laid back too, turning her head to look at me. "You don't have to figure things out alone, though. You have me."

I turned to look at her too and smiled. "I know, and I'm so grateful for you. Thanks for always being there."

Theo

AN UNEASINESS HAD SETTLED over me when I hadn't heard from Lux in several hours. I tried to distract myself, knowing how ridiculous it was to be missing her so profusely after a mere eight hours.

But she hadn't messaged me right away when she got back to Guelph. I'd texted to check in, and she didn't reply until after dinner, saying that she'd arrived safely. Nothing more, nothing less, and after that it was radio silence.

I felt that silence in my soul.

"Snap out of it, Theo," Talia demanded, drawing my attention back to her. We were hanging out on the back deck, playing Rummy. She was winning because I was so distracted.

Talia and I usually hung out and played card games when we were the only ones around. Normally, I was focused enough to hold my own. Tonight, though, my mind kept wandering back to Lux, wondering how things were going back home. Had she told her family she was moving yet? Was her sister giving her trouble?

"Sorry," I dropped my cards, gave up, and rubbed my head, trying to ease the tension headache.

"Wow, Lux really does have a spell over you," Talia's brow

arched, and she set her own cards down, revealing another winning hand. "I've never seen you like this before. Usually, you're unflappable."

It was true, I'd never felt this way before. Like a part of me was missing, and I knew exactly where it was, but it was too far away for comfort. Instead, I felt unsettled.

"Yeah, well. There's a first for everything I guess."

"You must really be into her," Talia tilted her head, appraising me.

"I am," I admitted. "I wasn't expecting to fall so hard and so suddenly for her, but it happened. A few years ago, I would have run from those feelings. I wouldn't have been ready or mature enough to handle the importance of them. But now, I feel ready for them, and I'm worried she's not."

"Are you forgetting the mess she left at home? She's probably busy dealing with sister drama. You are in a place for this, she might not be yet—and you've got to accept that. Either way, you won't know until you talk to her."

"You're right, I know," I sighed.

"If I'm right, why are you still moping?" Talia demanded.

"I have an uneasy feeling. I don't know," I ran my hand over my face, trying to wipe away the troubled feeling.

"Call her."

"I don't want to bother her."

"Then text," Talia countered, lifting her beer for a sip. She paused before taking a drink, eyeing me with a challenge. "Don't be a chicken shit, Theo. You're going to feel all mopey and distracted until you talk to her, so talk to her."

"I'll call her later…" I said, watching while Talia finished her beer.

"Call her now, I'm going to go to bed. I've got an early day tomorrow; Eliza and I are going hiking." Talia stood up, saluting me before she headed inside with her empty bottles.

The sliding door closed behind her, leaving me alone with

only the sounds of crickets chirping and the occasional car driving by.

It wasn't that I was worried she'd changed her mind about us—we'd parted on a pretty good note, with a kiss that I knew rocked Lux to her core as much as it had rocked me. But I knew the mental landmine she was walking into by returning home to that situation with her sister, and her short answer and radio silence wasn't a good sign.

Not that I knew how she communicated via text, since we hadn't done much of that in the past week, but I had a hunch.

Huffing in aggravation, pulling my phone out of my pocket. Talia was right, I wouldn't be able to stop thinking about it until I talked to her. I clicked her contact information, listening as the phone rang.

Lux picked up after a couple of rings. "Hello?"

"Hey," I said, feeling nervous. "Hope I'm not interrupting anything..."

"Oh, no. You're good. Jasmine and I were talking," Lux replied.

"Hi, Theo!" Jasmine's voice was muffled, like she was nearby but not speaking directly into the speaker.

"Oh, you're with Jasmine?" This news made me relax marginally, because I knew that Jasmine would make sure she was okay.

"Yeah...things at home didn't go so great. So...I'm staying the rest of the weekend with Jasmine at her parents, then I guess I'm heading back to Sudbury a few weeks earlier than antici-pated. Surprise?" Lux didn't sound so enthused about the situa-tion, not that I blamed her. If it was bad enough to merit leaving after not even being home for a full day, it was pretty bad.

Still, I couldn't help the excitement I felt over having her come back sooner. I was dreading waiting until the end of the month to see her again. If she came back with Jasmine on Sunday, I'd get to see her again before I travelled to Peru.

"Hey, you know you're welcome here whenever," I assured her.

"I know," Lux said quietly. "Thank you."

"Want to tell me about it?"

"When we get back. I want to not think about it for a bit," she admitted.

"I understand. Whenever you want to talk about it, I'm here," I said. "And for purely selfish reasons…I'm glad I don't have to wait several weeks to see you again."

"Yeah, I guess that's one bonus to it," Lux laughed lightly.

"There's plenty of bonuses!" Jasmine interjected, her voice sounding distant. "You set boundaries! Hooray!"

"Setting boundaries is good," I said in agreement.

"Not with my family, but it had to be done," Lux sighed. "Anyway, Jas and I are going to crash now. Big day tomorrow—her family's having a huge birthday dinner for her sister."

"Have fun! Gonna miss you in my bed tonight." I told her.

"I'm gonna miss being there, Jasmine hogs all the bedsheets."

"I do not!" Jasmine protested, and then something collided with Lux, knocking the breath out of her, and muffling her laughter.

Hearing her laugh eased the unsettled feeling completely.

"Goodnight, Theo," she said, still giggling.

"Night, Lux," I smiled.

$\mathcal{L}$ux

Since moving to Sudbury, I'd gotten a full-time job as a radiation technologist at a private clinic in town. I was loving rooming with Jasmine and Talia, even if I spent a lot of time over at Theo's house and in his bed. We crashed at my place sometimes, too.

In my time in Sudbury, I'd become even closer to Jasmine's group of friends. We all hung out whenever we could, and I got to attend Zoey and Kai's wedding as a guest, not just as Theo's plus one. It was at a small but beautiful venue in Sudbury, with only their closest friends and family in attendance.

Although Theo and I had made things official between us before I'd even moved in, a part of me had tried to keep my distance, fearing things would fizzle out. But Theo remained steadfast, proving to me with his every action and word that they wouldn't. And they *hadn't*. My feelings for him had only grown and continued to grow every day.

He went out of his way to romance and woo me, taking me out on dates every chance we got. Even our nights in were romantic and cozy, full of connecting with one another on a deeper level. Not only did he make me laugh, but he also made me feel seen and appreciated. Understood on a level in which I'd never experienced before.

Theo knew I was dealing with a lot of strain from my family, and he was so supportive. I didn't often speak to my mom, but when I did she made sure to guilt me about how I'd left things with my sister. Brinley had yet to apologize for her part in anything, and I'd learned in my time away that I didn't need to apologize for setting boundaries.

My mother's insistence that I forgive Brinley despite never receiving an apology only added strain between us.

My father was the only one who'd come out to visit me since everything went down. He'd appeared at my door five weeks after I moved in with a housewarming gift and an apology. He hadn't learned the true depth of Brinley's actions until around then, because that's when Brinley announced to the world that she was expecting a baby with Scott, and it had become impossible for her to hide the truth from him.

He understood completely where I was coming from, and although he hoped that Brinley and I would one day be able to resolve our issues, he knew a lot of that rested on her.

I had mixed feelings about Brinley's news. I knew I should feel excited to become an aunt, and I was really hoping that the baby changed my sister for the better, but I couldn't help but worry about how Brinley would handle the impending stresses of becoming a mother.

I was nowhere near emotionally ready for that venture, and I worried that my parents would end up having to raise the baby. But, as Jasmine constantly reminded me: not my monkey, not my circus.

Christmas was another source of tension. My dad had asked

me several times if I'd be coming home for the holidays, and while I'd gone back and forth on the matter a thousand times, I'd ultimately decided to stay in Sudbury.

Partly to protect my own mental health, and partly because Theo's family had extended an invitation for me to join them for their Christmas dinner. I'd met his parents a couple of times, but it would be the first time I'd be meeting his sister, Olivia. She'd flown out Christmas Eve and was staying until the new year.

Dad seemed to understand my reasoning, but my mom was hurt about my choice since I'd never missed Christmas with my family before. I compromised by telling her that Theo and I would make it out in the new year.

I wasn't exactly looking forward to it, but I did want my parents to meet Theo, and I couldn't avoid Brinley forever—especially not with my mom putting pressure on me to help her with the baby shower she was planning for April.

Theo told me we'd rent a hotel room so that I wouldn't have to be under the same roof, and we could make a weekend trip out of it.

"You ready?" Theo asked, leaning against the doorframe of the bathroom where I was curling the last bit of my hair.

"Almost!" I replied. My makeup was done, and I was dressed in an emerald green velvet dress that hugged my curves. Black stockings and black floral mesh block boots completed the look.

"Woah, you look incredible, " he remarked, his voice taking on a reverent cadence as he stepped toward me and put his hand on my hip, gently squeezing it.

"Thank you," I said, putting the curling iron down and making sure it was turned off before giving myself a final examination in the mirror. I'd styled my hair in a flirty ponytail with a few strategically placed pieces framing my face. I'd curled it so that it felt a little more elegant. "I don't know why I'm so nervous."

"You don't need to be. My parents already love you and my sister's going to, too." Theo shifted so that he was standing behind me and wrapped his arms around my waist, glancing at our reflection in the mirror with a devious grin. "But hey, we could always skip the dinner and get lost in each other's bodies. You'll hear no complaints from me." His words made my core clench with desire, but I shook my head, smiling.

"We can do that when we get back," I assured him. "We have to go, we're already late."

"Fine," Theo sighed dramatically, like it was the last thing he wanted to do. But his smile told me he was looking forward to it.

I grabbed my clutch and made sure my phone was in it before grabbing the tray of baked feta bites I'd prepared in advance. I hadn't wanted to show up empty-handed, but Theo had insisted his mother would cover the traditional dishes, so I settled on my favourite appetizer, courtesy of Maria.

While she hadn't taught me this exact recipe, she'd made this appetizer several times for my family back home, and I loved it. It was always a hit at dinners and parties. I'd found a recipe online and hoped it came close to Maria's.

Theo took the tray with one hand and helped me into my jacket with his other before we stepped outside. I made sure to lock up, since Talia had gone to Eliza's for dinner, and Jasmine was at her parents for a few days. I slipped my keys in my clutch and took Theo's hand, letting him lead me to his car. He'd already cleaned the snow off it and had remote-started it so it would be nice and warm when we climbed in.

I buckled up, then Theo handed me the tray before closing the door and walking around to the driver's side. He grabbed my hand, pressing a kiss to the back of it before releasing it.

We made our way up the interlocking stone driveway to the stairs leading to the front door. It swung open before we'd even had a chance to knock, revealing a girl who looked like a younger version of Theo's mom. Dark blonde hair, mossy green eyes, and a wide smile reminiscent of Theo's greeted us.

"'Bout time you arrived; Mom was about to send out a search party!" she said.

Theo hugged her, then stepped aside to introduce me.

"Olivia, this is Lux. Lux, this is my sister, Olivia," Theo introduced, guiding me into the house with his hand on the small of my back.

"It's nice to meet you," I told her, smiling as Theo closed the door behind us.

"It's nice to meet you too. Can I ask: what do you see in my nerdy brother? You're way too hot for him," Olivia said teasingly.

"I guess he's hidden his nerd side from me pretty well," I joked back, smiling at him over my shoulder.

Olivia laughed, taking the tray from me with a crooked grin. "Oh, I like her already. What's this?"

"Baked feta bites," I replied.

"Oh my god, she cooks too?" Olivia's eyes widened. "Yeah, you scored the jackpot, brother. Try not to mess it up."

Theo chuckled, helping me out of my coat while Olivia darted toward the kitchen with the tray. He palmed my ass, giving it a teasing squeeze before lifting his hand to the small of my back, guiding me forward.

"She's right, I did score the jackpot," he murmured into my ear before we joined the rest of his family in the grand kitchen.

Jacqueline Whitmore was standing in the kitchen in a cherry Christmas apron. "Merry Christmas, you two. Olivia tells me you've brought baked feta bites?"

"Yes Mrs. Whitmore, and Merry Christmas to you too," I replied, standing on the other side of the counter with Theo beside me, his hand still on the small of my back.

"I told you, call me Jackie," Jackie waved away my formalities with a manicured hand. "We need to heat them up, right?" she asked, plopping them in the oven before straightening.

"Yep, ten minutes should do it," I answered.

Theo pressed a kiss to my cheek before he dropped his hand and moved around the counter to hug his mom.

"Where's Dad?" he asked.

"In the family room, with Olivia's boyfriend watching the football game."

"Oooh, you brought a boy home?" Theo grinned at his sister, who was stealing a piece of cheese from the charcuterie board on the counter. Olivia narrowed her eyes while she chewed.

"Why do you sound so surprised?" she demanded once she'd swallowed.

"Just shocked someone could put up with you," Theo teased, mussing her hair as he walked past. "Let's go say hello, shall we?" he stopped long enough to take my hand.

"Take the charcuterie board with you," Jackie called out, and Olivia turned around to grab it before trying to catch up with Theo and me.

"Don't say anything embarrassing," Olivia hissed. "Or I'll tell Lux all about your Amtgard—"

"Fine, fine," Theo cut her off with a hard look, and I giggled. I already knew all about his Amtgard phase. I'd seen the photographic evidence, thanks to the photos Desmond still had of them from their LARPing days when they were preteens. He winked at me, giving my hand a gentle squeeze.

Theo

Lux was practically vibrating in her seat beside me with nervousness. We were about ten minutes away from her house, according to the GPS. She hadn't said much on the drive, and I knew she was working over everything in her head.

I reached over, placing my hand on her thigh. Lux was dressed in a pair of form fitting jeans and a cream sweater. Her hair was down and curled around her shoulders, her makeup subtle yet enhancing all her beautiful features. Those plump lips that I loved kissing, those magical grey eyes I loved looking into and getting lost in.

She looked put together and poised, but I knew she felt anything but inside. I gave her a gentle squeeze, and she glanced at me, her eyes a riot of emotions.

"We'll have dinner, cut out as soon as it's polite and go to the hotel," I assured her. I'd booked a hotel room in Toronto, near the aquarium I planned on taking her to tomorrow. Even if I couldn't control what happened at Lux's parents' house in the coming hours, I could make sure our weekend trip ended on a high note.

"That sounds good," Lux sent me a small, relieved smile. "I'm sorry in advance for how weird it's going to be."

"Meeting your parents for the first time while having dinner with your ex-boyfriend and your pregnant sister, how could that be weird?" I teased.

Her mouth twitched as she fought to suppress her smile. "Ugh, this is going to be a disaster," she shook her head.

Grabbing her hand, I pulled it to my lips for a kiss. "Even if it is, we'll be okay. *You'll* be okay."

Lux sent me a thankful smile as the GPS chimed in. "Turn right. You have reached your destination."

"Well, here goes nothing," Lux said, preparing herself as I parked in her parents' driveway.

I opened the door for Lux, holding my hand out to her to grab. She took it, stepping out onto the driveway and peering up at the house with a solemn expression.

I stepped closer, tilting her chin toward me. "Say the word, and we'll leave."

"Okay, let's go now?" Lux teased, her lips pursing as her eyes fixed on mine.

"I mean…we could. But I think you'd be mad at yourself if we left before even going in."

She sighed. "No, you're right. Let's do this."

Lux stepped out of my embrace and grabbed my hand before we walked up to the front door. She hesitated on the front porch for a moment before reaching out and ringing the doorbell.

Several seconds passed before the door opened, revealing a woman that I could only assume was Lux's mom. She was gorgeous, and it was easy to tell where Lux got her delicate bone structure from. "You're here!" the woman said, tugging Lux into a hug.

"Hi, Mom," Lux said, hugging her back for a moment. She stepped back, angling her body toward me. "This is Theo. Theo, my mom."

"Theo! It's so nice to meet you," Mom cooed, immediately pulling me in for a hug. "I can't say we've heard much about you, since Lux has been keeping her phone calls home short and sweet, but we're happy to have you joining us."

She released me and stepped back, sending an impervious look to Lux, her words meant to be a dig at Lux's distance.

"It's nice to meet you too, Mrs. Kennish." I said politely, biting my tongue on everything I wanted to say.

"Please, call me Diana. Mrs. Kennish makes me feel like my late mother-in-law, and I'm not nearly as stuffy as she was," Lux's mom—Diana, chuckled airily, standing aside to let us in.

I followed Lux inside to the grand foyer of their luxury home.

"Let's take those coats," she added, grabbing them off us and hanging them up in the front hall closet. "Can I get you both a drink? Theo, a whiskey?"

"Water's good, thank you," I replied.

"Are you sure? We have Glenfiddich 21 Year Gran Reserva, or—" Diana began.

"Water is fine, Mom," Lux answered. "For both of us."

"Alright, if you insist. Go on into the living room and I'll be right there." Diana gave us a tight smile before disappearing toward the back of the house. Lux took a deep breath.

I took the opportunity alone to tug her toward me, pressing a kiss to her forehead. She looked up at me with a thankful expression, and then led the way to the living room.

We heard their voices before we reached it, a man's voice—Lux's father, Mark Kennish—talking about the importance of a good, stable job. A couple sat on the couch, looking unimpressed and irritated.

"I have a job, Daddy," she huffed, tilting her chin up.

"Social media influencing isn't a real job, at least not when it doesn't pay the bills and save for the future," he said sternly, his gaze moving from her to the guy sitting beside her who looked like he'd rather be anywhere else. "And being a part-time student doesn't pay the bills either, Scott. You guys have less than five months to figure things out. The clock is ticking."

I knew Lux's sister from her haughty posture, and the familial resemblance. Where Lux had red hair like her father, her sister had her mother's fair hair and contemptuous expression. She was scowling at their father with her arms crossed, seething with anger, and didn't realize we were in the doorway.

Awkwardly, we lingered, not wanting to interrupt their conversation. Lux's ex/Brinley's current boyfriend, Scott, noticed us first. He seemed to perk up when he caught sight of Lux, then deflated when he saw me beside her.

Lux's father stopped talking when he followed Scott's gaze

and spotted us in the doorway, his expression softening when his eyes landed on his daughter.

"Lux, Theo! Glad you're both here." He stood up from his armchair with a grin, walking over to hug Lux.

"Hi, Dad," Lux said, squeezing him back with more ease than she'd hugged her mother.

"How was the drive?" he asked, shaking my hand with an air of familiarity. We'd met briefly when he came out to visit Lux.

"It was good, a little bit of traffic, but the weather was okay," I replied.

Brinley watched our exchange through narrowed, calculating eyes, her lips pursed in disdain. The jealousy rolling off her in waves was enough to floor me, although I didn't show it. I'd been warned; I hadn't expected it to be so obvious.

"We were sorry to miss you at Christmas, but I hear your sister was visiting from out of province?" Mark asked, sitting back down in his armchair, and picking up the tumbler of whiskey on the end table beside him.

"Yes, she was. She lives and works in Bonnyville, Alberta, and doesn't get the chance to come home often," I replied, sitting down beside Lux on the loveseat across from her sister and Scott.

"What does she do there?"

"She's the manager of parks and recreation," I answered politely. I could feel Brinley and Scott staring.

"That would be a fun line of work," Mark said, his eyes twinkling. "And Lux tells us you're an environmental geoscientist?"

"Sure am," I nodded politely.

"Do you travel a lot for work?"

"Ugh, can we stop talking about jobs and work please? It's making me nauseous," Brinley complained, throwing her hands up in aggravation.

"Everything makes you nauseous," Scott muttered, rolling his eyes.

"Uh, duh, because I'm *pregnant,* or did you forget?" Brinley snapped with irritation.

Sensing Lux was uncomfortable, my arm went around her shoulders. Scott tracked the movement a little too closely for my liking. I got the sense he wasn't quite over Lux, or that he was regretting his choices in life and where they'd led him. Couldn't blame him, really. I was only getting a small taste of Brinley, and I wasn't a fan.

I'd hoped there would be some redeeming qualities in her, but they remained yet to be seen.

"Congratulations on the baby," Lux said, her tone gentle and kind. "Do you know what you're having yet?"

"A boy," Scott answered, putting his arm around Brinley.

"Really? That's exciting," Lux smiled at her sister.

I had to give her props for that, for not letting the reality of the situation—her ex-boyfriend knocking up her sister—cloud her reaction with bitterness.

"I can't picture you with a little boy."

"Neither can I. *I* wanted a girl," Brinley rolled her eyes.

"You don't get to choose," Mark chuckled.

"I know that," Brinley huffed, her aggravation clear as day.

DINNER WAS AN AWKWARD, strenuous event, despite how hard Lux tried to not cause friction. Lux's very presence set her sister off, making her surly. By the time dessert was brought out, we were more than ready to leave.

Any time the conversation had drifted from Brinley's pregnancy and the baby to Lux and how she was thriving at her new job or about her life in Sudbury, Brinley would get agitated, and Lux's mom would work double-time to bring the topic back to her. I don't even know if Diana was conscious that she was doing it, or if she'd done it for so long, it was second nature.

"We'll be having the baby shower here in April," Diana informed Lux over dessert. "I'd like you to be here a few days before, helping me decorate and prepare. I've already gotten a guest list from Brinley and have started the invitations. We've decided to go with a nautical theme, haven't we Brin?"

Brinley nodded demurely, pleased the topic had gone back to her.

"I'll be here for the shower, of course, but I can't book time off work, especially during the week," Lux answered carefully. Her mother frowned, looking as if she was about to say something.

"That's understandable," Mark cut in before Diana could say whatever was on her mind. "If you need extra help decorating, Diana, just hire someone."

Lux shot him a thankful smile.

"Well, I could always see if Camellia's available to help."

"I told you, Camellia and I aren't friends anymore, Mom," Brinley rolled her eyes. "She hasn't even congratulated me." She stabbed at her desert with her fork. "Lux probably had something to do with that," she muttered under her breath, bringing the forkful to her mouth, and chewing aggressively.

Lux heard her and stiffened beside me. I reached under the table, giving her thigh a gentle squeeze. She drew in a stabilizing breath. "Camellia is busy with university and her internship."

"That's right. Can't fault a girl for focusing on her education," Mark said diplomatically, sending a stern look to Brinley. "If you'd done that, you wouldn't be in this…situation."

Brinley's mouth tensed, and her eyes filled up with tears. Before they could unleash, she pushed back her chair and stormed from the room. Scott rolled his eyes, pushing his own chair back to go after her—though I didn't miss the languishing look he shot in Lux's direction before he went.

"Mark!" Diana scolded, her eyes widening. "That was uncalled for."

Lux's father heaved a heavy sigh. "I'm sorry, you're right. What's done is done, all we can do now is focus on the future. But in order to give this baby the best future, Brinley and Scott have to get serious about theirs."

"This is not the time or the place for this discussion," Diana said lowly, gesturing with her head to me and Lux.

"I think we're going to head out now anyway, we've got a long drive ahead of us," I said, glancing at Lux. She nodded in agreement.

"I thought you guys were spending the night?" Diana exclaimed, trying to mask the hurt.

"Why would they want to spend the night? That'd be awkward, Di. Scott's living here now, and I'm sure Lux would rather not have to spend any more time than she has to around him." Mark pointed out, shaking his head. "When did our lives become an episode of Maury?"

"He's Brinley's boyfriend and the father of our soon-to-be grandchild," Diana countered. She turned to her daughter, giving her a disappointed look. "You're going to have to accept that, Lux."

My jaw dropped. Lux had been nothing but gracious given the situation. She'd been polite and tried her best to engage with her sister. Now that I was seeing it firsthand, I understood what Lux had to contend with. At least her father seemed somewhat on her side.

"I do accept it," Lux frowned at her mother. "But Theo and I have plans, so we aren't staying here tonight. Thank you for dinner, it was great seeing you all again, but Theo's right—we should get going."

Lux and I cleared our plates from the table before heading to the front foyer to put on our coats and boots. I could hear Lux's parents talking in the dining room, it sounded like they were arguing. Only her father joined us in the foyer to say goodbye.

"I apologize if the evening was a little more dramatic than

anticipated, but we are thankful you both came. It was great seeing you again, Theo," Mark said, shaking my hand firmly.

"I understand that tensions are running high right now," I said diplomatically.

"That's no excuse," Lux's dad said, sighing heavily. He glanced at his daughter. "Lux, I'm so sorry for the way your sister—and your mother—treated you this evening. It wasn't fair, and you didn't deserve it. I want you to know I'm proud of you. You're doing good, kiddo."

He hugged her tight, and Lux closed her eyes as she hugged him back, a tear escaping down her cheek. "Thanks, Dad. That means a lot."

He pulled back, keeping his hands on her shoulders. "Don't you worry about things here; I'll handle your sister and your mother. You focus on you, alright?" Lux nodded, and he kissed her forward. "I love you. Drive safe and enjoy the rest of your weekend."

When we were in the vehicle, Lux let out a stabilizing breath, recentering herself.

"You weren't kidding," I scratched the back of my neck. "That was...wow. Are your mother and sister always like that?"

"Pretty much," Lux sighed.

I nodded, reaching over to take her hand. I brought it to my lips, kissing the back of it. "Well, you heard the man. Let's go enjoy the rest of our weekend..."

PLAYLIST

For the full playlist, click here.

1. Meet Me in the Woods by Lord Huron
2. Rain Clouds by The Arcadian Wild
3. Relatively Permanent by Chris Staples
4. Ripple Effect by Scott Helman
5. Lay It on Me by Vance Joy
6. Coastline by Hollow Coves
7. Winterwood by Steph Cameron
8. Wells by Joshua Hyslop
9. The Night We Met by Lord Huron
10. 82 Fires by The East Pointers
11. Ship To Wreck by Florence + The Machine
12. Too Sweet by Hozier
13. Something in the Orange by Zach Bryan
14. Northern Attitude (with Hozier) by Noah Kahan
15. FAMILY TREE by RØRY
16. Tomorrow by Silverchair
17. Fireflies by Jonathan Young & Lee Albrecht

If you enjoyed this story (or if you didn't), please take a moment to **post a review** on Goodreads, your blog, or whichever platform you use. Reviews help other readers find books, and I appreciate any and all reviews!

Sign up for my newsletter to receive exclusive stories, sneak peeks, and updates: https://landing.mailerlite.com/webforms/landing/q1r0x0

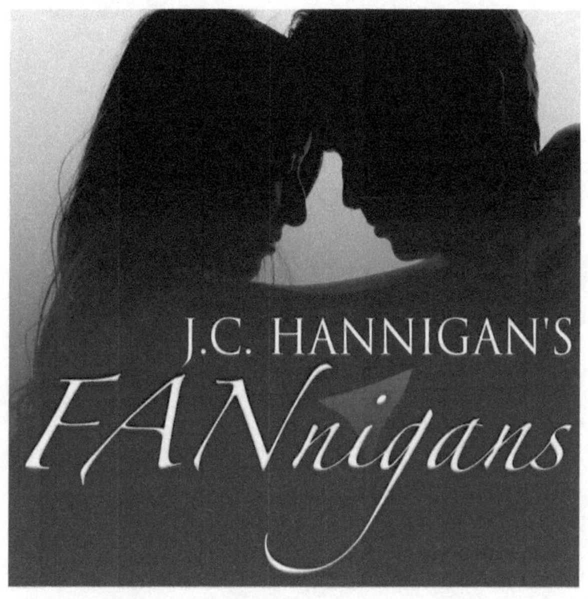

And if you like shenanigans, join my readers group J.C. Hannigan's FANnigans! There are exclusive giveaways, monthly live video events, and tons of other perks of becoming a FANnigan!

https://www.facebook.com/groups/FANnigans/

ABOUT THE AUTHOR

J.C. Hannigan lives in Ontario, Canada with her husband, their two sons, and their dogs. She writes swoony contemporary romance stories with compelling characters and vibrant plots. Her stories are based on small Canadian communities which are well received by readers craving a more familiar locale. Her writing has been described as romantic, bold, and poignant.

Website: www.jchannigan.com

ALSO BY J.C. HANNIGAN

Collide Series

Collide

Consumed

Collateral

Damaged Series

Damaged Goods

Reckless Abandon

Rebel Series

Rebel Soul

Rebel Heart

Rebel Song

Rebel Christmas

Standalones

The Key to 19B

Coalescence: A Welder Romance

Riverside Reverie

Forgotten Flounders Series

Off Beat

Off Limit

Off Balance (Releasing 2026)

Hartwood Creek Romance

Wood You Knot

Last Resort (Releasing 2025)